STRONGHOLD
OF HAPPINESS

Devina Symes

Tim Saunders Publications

TS
Tim Saunders Publications

Cover design: Support for Russia by Barry Weekley

To my dear father, Leslie Burt (1921 to 2016).

The peasants are the great sanctuary of sanity, the country the last stronghold of happiness. When they disappear, there is no hope for the race.

VIRGINIA WOOLF

CONTENTS

FOREWORD

Stronghold of Happiness is set on the south coast of England just before and during World War II. Although mainly a love story there is so much more to it, including the village evacuation of the two central characters, and the true story of the first Arctic convoy during WWII.

The book is fiction based on fact, and almost all of the country characters are based on people I knew as a child, whose language and routines have spanned the generations. Little did they know they were standing on the cusp of a vanishing world.

Much of the story is based on information from my late father. It has also been adapted into a screenplay and stage play.

Devina Symes

CHAPTER ONE

November 1942

Waterloo station was heaving with people and awash with colours of the multifarious uniforms of servicemen travelling to and from various war zones.

In between disjointed train announcements, *Don't Sit under the Apple Tree* and other wartime songs were reverberating round the stone walls. The atmosphere was thick with the cloudy swirl of steam, and amid the throng of people the Red Caps[1] could be seen randomly stopping servicemen to check their passes.

As he scanned the platform for his southbound train, Sergeant Peter Samways accidentally bumped into his old Sergeant Major, Edward Spencer, who swung round in surprise.

'Well, I'm dashed! Samways isn't it?' He glanced at the young man's upper arm. 'Well done on the stripes.'

Peter blushed modestly. 'Thank you, sir. How are you?'

'Pretty good thanks.' His eyes sparkled. 'How is that girlfriend of yours? Have you made her your wife yet?'

Peter smiled. 'Not yet. I'm on my way to Downside Alley now actually. And, er, I have a ring in my pocket!'

'Good for you, Samways. I'm going to your part of the world, too. The old man passed away a few months ago. This is the first chance I've had to get to the house, what with the war and everything.'

'Oh, I'm sorry to hear about your father.'

Edward put his hand on Peter's shoulder. 'No need to be... you see I, er, never really knew the old devil: sent away to school at seven, then straight into the military. Rather different from the childhood you were telling me about, eh?' Peter smiled, remembering the conversation.

The shrill whistle of a departing train interrupted their exchange. Both picked up their kit bags and walked quickly to the already slowly moving train. Once on board, Edward turned to Peter and shook his hand. 'Good luck, Samways. Look after your soon-to-be wife. And make the best of life, eh?' With that he turned and made his way towards the first-class carriages.

Finding no available seat, Peter stood in the already packed corridor where many servicemen were smoking and sharing jokes. Like him, they were simply elated to be going home. By the time the train reached Southampton a few seats were free and Peter was thankful to sit down. He felt far too excited to sleep, but closed his eyes in a bid to picture his darling Ella. He had not heard from her for over ten months and tried to push any feelings of doubt from his mind. He recalled their last meeting and tender words when he had been on a brief leave twelve months before. It was now four years since they had first met, and the initial obstacle, which had sought to keep them apart was no longer there.

As his thoughts lingered on Ella's beautiful face, in spite of wanting to stay awake, the motion of the train and the heat of the carriage soon sent him to sleep.

Sometime later Peter was woken by the lurch of the train as it screeched to a halt, mid stations. There was lots of murmuring and speculation as to what had happened, but no one really seemed to know what the problem was until the rather rotund, red-faced ticket collector came round. Feeling quite important, he was pleased to inform everyone that a cow was on the line but it was now being removed by the farmer and the train would soon recommence its journey. Peter mused to himself that most of the men on the train had been flung into the horrors of war with all its atrocities, but the ways of country life continued as ever.

Checking his watch he realised that they must be near Sandham, the closest town to Downside Alley and his destination. Although, due to the threat of invasion, the station names had been removed, he recognised the fields and backwater as the train approached his home town. He gathered his bag and rucksack, squeezed by the soldiers, then alighted as soon as it was safe to do so.

The station was packed, many were mothers and wives anxious to see their sons and husbands, and Peter was surrounded by tearful reunions and squeals of delight.

No one was there to meet him because no one knew of his return. He wanted to surprise them and couldn't wait to see their faces when they opened the door.

He could have taken a taxi for the four-mile journey but decided the walk would be good to clear his head and, besides, any spare money he had was to go towards the wedding: the wedding that Ella's father was so vehemently against. But that was when he, Peter, was just a farm worker. Now everything had changed.

Ella's father, Godfrey Harvey, was the doctor for Downside Alley and the estate. He had tragically lost his wife to cancer in 1938 and decided to leave London for the country with his only child, Ella, a pretty teenager with chestnut-coloured hair.

Godfrey was a bit of snob and had warned his daughter not to mix with the peasants, a term he loved to use for the locals. With such indifference towards the villagers, Ella wondered why he had chosen to come to the country in the first place. However, she was to learn later that her father had acted on the advice of a good friend, one of the top surgeons at St Mary's Hospital, who had assured him that the long speculated over war was imminent, and that with a young daughter to consider, London was no place to be.

As he took in the familiar rural views, Peter reflected on his first meeting with Ella at the harvest dance in the late summer of 1938. The annual fete, which was held on Farmer Cooper's lawn, consisted of the usual skittles, greasy pig, beer tent and children's games, but as the sun sank over the hill, the paraphernalia of the day was packed away and the local band assembled.

The John Jarvis Band came from Sandham and took their name from their multitalented pianist and organiser. Collectively they played in many village halls around the area and had quickly gained a following when they had formed in the mid 1930s.

All were smartly dressed in suits and bow ties, and their repertoire was extensive – from swing jazz to classical. Many a romance was started as couples swayed sexily together to the rhythm of the latest hit, which was so smoothly sung by Don Gibbs, the tall, suave singer.

Peter, who had been helping with the skittles on his half day off, was ready to go home after returning the skittle alley to the stable where it was stored.

It was his older brother Joe who persuaded him to come back for the dance after he had freshened up. Peter, like his mother, was more reserved than Joe, but both had their father's humour, and although Peter's hair was as dark as Joe's was fair, both had ruggedly handsome faces with the same charismatic smile.

And so, just after eight that evening, Peter had joined Joe in the beer tent. The band was playing *Tiger Rag* and the green was alive with dancers and laughter.

Joe put an affectionate hand on his brother's shoulder. 'Glad you changed your mind, Pete. They're a great band, don't you think? Bit different than the old codgers who used to play in the village hut, eh?'

Peter grinned as he remembered when the two brothers had stood at the back of the hall all night making fun of the old Victorian folk who shuffled round the floor together.

'Oh my goodness! Remember Mr and Mrs Brine? He with his hunch back and she with her massive bottom! Honestly, what monkeys we were to mimic them at home: you with a cushion on your back, and me with one on my bottom!'

'Mother was that mad when she caught us doing it,' Peter grinned.

'Yeah, stopped our cocoa for a whole week! Come on, let's grab another beer and get a load of this kooky music.'

The beer tent was packed but eventually, after being served, the brothers walked out onto the well-manicured lawn.

It was a perfect early autumn evening, the sun still had some warmth in it and the dancers were able to take off their jackets and gyrate freely to the marvellous rhythm.

The dance had been well advertised, and although most of the faces were familiar, some were new. Joe was completely relaxed as he tapped his feet to the music, glad to have escaped the hum-drum of farming life, if just for a while.

'Don't you feel like this is a new era, Pete? I mean, I know we are still tied to the land just like our father and so on, but there seems to be a buzz around, and I feel we could escape the old ways and have a new life, if we really wanted to.'

Peter did not answer his brother; he was distracted by two girls who had just walked onto the green. One was Hannah Butt, whose mother was housekeeper to the village doctor; the other, a stranger.

'I don't know about you, but I think my life has just changed forever!'

Joe followed Peter's line of vision. 'Whoa! That sounds pretty heavy. Which one has taken your fancy?'

'Not my fancy. My heart! The brown-haired girl with the very pretty eyes.'

'Ah yes. Miss Harvey. Her father's the new doctor. Father dug the grave for Doctor Sniffy

Smith last month. Remember?'

Peter was entranced and could not take his eyes off the vision of beauty. Joe realised his brother had fallen under some sort of spell and waved his hand in front of his face, as if to break it.

'Well, there's only one thing for it, Pete. Let's go over and introduce ourselves.'

As the two boys already knew Hannah, the introduction was easy.

'This is my friend, Ella,' Hannah said, and smiled brightly at Peter and Joe.

Ella smiled shyly as her eyes met Peter's, and her heart leapt at his mellifluous tones as he said, 'That's a pretty name, it suits your face.'

Gazing into his attractive face with magnetic smile, she was instantly captivated. And in an almost fairy-tale-like way the band began to play *The Very Thought of You.*

Before they knew it, Peter and Ella were dancing intimately on the green, oblivious to everything and everyone. Joe and Hannah watched as the young couple danced to successive songs; fast or slow, they continued to hold each other, spellbound. When they finally joined Joe and Hannah it was obvious to the latter that the young couple had fallen for each other in a big way.

Peter led Ella by the hand as the four made for the beer tent. But before they had time to place their order, Farmer Cooper barged into the tent.

'Pack it in now. We've got a busy day tomorrow.' Everyone looked at each other in dismay.

'What!' Joe cried. 'We've just got going.'

'Maybe, but sore heads won't help in the morning. You've had your fun.' He turned to look at Peter. 'Some of you shouldn't even be drinking.' With that he stomped out of the tent.

'Miserable old so and so,' Joe remarked. 'Not like him at all. Must have had an argument with his missus I reckon.'

Peter nodded. 'Or maybe he's just sore at having to settle the harvest money.'

Joe laughed. 'Yea, always hates parting with his cash.' Turning towards Hannah and Ella he continued, 'Well, the least we can do is walk these young ladies home, eh Pete?'

Peter looked at Ella adoringly. 'It will be my pleasure.'

Once the four of them had left the green, Joe and Hannah separated from Peter and Ella and drifted into Downside Alley and along the lane.

After leaving Joe and Hannah, Peter and Ella had taken the longer route over the stile and across the field to the doctor's house. The evening had grown chilly and Peter took off his jacket to put around Ella's shoulders. As he did so, he pulled her close to him, then bent down to kiss her.

'I've been wanting to do that all evening.'

'And I was hoping you would,' Ella whispered.

'Oh, my darling, beautiful, Ella.' Peter kissed her again. This time fuller and for longer. Their passionate kiss left them almost breathless, and both felt as if they were floating on air. As he cupped her face gently in his hands, he whispered, 'I love you, Ella. I, I know that sounds crazy... we've only just met... but...'

This time Ella pulled him towards her. 'I feel just the same. My heart feels as if it's about to burst. Oh Peter!'

The two held each other tightly until Peter pulled away. 'I don't want this evening to end... but I know it must. When can I see you again?'

Ella looked into his face, her large blue eyes sparkling with happiness.

'Soon. Very soon... please.'

And that is how it had all started. Both knew their lives would never be the same again.

CHAPTER TWO

It was now 1942, three years since the young couple had first met. Peter was standing in a field, gazing up at the sky. The all too familiar noise of exploding shells was quickly followed by a low-flying aircraft, which interrupted Peter's reverie. He recognised the Focke-Wulf Fw 190 and muttered, 'Bloody Germans!' The aircraft was so low that Peter could clearly see the pilot, whose blonde hair contrasted with the darkness of the plane. The latter waved and smiled mockingly at Peter, then accelerated and headed towards the coast.

As Peter brooded on the madness of war, the long-threatened rain began to fall. He scanned the surrounding countryside and soon noticed a badly bombed cottage and decided to shelter there. Although it had lost its roof, the stone porch was intact, and he was thankful to sit down on the stone seat, out of the now heavy rain.

Being alone in the silence of the ruin, once more his mind drifted effortlessly back to those early days when he and Ella had first met.

They had not been seeing each other very long when, one evening Ella had arrived at Peter's house unexpectedly. As soon as they were alone she tearfully told him that her father had heard she was seeing him and was horrified. He had told her that, as a farm worker, Peter was not good enough for her, and forbid her to see him any more.

Peter had feared this may happen as, on their first date, Ella had confided in him, saying that ever since their arrival her father had been trying to get her to agree to go to Downside House and officially meet the squire's son, Charles. Ella said that she had already seen him briefly at a young farmers' meeting and had taken an instant dislike to the man.

On this particular night when she had turned up out of the blue, as she blurted the story to Peter he had taken her in his arms and told her not to worry. He would think of an answer, and that nothing was going to keep them apart.

Ella had gasped, 'But he won't give up. I know him too well. He likes to get his own way. This is so horrid.'

Peter had taken charge of the situation and told her, 'I will think of something, my darling, I promise. Now, no more tears, eh? Let's wind up the gramophone, put on some records and dance our cares away. What do you say?'

Ella had blown her nose, then smiled gratefully at him.

'That's better.' He had taken her in his arms and cuddled her tenderly. Moments later he chose a record for them to dance to.

'Ah, this is perfect.' The two were soon

dancing to Hoagy Carmichael's *Georgia on my Mind*. Swaying intimately together, Peter looked deep into Ella's eyes.

'I think we should call our first daughter Georgia. It's such a beautiful name... just like you.'

Ella's eyes flashed in mock indignation.

'Our *first* daughter! How many are you planning on having?'

Peter laughed at her semi-cross face. 'As many as you plan to give me, my darling.'

The two continued to dance in silence. Neither wanted this blissful time to end. But a knock to the sitting room door brought them sharply from their reverie. It was Jane, Peter's mother.

'Peter. Sorry to interrupt, dear. Hannah wants a word with Ella.'

'That's alright, Mum. We were... eh, just coming out anyway.'

'No need to. I'll send her in, shall I?'

'Thanks Mum.'

A few moments later Hannah joined them in the sitting room.

'Hi you two lovebirds. Sorry to barge in like this. It's just that Ella's father is asking where she is. Or rather he asked my mother if she knew your whereabouts.'

Peter and Ella exchanged glances.

'Thankfully, Mum said you were with me, and that she would tell you that your father wanted you.'

Ella sat down on the couch and looked up at Peter. 'He's never gonna stop hounding us!'

Peter sat next to her, taking her hand. 'I said I would think of something, and I will.' He turned to Hannah. 'Thanks so much for coming, and, er, thank your mum too. She's a star.'

'Well, she quickly realised what he was like!' She looked at Ella. 'And we had a conversation with her last week, didn't we, El?'

Ella nodded her head. 'Yes, thank goodness we did.'

Hannah smiled at them both. 'I'll wait for you outside then. Best we walk home together,' she laughed, 'just in case he's looking for you in the Alley, eh?'

Ella stood up. 'Sure. Thanks Hannah. You're a real friend. I'll see you in a mo.'

After a tearful goodbye, Peter sat, thinking long and hard. Silently he prayed for some inspiration to guide him as to which way to go. His mother brought him in a cup of coffee, thinking this would help cheer him. And as he sipped it he reflected on various options he had recently thought about. He knew he did not want to work on the farm all his life. That said, he liked it well enough, and when it was time to leave school there was no other option. Farmer Cooper had told him on his last day of education that there was a job at the farm for him and that he would see him on Monday morning at six o' clock. As his parents always needed extra money, the decision was made. And until he met Ella he had not questioned it too much. But now that Ella's father had dictated in this way, it was time to be proactive.

As he churned thoughts over in his mind, he recalled that one day not long before he had met Ella, when he had a few hours off work; he thought he would explore the area and had borrowed his uncle's bike and rode to Parwell, a village west of Sandham. Just outside the village he came across an aerodrome, and as he watched the RAF men walking round the station the idea had occurred to him that maybe he could do that.

But since that day he hadn't given it any serious thought. Now with Ella, in his world everything had changed. He would go to the ends of the earth for her and their life together.

Later that evening when he and Joe lay on their beds he told his brother of his idea. After staying silent for a while, Joe had puffed on his woodbine, then, as he blew smoke circles in the air, said, 'Just a thought, Pete, but when old Digger Dave was looking for work and wanted to move away... you know, with all the family trouble he had, well he told me he eventually found a job in the Army through an advertisement in the *News of the World*... gotta be worth a look.'

Peter perked up at this. 'Any idea who takes it?'

'Sorry, bro, I don't. Ask Mum, she'll probably know someone. If not, buy one. Could change your life, you know.'

Peter looked across at his brother and felt as though his words were some kind of a sign. 'I will... I will. Thanks Joe.'

As he stubbed his cigarette out, Joe said, 'No problem, Pete. Maybe you can return the favour?'

'Sure. What's on your mind?'

'The night of the dance, when you and Ella fell head over heels... as you know I walked Hannah home.'

Peter grinned at his brother. 'I remember it well!'

'Yea, well, when we got to her house I kissed her goodnight, and, oh boy, it was phenomenal. She felt it too, I know.'

'Oh, and you want to know what to do about it?'

'Well, yes. I'm seeing Mary as you know, and I do love her, but my mind is in such a whirl about Hannah.'

Peter rested his head back on his hands. 'Were you happy with Mary before you kissed Hannah?'

'Yes. Very.'

'Well then, I suggest you put the one lone kiss out of your mind, at least for, say, a month. See how things are going with Mary, and then make a decision.'

Joe felt relieved at Peter's clear-headed

advice, and answered, 'Thanks, Pete. I knew you could put a sensible spin on it. I'll see what the next month brings then.'

Much to Peter's surprise, he found that their neighbours, the Cutlers, took the *News of the World*, and Gran Cutler was only too pleased to let Peter borrow it. Sure enough, the Sunday paper held an advertisement asking for young recruits for the RAF.

The next time they met, Peter told Ella of his plan to impress her father, and also to give them a stable start to their life together. Adding that, in anticipation of her approval, he had already sent the form away. But Ella was hesitant at first.

'Oh Peter! You would do this just for me?'

Peter took her hand in his. 'My darling, surely you know by now! I would do anything for you. So, do I have your blessing?'

'Well, yes, yes, of course. But what if you do this and my father is still against us?'

'Then, my darling Ella, we shall live together until you are old enough to get wed without his consent.' Totally unexpectedly Peter got down on one knee. 'Miss Ella Harvey, will you do me the great honour of becoming my wife?'

Ella's face beamed. She had no idea that this was going to happen right now, but had secretly prayed that one day they would get married.

Although she was bursting with happiness, she calmed herself down before answering.

'Yes. Yes. Oh, my darling Peter.'

'Do you promise?'

'Yes, I promise.'

'A promise made is a debt unpaid, you know.'

'Ah! You've read Robert Service[2], too! Then, my darling Peter, I am in your debt forever.'

Peter pulled her close to him. 'Thank goodness for that. I couldn't bear to live without you now.'

Peter lifted Ella up and carried her to the rather shabby horsehair couch. The two embraced and kissed passionately until Ella broke away and sat up.

'I s'pose you'll have to go away? Oh, God!... I'll hate it!'

Peter gently touched her cheek and said, 'If I am successful, I will have to go on a training course.'

'Well, I hope you are accepted... but with you away... well, how shall I exist?'

Peter laughed. 'It will quickly pass, my love, and then we'll be together forever!'

Within a short time Peter was asked to go to Bristol for an examination and medical. His rounded education and sharp brain meant that his exam went without a hitch. His medical went equally as smoothly and he was soon on his way to West Drayton to get kitted out, where he stayed overnight.

The speed with which everything had happened was astonishing. He was then sent to Uxbridge for twelve weeks' training and did not come on leave until Easter 1939. Once settled at Uxbridge, Peter wrote to Ella, telling her of his three months' training. In her reply, which came by return of post, Ella wrote of her distress at not being able to see him for twelve whole weeks, which she followed with loads of exclamation marks, adding that to keep her sane she would write to him every day.

In that first missive, because Ella had not realised that Joe had already confided in his brother, she told Peter that one evening she and Hannah had had a heart to heart, and Hannah had told her that she had the hots for Joe after a goodnight kiss. But as he was now spoken for, it made it even harder for her, forbidden fruit and all that, but after a glass or two of sherry and some friendly advice from Ella, Hannah had concluded that she would never do anything to come between Joe and Mary.

At the end of her letter Ella had said how fortunate they were that it was only her father's ignorance that kept them apart, and somehow they knew they would overcome that. As Peter had so often told her, nothing in the world would stop them getting married, and that magical thought and Peter's loving letters kept her focused and happy.

After his training, Peter was sent to Calshot near Southampton. Over the next couple of years letters between the young couple were a lifeline, and his leave was very precious to them both. He was amazed how everything had fallen effortlessly into place regarding the RAF. All meant to be, he supposed. Joining as an AC2, he had been quickly promoted to Corporal, and remembered when he had surprised Ella on leave in 1940, and how she had beamed when he had taken off his greatcoat to reveal his new stripes.

'Oh my! You'll have all the girls after you now.'

Peter had taken her in his arms and kissed her, saying, 'There's only one girl in the world for me, and that's Miss Ella Harvey.'

Back in the present, as he looked round the cobwebbed porch of the dilapidated cottage, he reflected on the day that had changed his life, along, of course, with millions of others. On Sunday September 3, 1939 came the awful announcement by Prime Minister Neville Chamberlain that the country was at war with Germany.

Peter had been at home that weekend and on the Saturday morning had gone to Brian, the butcher, to buy some sausages for his mother. As usual there was a queue, and as Peter and two others joined it, Brian, who liked to think he was the font of all knowledge, greeted his newest customers: 'Mornin'. Have you heard the latest news, folks?'

As no one ventured a reply, Peter had spoken up. 'No. What's that then, Brian?'

Brian thumped his cleaver down on a piece of brisket, then wiping his nose on a rather grubby handkerchief, said, 'Well, I heard on the wireless yesterday that Germany 'ave marched on the Poles.'

One of his customers, Mrs Burden, a slow, bucolic lady, whose son's job was to maintain telegraph poles, said, 'Cor, our Stan do work wi' they!'

Along with Brian, many of the customers had struggled to conceal their laughter, and later that evening when the family were gathered round the fire, Peter relayed the story of Brian delivering his latest news and the innocent remark made by Mrs Burden.

As everyone laughed at the old lady's naivety, Peter looked round at their smiling faces. The thought struck him that Britain and France had made an agreement to protect Poland against any threat of war. The very worrying fact that the Prime Minister was going to address the nation the next day, on Sunday morning at quarter past eleven, could mean that this might be the last time for some while that a happy anecdote was shared between them all in a carefree atmosphere.

Peter's fears were confirmed when, the following morning he and his family had gathered round the wireless to hear the devastating news that their country was at war with Germany. Air raids were expected imminently. Everyone had been shocked into silence; the long speculated over war was now a reality. As his mother began to cry, his father had put an arm round her shoulder; then, looking at the concerned faces of his family, and to boost their morale in this darkest hour, he spoke up.

'Your mother and I have been through this before, my dears, an' no doubt there will be trying times ahead, but if we stand firm and face the storm, we'll come through it all.'

As she wiped her eyes, his mother Jane put on a brave smile and continued with the preparations for the Sunday dinner. After digesting his father's words of encouragement, Peter realised that it was indeed an uncertain future, but consoling himself with the fact that his family was known for their indomitable spirit, he knew that with each other's support, they would all somehow cope with the challenges ahead.

As the rain began to ease and a few rays of autumn sunshine broke through the open porch, Peter decided to continue his journey and smiled to himself as he remembered the last night before his posting abroad in 1941.

He and two of his newly formed friends were enjoying a drink in the NAAFI₃, and were discussing their situation. Jim, a young cockney lad, said he was worried about his wife who was pregnant with their first child. Arthur, the older of the three, said there was no point in worrying and suggested another drink.

Peter declined the offer, saying that he was off to the barracks to write to his girlfriend. Just as he said that, Edward Spencer, the most pompous of the Sergeants billeted with the young men, strode over to their table. The three men stood up immediately.

'Good evening, lads. Good to see you relaxing.' He looked at Peter who had already left the table. 'Not leaving already are you, Corporal?'

'Yes, sir.'

'What's your name, lad?'

'Peter Samways, sir.'

'Well, Samways, why not have another drink?'

'No thank you, sir.'

'Come on. Tonight is the last before your

posting. Try and relax a bit, eh?'

'I'd rather just go, sir.'

'What can be more important than drinking with your mates?'

'I thought while I had the time, sir, I would write to my girlfriend.'

'Girlfriend! What's your problem, Samways? This is wartime. No bloody time for girlfriends. Get out there and sow your wild oats. The women are mad keen for young, handsome men in uniform. You can oblige, I'm sure. War is not only for fighting you know, it's for something more pleasurable, which also begins with 'F'.' Twirling his waxed moustache, before walking away with a broad grin on his face, he added, 'Well, goodnight lads. Have fun.'

Jim looked at Peter. 'Don't take any notice of him, mate. You do what you want.'

'Yea, Jim's right,' Arthur said. 'Seems to me he's the one with the problem.'

'Umm. With an attitude like that I reckon he missed out on his childhood.' Peter drank the last drops from his glass. 'Well, I'll be off then. See you both later.'

A few minutes later Peter was writing to Ella. He told her how much he missed her and that it was only the thought of being with her that kept him going in this strange world. And even though the war had interrupted their plans, it wouldn't be long before they would be together for always. He said that he was awaiting news of his posting abroad and would write as soon as he could, adding that she must never forget the promise they had made to each other, and that one day they would be blessed with Georgia and her siblings.

He sealed the letter and went to put it in the post box. It was an amazing night, with clear skies and a multitude of stars. As he looked up at Orion he wondered if maybe Ella was looking at it too from Downside Alley. All was quiet, then suddenly the silence of the camp was broken by a loud clattering sound followed by various expletives. Peter followed the direction of where the noise was coming from until he came across a man lying on the floor with a heap of tin helmets surrounding him. The man looked up.

'Help me up, old man, will you?'

'Of course, sir.' It was Sergeant Spencer. As Peter helped him to his feet, the Sergeant yelped with pain.

'Damn it. My ankle has twisted.' He looked at his rescuer with keen eyes. 'It's Samways, isn't it?'

'Yes, sir.'

'Well, Samways, can you can help me back to my quarter?'

'Yes, sir.'

With Peter's help the Sergeant hobbled to his room and sighed gratefully as Peter eased him on to his bed.

'Thank you, Samways. I appreciate your help.'

'No problem, sir. Is there anyone I can contact for you, sir?'

The Sergeant exclaimed loudly, 'Hell! I'm supposed to be on duty, and I've, er, had a drink. Strictly against the rules you know.'

'I could say you have gone down with that twenty-four hour flu that's been going round, sir. Your ankle should be easier in the morning: so no need for anyone to know, sir.'

The Sergeant looked long and hard at the young Corporal. 'Thank you, Samways. I've misjudged you.'

'Something we all do, sir.'

'I like your thinking, Samways. Where were you moulded?'

'I believe we are shaped... or moulded, if you like, by our childhood years. My grandfather often talked of some wise sage who said a man is made out of a boy.'

The Sergeant swallowed hard and cleared his throat. 'And where was your childhood spent, Samways?'

'Oh, on a remote estate on the south coast, sir: it's called Downside, and I live in Downside Alley.'

'Well, I'll be jiggered! I flew over there in 1937. My father had just inherited a small estate from his older brother, who had died suddenly without issue. It's called Woodleigh, and in fact I think it is very close to where you live. Small world, eh?'

'It certainly is, sir.'

'Well, Samways, I'll say goodnight to you. And good luck with your posting.'

'Thank you, sir. Goodnight.'

Peter, who by now was part of the 151 Wing[4], was awoken later that night by a tap on the shoulder, and along with his fellow airmen had to scramble his things quickly together. After a train ride to Liverpool he boarded the Llanstephan Castle, a small mail boat. From there he journeyed to Scapa Flow and then to Iceland, where the first Arctic convoy assembled. Like his fellow airmen, he had no idea where he was going. Then one day during the three-week journey came a notice in the dining room, stating, 'Lessons will be given in Russian'.

With his thoughts preoccupied, the last mile or so had passed very quickly, and as he headed for the lane that led to Downside Alley, Peter's excitement grew. He was almost home! With the mission being completed he had returned from Russia early in December 1941, and after a short leave was posted to a secret base in England. He had been there ever since. It had seemed forever when he was away and he wondered at times if he would ever return home.

Then, as he rounded the corner he stopped abruptly, and simply could not believe his eyes. Before him and barring his way to Downside Alley were rolls of barbed wire. A large sign read, VILLAGE CLOSED – KEEP OUT!

CHAPTER THREE

Early Autumn 1938

The dark, heavy sky seemed to echo Ella's mood as she packed her belongings. Apart from the day of her mother's funeral, it had been the hardest day of her life. And worst of all, it had happened so quickly. Ella's father, Godfrey Harvey, had announced at breakfast only two weeks before that he had been offered the position as doctor on a country estate on the south coast, and had had no hesitation in accepting.

The previous doctor had died suddenly while reading the lesson at church, leaving the inhabitants of the Downside Estate without a medical practitioner. In truth, the doctor was really employed to attend to the medical needs of the squire and his family. But the locals were able to call on his medical skills when the need arose, if they had the sum of two shillings to pay him.

Ella had decided that her eclectic collection of books would be the last thing to be packed, and before she consigned them to the ancient packing case, she thumbed through the various tomes to seek words of wisdom and comfort from one of her favourite authors. It was her mother, Grace, who had educated Ella, who introduced her daughter to the classics. And authors such as Austen, Brontë, Hardy, Woolf and Dickens had filled the young girl's shelves since she was ten or eleven years old.

Grace, whose name aptly reflected her poise and elegance, had always told her daughter that those books laid out a guide for life, highlighting the pitfalls to be aware of and also the goodness that existed in most people. Not forgetting the age-old story of the twists and turns of love, unrequited or otherwise.

As she packed the last of the Hardy novels, Ella wondered what her mother would say to her now as she embarked on a journey into unknown territory with strangers around her. As if in answer to her probing thoughts, a piece of paper fluttered from the pages of *Far From the Madding Crowd*. Before Ella picked it up she recognised her mother's handwriting. It was part of an assignment that Grace had set her daughter a year or so before. Ella had, of course, read it at the time, but today her mother's words seemed to answer the questions that Ella had silently asked for that very day.

> *...Well done for your observations on all the main characters, especially Gabriel Oak. His steadfast character reveals to us that we should always go by our instincts, and that whatever happens we must be patient, brave and strong in order for good to prevail.*

And as for true love, well, my dear Ella, never compromise on that. Once you have found it, and you will certainly know when you have, hold on to it tightly; in this world it is the most precious gift that you can have.

Life is a huge adventure and we must make the most of it. Well done again. I look forward to reading your next paper on Wuthering Heights!

As Ella reread the words, the ache she had felt in her heart since her mother's passing seemed to pierce her very soul, and she cried bitterly. Then, through the blur of tears, she read the message once more. The words – *brave* and *strong* – leapt up at her and she knew that that was her mother's wish. She wiped her eyes and put the Hardy novel in the box, and as she sealed it up, whispered, 'I must do as Mum has asked me to.'

Grace had been diagnosed with an ulcer of the breast on midsummer's day in 1938, when the roses in their suburban garden were in full bloom; their splendour and perfume seemed to mock Ella's heartbreak. Sadly, Grace's husband and his contemporaries could do nothing for her and within twelve weeks she was dead and buried. And now three weeks later Ella was leaving her London home for life in the country.

The doctor's house was one of the lodges on the estate and stood at the southern end of Downside Alley. It was a square, whitewashed dwelling with sash windows and tall chimneys. Part of the condition of the doctor's employment was that the house would be painted throughout, and when Ella and her father had arrived at their new address they were delighted to find their home fresh, airy and light. The journey down to Downside had been a pretty one. The countryside was amass with the golden tones of early autumn and as they drove the Baby Austin through the New Forest with the sunshine glinting through the myriad of trees, the omens looked good for their new life.

The two had hardly spoken on the journey, both engrossed in their own thoughts. Although Ella had always respected her father, she had never spent much time with him, always being much closer to her mother. Those last few weeks of Grace's life had given her a chance to try to bridge the gap between Ella and her father, and many tender, poignant moments had been shared between mother and daughter. Grace unselfishly put the welfare of her daughter above everything else, and Ella, wanting to please and assure her mother as much as she could, vowed to try to have a closer relationship with her father. After all, he was her only living relative.

Ella had often wondered how her mother

had fallen for her father. Grace was so elegant, beautiful and gentle. Godfrey, on the other hand, was rather haughty, and often withdrawn and curt. On one occasion when he had spoken rather sharply to her mother, Ella had asked her why she put up with it. Grace had smiled sweetly, saying that although his manner was often abrupt, he meant nothing by it, and that he was a real softie underneath with a very kind heart. Ella supposed this was true for she had once, on holiday, watched as her father picked her mother up, twirled her around and told her that he loved her. This was on one of the family holidays. Grace always chose where they would go for their annual break, and Godfrey was happy to go along with her.

With Grace's love of the classics and English heritage, their trips often took them to very historical, romantic places such as Stonehenge, Bath and Glastonbury, but their holiday in 1932 was the most romantic of them all.

One of Grace's friends had a friend who had moved to south west Cornwall in the 1920s. Details were sketchy at first, but it seemed that the lady, Rowena Cade, had started a local drama group and actually built an incredible stage into the cliff edge. In the year of Ella's tenth birthday, the local theatre was staging Shakespeare's *The Tempest* during the summertime.

Thinking about it now, Ella realised that this was the holiday that had unlocked her love of the sea. The journey down to Porthcurno was long and tiring, and in fact the longest the family had ever taken. Refreshed after a night's rest and a full English breakfast, the three of them walked down to the almost Mediterranean-like beach of Porthcurno and were entranced by the turquoise sea and the beach's wild beauty.

It was there on that remote sandy bay that Ella witnessed that most romantic gesture between her parents, and as she shyly looked on, she couldn't help but smile at the two of them laughing as the waves lapped over their feet. That most amazing day would be etched in all their memories forever, and not least because of the spectacular evening to come. As they walked down the gorse-lined path to the theatre, with the moonlight glistening across the bay, the three of them, even Godfrey, were spellbound. They had picked their tickets up from the house as they had been told to and made their way down the cliff to the open-air theatre. Once seated, they had a chance to really take in the spectacular situation. They were quite near the edge of the cliff from where there was a sheer drop to the Atlantic. The whole evening was magical and, though Ella was only ten, she took it all in, taking a photograph of the stage and actors in her mind.

But even though Ella had witnessed some loving actions by her father on that holiday, the two sides of his nature still confused her, and as a growing child she was hesitant to show her feelings to him.

And another thing that puzzled her, ever since she had been introduced to the world of books, in complete contrast to her mother, he had told her not to read such rubbish and that the real world was nothing like the slushy tales in those novels. Grace had heard him admonishing her one day and later told Ella to take no notice, adding that he was used to reading *The Lancet* and other medical journals and had not the inclination or interest to indulge his emotions in fiction.

As the miles sped by, Godfrey found himself reassessing his situation. Although Grace's death had turned his world upside down, leaving him heartbroken and vulnerable, he was sure that the move south was the best one for both him and Ella. The threat of war seemed to draw ever nearer, and at least in the country they would be out of harm's way. Although his colleagues at St Mary's Hospital did not want him to leave, they understood his reasons. They all knew Grace, as she had trained at the hospital, and in fact that is where the couple had met twenty years earlier. Everyone sympathised with Godfrey's loss. As the car purred its way towards the Downside Estate, Godfrey recalled the euphoric time of their first encounter and felt that his marriage to Grace was the best thing that had ever happened to him, although it had not been easy at first.

Grace's parents were business people and, owning a very successful London department store, had high hopes for their only daughter. But Grace had different aspirations. Since childhood she had an innate urge to care for people and had always known that she wanted to be a nurse. In spite of her parents' objections, her determination won through. She had not long qualified when she fell deeply in love with, Godfrey Harvey, a trainee doctor.

Grace's parents, rather like the infamous Mr and Mrs Bennett in *Pride and Prejudice*, hoped she would marry one of the landed gentry with whom they mixed with socially, but this was not to be. When they forbade their daughter to see Godfrey again, Grace became so withdrawn and thin that they reassessed their ideas and both agreed that their daughter's happiness was the most important thing. And so the young couple were married in 1921 and when they were blest with a daughter one year later their happiness was complete.

The wrongly perceived stability of Grace's parents' finances offered the young couple a financial cushion and they decided to rent a large Edwardian house in south west London. But before Ella was two the up-market department store, which had flourished in the early part of the twentieth century, was feeling the hard knock of the depression and finding it almost impossible to compete with new cheaper stores, which many of the lower and middle classes were flocking to. Very sadly, by the early 1930s the business was bankrupt, and its demise resulted in the failing health and early deaths of Grace's parents.

This had been a terrible blow for Grace, Godfrey and Ella, but fortunately their financial outlook was not so bleak because by then Godfrey's wage had risen to a substantial rate, and Grace, once recovered from the shock, put all her efforts into making their holidays and time together as special and as memorable as it could be.

When they broke their journey for a leg stretch and tea break, Godfrey had opened up to his daughter, discussing various aspects of their new life, and especially his hopes for his daughter's future.

'Well, my dear, not long now and we'll be opening the door of our new life. How are you feeling about it all?'

'A bit nervous really, father.'

Godfrey smiled kindly. 'Only natural, my dear. But no need to be. Mrs Butt, our housekeeper, has a daughter the same age as you. Hannah, I think she's called. And I'm sure you will find a good companion in her.' This was news to Ella. Good news. 'Of course, she's had an inferior education to you, my dear. But no worry, I expect you'll be able to educate her.'

'As long as she's a nice person, that's all that matters, father.'

'Well, yes. That's true. But don't get too close to her. Use her to find your way round the village. And I'm sure before too long you will meet some of the local gentry, and they are bound to have daughters your age, too.'

'Oh, Father. How you keep on about the gentry. We're not gentry. We are who we are... just... ordinary people.'

'That's not quite true and you know it. Look, all I'm saying is don't get too involved with the, the....'

'Peasants, I know.'

'Precisely.'

'And I don't care what you say, I am just the same as them. Yes, I had the benefit of a better education. But that's not everything, father. I just want to get on with folk. And living in a small village, which I presume Downside Alley is, that is what we have to do, or at least try to do.'

Godfrey conceded defeat. He decided to bide his time and felt sure his daughter would come round to his way of thinking in due course. For the moment he was just glad to be opening a new chapter on their life in Downside Alley.

Thinking of her mother's wish, Ella felt a bit guilty for having clashed with her father. But with the dichotomy between them being so huge, bridging it was going to be difficult if he persisted with his snobbish ideas.

Pushing aside the negatives, Godfrey smiled at his daughter's rather stern face. 'Cheer up, my dear. Soon be there now. Mrs Butt assured me that she will be waiting for us with a fresh cup of tea and homemade scones.'

Ella had to admit that when her father was in a good mood he was utterly charming. But she never understood how quickly he could change from grunt to grin, and this irked her all the more.

Sure enough, as they drove up the short drive to Downside Lodge, Hilda Butt was there on the doorstep to greet them. Her open face and broad smile made the two newcomers feel immediately at home, and as if they had known her for years.

'There we are then. Come on through. Hannah and I will fetch your bags in a minute.'

Godfrey held out his hand. 'Godfrey Harvey. Very pleased to meet you. And this is Ella.'

Unused to this kind of formality, Hilda blushed as she shook his hand and then in turn Ella's.

Any awkwardness was broken by the appearance of a fresh-faced teenage girl with thick wavy blonde hair. She grinned broadly at Godfrey and Ella. 'Hello. I'm Hannah. Welcome to Downside Alley. Can I help with your bags?'

Ella beamed at her new companion. 'Thanks. That would be great. But I'll come with you.'

'Sure, whatever you want. How was your journey?'

The two girls chatted happily as they made for the car. Hilda led Godfrey into the dining room where she took his jacket and poured him a cup of tea. 'I'm sure you'll be happy here, sir. It's a nice village.'

Godfrey drank his tea and munched the warm scone, topped in cream and jam, which Hilda had offered. 'I'm sure we will, Mrs Butt.' There came the sound of laughter from the hallway. 'Looks like the girls have hit it off well.'

'Yes. Well, teenage girls have a lot in common, sir.' Remembering the tragic circumstances of the doctor's move, she continued, 'I think it will be good for you both that you're here.'

Godfrey wiped his mouth on the damask serviette. 'I'm sure you're right.' He helped himself to another scone. 'Delicious, Mrs Butt. All your own?'

'Oh, yes, sir. Everything is homemade in this house.'

'Good, good.' And with a twinkle in his eye, he added, 'I've come to the right place then!'

Hilda was pleased. Cooking was her passion. She had trained at the Royal Bath Hotel in Bournemouth, or rather was in the middle of training, when her mother had become ill and she had had to return to Downside Alley, where they rented a cottage off the estate, to look after her. Unfortunate as this was, she had been in training long enough to master the meals that would be required of a cook and housekeeper. At first, while still caring for her mother, she would cook meals for the local gentry when they entertained their guests. This gave her a lucrative income, which she further enhanced by making jams, honey and cakes to sell at Sandham market.

Her husband had died years earlier while working on the roads, leaving her solely responsible for looking after herself and Hannah. Although her parents had tried to put her off going to the Royal Bath Hotel at Bournemouth, quite a distance away, to train, Hilda often reflected what a blessing it was that she had persevered, and how great the dividends were. She had always loved cooking, and, as a child, used to help her mother make the bread and cakes. Like most folk in Downside Alley, Hilda was always looking for a way to earn an extra shilling or two, and was encouraged by her parents to save. During the period in between leaving school at fourteen and her training at Bournemouth, she was not too proud to turn her hand to anything.

One such a job was helping the Ryder sisters, two elderly spinsters who lived in a detached cottage in Downside Alley, which was right on the roadside. Since their father's death some years before, the two ladies had managed to pay the rent by taking in lodgers. But now both in old age, they were frail and in need of help. When Hilda's mother had met one of the sisters on the common trying to milk a goat someone had given them, she had suggested that her daughter might be able to help out.

And so Hilda started her first job. In order for the ladies to continue to take in lodgers, the house had to be kept clean and tidy, and this was one of young Hilda's main tasks. After being there a while the young girl decided that the elderly spinsters must have some private means of finance, as they ate well and paid Hilda well, especially for the extra task on Saturdays when she would empty the earth closets for them. For this one job the ladies paid her two shillings and sixpence, and, in all honesty, Hilda could not wait to get to work. Although she gave her mother most of her other wage, the money from her Saturday job was saved, and how glad she was to have a tidy sum put away when she embarked on her training at Bournemouth.

Saturday was traditionally the day when the earth closets were emptied in Downside Alley, usually in the evening, and usually by the men folk. It was a ritual that they engaged in together, and as they carried the large galvanised buckets on their shoulder, the banter would flow freely between them. One of the older men in the village used to light up his pipe, to keep the smell at bay, and say to his neighbours, 'Come on then, lads, let's toss these sailors out.' No fuss, no moaning, just another job to be done. Each dug a large hole in which to tip the contents, and when it was very cold in the winter, would cover the space next to the newly filled-in hole with straw, so that the ground would not be too hard for digging the following week. Some, like Archie, Peter's father, would put the contents on their garden to be used as manure.

When Godfrey and Ella settled down for their evening meal that first night, both felt that the move to Downside Alley had been the right thing to do and that Grace would have approved. Mrs Butt and Hannah were both very decent people, to mention nothing of the supreme food produced.

Ella had had a good talk with Hannah and the two girls were meeting up the next day to find something worthwhile for Ella to do with her time. They had bonded straight away, both being gregarious with a good sense of humour. Hannah liked reading too, but did not have many books. So, Ella immediately offered her the use of her collection whenever she wanted it.

Godfrey was to be on duty the following

day and later that evening familiarised himself with his study and surgery. Both were more than adequate and comfortable. He didn't think that many would come to the surgery, due to the lack of finance, and guessed that regarding the squire and his family, he would visit them at their house.

By coincidence, just as he was thinking this, Mrs Butt came in to announce that Squire Harrington was in the sitting room and wished to see him. The two had spoken on the phone but had never met, and as Godfrey entered the room, the two men weighed each other up.

'Welcome, Doctor Harvey. I trust the house is to your liking?'

'Thank you. Yes, everything is fine. Ella and I like it very much. It's a very nice spot you have here.'

As Squire Harrington smiled, his eyes disappeared into a narrow line. 'Good, good. We like it. Now, I hate to pounce upon you so soon, but the fact is my daughter has sharp pains in her stomach: quite bad actually. Could you come up to the house, do you think, and take a look?'

Godfrey had not expected this, and had just been thinking of retiring for the night. But this was his job, and the squire paid his wages.

'Of course I'll come; so sorry to hear that. Has she eaten anything different, do you know?'

The squire gestured Godfrey through the door and onto the driveway where his Buick

Eight was parked. 'Not that I know of, but Sophie will tell you more.'

A few minutes later the two men arrived at the manor house, and as he looked at the huge building before him, the ornate chapel to the right of it and the ruined abbey a few hundred yards away, Godfrey quietly said to himself, 'These are big people.'

Half an hour later he was enjoying a glass of whisky with Hugh Harrington and his son, Charles. Godfrey's initial thoughts proved correct. Sophie had gone to a harvest ball in Sandham the night before and after Godfrey had questioned her closely as to what she had eaten, it turned out that part of the ten-course menu included shellfish, which, after examining her stomach, Godfrey concluded had probably given her mild food poisoning. Rest and plenty of water being the only cure, Sophie had taken to her bed with a wan smile, which vaguely brightened up her pale, delicate face.

As he undressed that night, Godfrey thought that the introduction with his new boss and family had been providential, and had put their relationship on a firm and unbiased footing. Something he hoped to build on in the future when he would take Ella to meet Charles, who would soon take over the running of the estate.

Ella meanwhile was settling into her new bedroom, which was freshly painted in a pastel pink. She had put her books away and hung up most of her clothes. Snuggling between the sheets, she felt happy, especially at having Hannah as her friend. Drifting off to sleep, she looked forward to a tour of the village the next day, and maybe a paddle in the sea!

Godfrey and Ella settled into their new home and routine at an alarmingly fast rate. Although the day after their arrival the newspapers had printed the good news of the Munich agreement, and Neville Chamberlain's declaration that there would be 'peace for our time,' Godfrey remained concerned about the whole situation and was thankful to be away from London.

The whistle-stop tour that Hannah took Ella on was a great success and as they bathed in the sea in the late afternoon sunshine, with cormorants bobbing around, the two discussed what Ella could do with her spare time.

'The headmistress is always looking for extra help with the children's lessons. I know you are not qualified, but it sounds like your mother gave you an excellent education... not sure if she could pay you though.'

'That wouldn't matter. Maybe I could help with nature tours and outings. I think village schools have such classes on their curriculum these days.'

'Maybe. Best to speak to Miss Bowen; I'll have a word with her if you like.'

'Thanks, Hannah. That would be great.'

As it turned out, Miss Bowen was very

pleased to have the offer of help and Ella worked for two days a week in the classroom assisting the children when they had arts and crafts lessons, and reading stories to them. Also every lunch time she helped out in the canteen. This brought in a small wage, and she decided to save some and use the rest for records and trips out with Hannah when the two of them were free in between their jobs.

Hannah worked part time in the local grocery shop and also, being a good seamstress, did clothes alterations for people. She could run up a dress as quickly as others sewed a hem. The two girls would meet up in the evenings, play records, go for walks, chat and giggle. Ella had only been living at Downside Lodge for a short while when Hannah mentioned the forthcoming dance that was to be held on the village green, to celebrate harvest.

'Let's go, shall we? Be a bit of a laugh.'

'Yes, let's. My dancing is not too hot though. I never did master the Charleston properly.'

'Get on! I had you down as one of those flappers! Don't worry, my footwork's not too hot either. Let's practise this week at my place, eh? Mum won't mind.'

And so every night after their evening meal the two met at Hannah's house, played some jazzy tunes and tried to improve their Cha Cha, Tango and Charleston; all amid hilarious laughter.

Then came the evening of the dance. Hannah had called at Ella's and helped her choose a dress and matching cardigan. As Ella hung up the discarded clothes, the two girls decided that as the evening was dry and warm, no coats were needed.

At the dance, as the young girls sipped their lime juice, they were approached by Joe and Peter Samways. Hannah introduced Ella to the brothers and, like Joe, was quickly aware of the huge impact Ella and Peter had on each other.

CHAPTER FOUR

1938

Life in Downside Alley had remained largely unchanged throughout the centuries, with the daily rhythm of farming life following on from one season to the next. The surnames of the families that inhabited the Alley remained, with just a few exceptions, consistent and predictable. Due to the nature of their existence, the people, although independent, were approachable and neighbourly.

The clusters of pretty cottages, some built of cob walls with thatched roofs, while others were built of brick and flint with slate roofs, were, in spite of being mis-matched, picturesque. Overlooking the green was the ancient church with its Norman font and outside steps leading to the minstrel's gallery, where only fifty years earlier the Downside musicians had played. Further along the Alley stood the blacksmith's shop and village store, which had alongside it a workshop and one lone petrol pump, selling petrol at eleven-and-a-half pence a gallon. All clung tenaciously to the long narrow lane at the foot of this sheltered valley, with the school, pub, vicarage and Downside farm veering off towards the common and completing the northern end of the Downside estate. To an onlooker the verdant scene etched with green pastures and wildflowers offered a sense of well-being, which on the whole was felt by its farm-working community, who had a great acceptance of life and found comfort in abiding things.

Life was easier for the farm labourers than a century before, when the Tolpuddle Martyrs had pleaded for enough money to keep them and their families from utter degradation and starvation; the labourers' wage of thirty shillings a week then was scant enough to keep a family on, and many, as their fathers before them, resorted to other means by which to supplement their income.

From the vantage point of Downside Hill, Archie Samways looked down on the small settlement of Downside Alley. He could see his flint cottage with large garden where the vegetables grew and the chickens ran free. In one corner of his half-acre plot were his stables, one of which housed Jimmy, his donkey, and it was from there that the washing line ran the full length of the garden. He smiled contentedly as he watched the clean sheets and towels flapping and dancing in the westerly breeze.

Rumour was that the Alley had been added to the northern part of the estate around a hundred years before by the then landowner who lived at the manor house, also called Downside. This was after he began receiving letters that were meant for one of his many labourers in the village. And so the secluded village of Downside became known as Downside Alley – a small pocket of England where multiple springs trickled down through the ancient chalk hills, spewing clear crystal water in to the river Down, ensuring its inhabitants had an endless supply of sparkling, fresh water.

The relatively small acreage of the northern part of the estate merged into the larger more southerly area which included the Georgian manor house and ruined abbey, the latter having been built by Cistercian monks in the twelfth century. Although they abandoned it half a century later it is thought the monks left something of their spirit behind, a stillness, which pervaded the whole area and resulted in progressive generations referring to it as the tranquil valley. The whole estate was owned by Squire Harrington, with the southern acres leading down to a pretty sandy bay with rocky cliffs acting as sentinels either side of the bowl-shaped inlet.

Archie was gamekeeper for the estate, and on that particular autumn morning he was plucking some pheasants, a task he had undertaken countless times. Some would be sold to pay for any extras, which this week included new shoes for his wife, Jane. Although he was free to shoot pheasants on Downside soil, the rules of his job forbade poaching on adjoining estates. But when mouths needed feeding and Archie was in need of a beer, it was hard not to trap a rabbit or poach a pheasant. He and Fred, his younger brother, often pursued this wily activity together, and once, when questioned about a glut of rabbits he had, Archie had said, with a twinkle in his eye, it had been difficult to know whether the rabbits were from Downside or the neighbouring estate.

On that particular morning, as he looked around him, he admitted to himself what a lucky man he was. His job with the estate, and being able to keep a few cows, pigs and goats on the nearby common, kept him, his wife and four children in food and all basic necessities. He liked having family around him and, although some of his siblings had moved to other estates for work, he was pleased that Fred had taken on the smallholding at Downside Alley. They had both been born here and had no illusions about life. Working on the land like their forebears was enough fulfilment for them. Archie and Fred had served in the Great War, and after having been through hell in the trenches, were thankful to return to the soil, never mentioning their horrific ordeal to anyone.

Having his own family and some of his extended family living and working on the estate, Archie often mused to himself that Downside Alley was the Samways' ancestral home. His sense of humour and quick retort, inherited from his father, helped him through many a trial and tricky situation. Nothing or no one was going to get the better of him if he had anything to do with it.

As Archie plucked away at the hen pheasant, he suddenly winced and poked his finger in his mouth; the toothache, which had bothered him on and off for some time now, had returned. He vowed to himself that he must see Fred very soon and the two would do each other a good turn by pulling out each other's rotten teeth. Fred had said only recently that one of his back teeth was giving him jip, and so now was the time. They would take a bottle of whatever hard stuff was to hand and go and sit at the top of Downside Hill. After a few drinks they should be able to pull out each other's offending teeth. The only other so-called dentist in Downside Alley was the publican, who would sit the patient by his largest window, ply him with brandy and then, with a crowd of rowdy men watching, pull out the rotten tooth. Archie had succumbed to this type of dentistry once before, but as he had very strong teeth, after sweating hard for an agonising five minutes, the publican had to give up, and had left Archie in more pain than before. That was when Fred came up with the idea for the two of them to cure the problem themselves.

As he stood up, Archie flung the plucked birds into a sack and made his way home via the common, to check on his livestock. As he approached the gorse-filled common he heard a bleating and soon discovered his goat was caught in some of the sweet-smelling bush. After he freed the goat he checked on his few cows and pigs, and was pleased to see that all was well. He bent down to pick up his small stool, which he supposed Joe, his eldest son, must have left there after he had milked the cows that afternoon, something he often did to help Archie out.

Joe worked in the dairy, and Peter, who had worked as a farm labourer on the estate after leaving school at fourteen, was now a carter[6]. As he reflected on how good it was to have his son's help, Archie heard the rustle of feet on the heather behind him and looked up to see Peter. Archie always had high hopes for his younger son, who from an early age was inquisitive and was at his happiest when he was able to make notes and write stories.

Peter had a good brain and had passed for Grammar school, but unfortunately the journey to the nearest school was some distance and the rail fare too expensive. Although Archie was sad about that, he was pleased that Peter was in work, and greeted him with an affectionate slap on the back.

'Ah, Peter.'

'Hello, Dad. I thought you might be here checking the livestock.'

'Well, 'tis good to see you, son. How's the estate's newest carter getting on? Got used to all that walking yet?'

Peter sat down on the heather and rubbed his ankles. 'Eleven miles a day, six days a week, takes some getting used to. But I'm getting there!'

Archie sat down next to him. 'Well, it takes time, an' you've only been there a week. How do you, er, get on with the other carters? Treat you alright do they?'

'Oh, fine. Teased me a bit the first day when I made a mess of the horses' harness. But no, they're a good bunch really.'

'Most 'ave been doing the job for years. So they'll teach you right, son.'

'I'm amazed at their intuition of the horses' needs. The first morning we were up in Bull's Patch and had been working for some time when I noticed one of the horses getting restless. Carter Bill let the horse finish his line of ploughing, then he whistled, and blow me if the horse didn't start weeing!'

'Ah, 'tis a close bond between man and horse.'

'Sure is. I'm getting to know my two horses quite well now.'

Archie grinned. 'Something else for your notebook, eh?'

'I was just thinking about that when the carter from the Woodleigh estate gave a message to Bill, our carter, for Dan Bowditch this morning. Covering the ground as we do we often meet workers from adjoining estates and become sort of verbal postmen; saves the cost of a stamp, I guess.'

Archie, whose legs were now beginning to stiffen, stood up and arched his back. 'Ah, an' 'tis quicker. Funny you should mention Dan Bowditch. I 'ad a visit from 'im this mornin'. In a bit of a state he were.'

Peter looked concerned. 'Why? What's happened?'

'Well 'tis to do wi' our Joe. But I'd best tell yer mother first.' Archie paused, then said, 'I'm pleased that you're not finding the job too hard, son.'

'Well, after just a few days in the job, watching the sun rise over Eighteen Acre Field towards Downside Cove, even though my limbs were aching, I understood what you meant about life in Downside Alley being heaven and hard work. And, yes, it's good.'

The common was a great asset to the villagers of Downside Alley. They could all graze livestock there for free and, as well as being able to take the furze to light their fires, they could bury their rubbish there.

Archie's two cows, Spot and Daisy, gave them a good supply of milk and they were good natured animals. He usually milked them at five o'clock before going to work, and that morning had been no different. The only exception was that he had had an unexpected encounter with one of his neighbours, and he couldn't wait to tell Jane about it.

Before going inside, Archie washed his hands under the freshwater spring, which gushed out from the mossy bank. As he rubbed his hands round the carbolic soap, which stayed permanently on the grass, he heard the cottage door open and looked to see his twin daughters, Violet and Florrie, coming towards him.

'Ah, there you are my maids. And where be you going on this chilly day?'

'We're off to Ruth Joyce's party, Dad,' replied Florrie, the more prosaic of the twins.

'Yea, but Mum wouldn't let us go until we'd eaten all our dinner,' Violet added, disconsolately.

Jane stepped through the door, smiling. 'Well, I can't have Mrs Joyce saying that those Samways girls just come for a good feed, can I?'

Archie's eyes sparkled. 'No, my dear. That will never do.' He turned to his daughters. 'Well, off you go then... and have a good time.' The two sisters waved and were soon in the lane heading for the Joyce household.

Archie joined his wife inside the cottage and straight away tucked into the rabbit stew, which Jane had prepared that morning. The rabbit had been cleanly shot a few days before, and the stew, which also consisted of vegetables from the garden, would provide the family meal for a few days. As Archie enjoyed his dinner, Jane read a letter, which she had received from her sister, who lived in London.

'Listen to this, Arch. Our Lily says that Jack, her eldest, works for the BBC and is involved in making a radio programme about life in the country and country folk.'

Archie put down his fork and wiped his moustache.

'What do they script writers know about life in the country?'

'Well, Lily says they do research.'

'Research, my ass. They needs to get down here to Downside Alley. Then they'd know what country life was all about.' He fished round his plate for the last piece of rabbit. He stabbed it with his fork, and waved it in the air before gleefully gobbling it up. 'One whiff of cow dung and they'd be off, I reckon. Bloomin' foreigners ain't got a clue what country life be really like!'

Jane has seen her husband flare up many times and knew it would quickly pass. She poured him a cup of tea and pushed it towards him.

'Here, Arch, have a cup of tea and tell me what's on your mind.'

Archie scratched his head. 'Well, now you come to mention it, something has happened. But nothing we can't get over, my dear.' A few soothing words and a cup of tea had calmed her husband down as Jane knew it would. Archie was soon laughing as he recalled his early morning meeting. 'I'd just finished milking Daisy this morning when I looked up to see Dan Bowditch striding towards me with a face as black as thunder.'

'Dan Bowditch? The carpenter and wheelwright? What's he gotta be angry with you for? You paid him for your uncle's coffin, didn't you?'

'Yes, my dear. 'Tis nothing like that.' Archie smiled in remembrance of the encounter.

'Don't keep me in suspense then, Arch.'

'Well, he squares up to me like he wants a fight. Then changing his mind says, "Your son, Joe, 'ave got my daughter into trouble".'

'What! Our Joe?... Well, what did you say?'

'I scratched me 'ead and told him that our Joe is an awkward young devil. And that he broke my spade last week.'

Jane giggled. 'That must have been a red rag, Arch.'

'Ha, ha. I know. I thought he was gonna explode. Well, then he repeats the accusation and asked what I had to say about it. So I says, "I knows what to charge for the bull, and I knows what to charge for the boar, but I don't know what to say for the boy!"'

'Oh, Archie! You do know how to wind folk up.' Jane was thoughtful for a few seconds. 'So our Joe is going to be a father, eh? Ah well, 'tis only natural after all.'

Archie smiled in admiration at his wife, who after twenty years of marriage and four children was as pretty as ever.

'I thought that's what you'd say, my dear. You're an amazing woman, no doubt about that.' Jane blushed, which reminded Archie why he fell in love with her all those years ago. The reality of the situation suddenly dawned on Archie. 'Another generation, eh!'

'Umm, I know, my dear. So how did you leave it with Dan?'

'I told him to climb down and that we'd sort something out. And fortunately, he did. Looked a bit sheepish actually. I, er, invited him and his wife and daughter to come over for tea on Sunday.' Archie looked at his wife. 'I hope thass alright, my dear?'

'Of course 'tis. We must get our thinking caps on now as to what's to be done.'

'I've already been thinking about that. I must make some enquiries about a house for them. Then we'll talk about it on Sunday. But first thing to do is plant an extra line of spuds!'

Jane laughed. 'Thass your answer to everything.'

'Well, if you've got a spud, you've got a meal!'

'Thass what I love about you, Arch, you never worry.'

'No good to, my dear. There's always an answer. Our Joe will be alright. You'll see.'

When Joe learnt from Mary that he was to become a father, he realised that Peter's advice to him was salutary, and vowed to do his best for Mary and the baby, putting the momentary ardour with Hannah behind him.

Ella's mind was in a whirl of happiness. She had to pinch herself to know that it was real. She had met and fallen deeply in love with Peter Samways, a local carter. In her excitement and euphoria she had picked up her battered teddy bear and twirled round the room with him. A few minutes later, a knock was heard at the door; it was Hannah, her face beaming with happiness. She hugged Ella tightly.

'I'm so pleased for you. Pete is a lovely guy. He really is. When are you seeing him again?'

'As soon as we can... hopefully tomorrow... I do hope so. I miss him already!'

Hannah laughed. 'Golly, you've got it bad, El. Does it hurt that much? I've never been in love.'

Ella's eyes sparkled brightly. 'It's a wonderful feeling. I want to feel like this forever and ever. And no, it doesn't hurt.' She sighed. 'But there is a huge ache now he's not here.'

'Well, I'd better not stay too long now. Mother will be looking for me. Just wanted to see that you were safely home. Someone's got to look after you, you know.' Hannah grinned at her love-struck friend.

'Thanks, Hannah. I'm fine. Just still flying high at the moment.'

'Well, I'll see you in the morning when you've come down to earth. No doubt the school children will bring you down with a bump.'

'Oh, they'll be fine. Everything is fine now. Thank goodness you suggested going tonight.'

'Meant to be, see, El. Meant to be.'

Ella sat back on her bed as Hannah made for the door. 'Yes. I was meant to come to Downside Alley that's for sure. Night, night. See you tomorrow.'

'Yep. Sleep well… if you can!'

Ella slept very well, deeply and long, and was awoken by a sharp rap on the door. It was Mrs Butt telling her it was quarter to eight in the morning. She quickly dressed and went down for breakfast. Her father, who had finished his breakfast and had his head stuck in *The Times* newspaper, looked up as she came in the room.

'You're late this morning my dear. Everything alright?'

'Oh yes. Everything is just fine, Father. I must have been overtired.'

'Mrs Butt said you and Hannah went to the

harvest dance last night. Was it good?'

'Yes, very good. The band was excellent.'

'I'm pleased to hear that.' He looked at her over his half-rimmed glasses. 'I, er, hope you didn't fraternise with the local lads though. Remember my advice?'

'I remember, Father.' Ella started to boil up inside. Surely she was entitled to her life? She was not irresponsible. 'Hannah and I did dance with some local lads as it happens, two brothers actually. Peter and Joe Samways. They were both very respectful, and I'm meeting Peter again.'

Godfrey's face darkened. This was what he had feared.

'I don't care if they were respectful or not. They are farm workers, no doubt, and far below your expectations. I ask you please not to see Peter or any of the other local lads again. Do you hear me?'

'Perfectly well, Father. No need to raise your voice. Now if you'll excuse me, I have to get ready for work.'

Godfrey watched his daughter leave the room, then clenched his fist in exasperation. 'Confound it. She'll get over it. She'll just have to.'

Peter had not been back from the stables very long that afternoon when, to his surprise and delight, Ella turned up at his parent's cottage door. He took her through to the sitting room, which was reserved for special occasions only, and, as soon as the door was closed, embraced her.

As the two cuddled, Peter realised that Ella was not her bubbly self and relinquished his hold on her. 'Is everything alright, my darling?'

At this Ella began to cry and in between sobs told him that her father had banned her from seeing him. As Peter held her gently, he stroked her hair and reassured her that everything would be alright.

'How can it be?' Ella blurted. 'He won't give up. I know him too well. He likes to get his own way. This is so horrid.'

'Don't upset yourself, my angel. We've already said nothing will keep us apart, and that includes your father.' He gently lifted her face up towards his. 'Now, let me see that beautiful smile.'

Ella's face lit up. 'It's always alright when I'm with you, darling Peter.'

'And it always will be. Let me think about this. If I can get a better job, your father may look more kindly on me. He only wants the best for you. And I fully understand that. Now, no more tears, eh?'

True to his word, Archie wasted no time, and

the next day he made enquiries about a house for Joe and Mary. The ideal opportunity arose after the local mid-week shoot when Archie and the beaters joined the farmer, squire and other gunmen for some lunch. Cyril Cooper, the local farmer, was on the whole a genial man, who always listened to any concerns the farm workers might have, but he was also a businessman and therefore could not always bend to their needs.

But the matter Archie spoke to him about that misty, damp day did not concern money, rather property. Cyril listened to Archie's concern and the need for a house for Joe and Mary. Then, as he swigged down the last drop of beer, he turned to his gamekeeper and told him that he would leave some keys to the empty estate cottages in the farmhouse for Joe to collect the next day. This was the answer Archie had hoped for. He shook Cyril's hand and thanked him profusely. Cyril nodded happily, and added that as Joe worked for him it was no problem and he hoped the young couple would find something suitable.

Jane had been busy all morning in the kitchen. She had baked three white loaves, an apple cake, which she filled with the delicious Blenheim Orange apples from the orchard, some scones, topped with cream made from their own cow's milk, and a sponge cake filled to bursting with her homemade strawberry jam. Jane liked to cook but, as money was tight, did not often entertain on such a scale. But this was a special occasion, and as she straightened the table cloth out, she had to admit it all looked very appetising.

Dan and Agnes Bowditch arrived with their daughter Mary at four o'clock, as arranged. All three were dressed in their drab Sunday best, which seemed to match their rather sober faces.

Peter knew that his parents wanted to talk to the Bowditch family in private, and so had changed his plans for Ella to come to the house, and arranged instead to meet her at the nearby stile. As he turned into the lane, he could see Ella sat on the step by the fence and his heart leapt with happiness. Soon they were in a locked embrace, oblivious to the world.

Fortunately, as Godfrey was away for a day's golf, Peter and Ella had the freedom to walk around the countryside in Downside Alley, and after they crossed the River Down, they wandered into Shaberries Field where the sheep grazed. As they held hands, they laughed at the shepherd, who had recently lost his sheep dog and now rounded up his flock on his bicycle, panting like a dog himself.

'Just look at that, darling,' Peter said. 'It's resourcefulness like that, which made me want to write about the lives of the farm labourers, their wisdom and sense of nonsense, before it slips into obscurity.'

Ella put her arm around his waist. 'I didn't know you were writing a book, my love!'

Peter grinned modestly. 'Well, it's not a book, just some notes I've been making about life as it is today in Downside Alley, which I believe with the coming of the tractor, and other insidious changes, is gradually being eroded away.'

'Well done for you. I was just thinking that the countryside here with the men working away at their skilled labour was just the sort of place Virginia Woolf was talking about in her tribute to Thomas Hardy.'

'Oh, what did she say?'

'That the peasants were the last sanctuary of sanity, the country the last stronghold of happiness. When they disappear, there is no hope for the human race.'

'Whew! That's profound.'

'I know.' Ella kissed Peter. 'So keep writing your notes.'

'I will. Talking of which, shall we go and write our names on one of the ancient oaks in Downside woods?'

Ella's eyes sparkled as she cried, 'I'd love to! Do you have a knife?'

Peter smiled as he took out a small knife from his pocket. 'Oh, yes. Always have a knife, some string and a sixpence in your pocket, Granddad used to say. That way you can cut, tie and buy.'

'More of the wisdom you were talking about, eh?'

By now they are entering the woods and Peter held back a fallen branch so that they could get through the gap easier.

'Umm. As Granddad used to say, we scratch for our own worms. Self–sufficient, you see.' Peter looked around at the profusion of oak trees. 'Now, which one has the most pliant bark do you think?'

Ella skipped from one tree to the other, ecstatic to have such freedom with Peter. Finally, she ran her hand over a particular tree, and said, 'This one is perfect, my love.'

And so the two of them carefully carved their names on the side of the oak tree, which Peter then framed with a heart. After a brief kiss, Ella ran deeper into the woods, laughing as she called for Peter to find her. After some chasing, Peter managed to find the elusive Ella, who had hidden behind some holly bushes. As he grasped her firmly, he straddled his legs either side of her nubile body; both were breathing heavily as they kissed passionately and immersed themselves in their euphoric wonderland.

CHAPTER FIVE

1938

Jane answered the door with a bright smile and ushered the Bowditch family into the cottage parlour where she introduced them to her parents-in-law, Alice and Tom Samways, who lived with them.

For years Tom had been the head carter on the Sandham estate, but when he was badly kicked by one of the horses and unable to work any longer, he and his wife had to leave their cottage. Archie had asked Farmer Cooper about a cottage for them on the Downside estate, but any that were free at that time were kept for the workers. A very few were rented out, but with just a small pension the elderly couple could not afford the rent. Determined not to see them go to the workhouse, a place everyone dreaded, not least because the men and women were split up and sent to different wings, Archie looked about his few outbuildings and wondered if the disused stable adjoining the cottage could be converted. After speaking to Farmer Cooper about this idea, he was told that he had no objections to the proposal as long as Archie paid for the work himself. So, Archie, Joe and Peter set to and made the flint building habitable. A connecting door to the house was already in place, probably from when it was a coaching inn, which made it easy for Alice and Tom to enter Archie and Jane's cottage without having to go outside. The men worked hard on the conversion and it was soon a bright, comfortable dwelling for the elderly couple, who were thankful to be near their family.

Before long the tea was poured out and the two families were sat around the table. Florrie and Violet had been instructed to offer the food around, which they were rather nervous about. Then with a wink and half nod from her mother, Florrie handed the plate of bread and butter to Dan. Mary, who had been silent until then, spoke up.

'Father will 'ave some cake. We've plenty of bread and butter at home.'

Jane shot a quick glance at Archie, hoping he would not react to this, but he didn't. He was waiting to launch into the matter in hand when it seemed appropriate. By her last remark, Jane realised that Mary was not afraid to speak up and reasoned that perhaps that was a good thing. The food quickly disappeared and Jane thought it time to send the girls out so that the discussions could begin.

Finishing his second piece of apple cake,

Archie wiped the crumbs off his moustache and led the conversation.

'Well now, Joe and Mary, do tell us how you got on yesterday when you picked the keys up. I tried to get Joe to tell me before, but he said I must wait until everyone could hear.' Archie gave a mischievous grin. 'Young monkey!'

The young couple glanced at each other, smiling broadly.

'Mary and I were just amazed, Dad. There were four sets of keys.'

'Four?'

'Yes. And so we spent half a day looking at the different cottages.'

Jane turned and smiled kindly at them both. 'And have you chosen one?'

Joe had taken Mary's hand and squeezed it. 'We have. Mary will tell you the reason why we chose as we did.'

'Rose Cottage was lovely and had a nice garden, but it smelt very damp. So... no good for baby.' Mary blushed at mentioning baby and looked at Joe, who continued explaining.

'That's right. Then we looked at Grey's House. Although we liked it very much, it's a bit far from the dairy really. And what's more, it's huge!'

This inspired Granddad Tom to speak up. 'Hah. A big house never kept anyone.'

'Quite right, Granddad,' Joe said, 'and thinking about what we need every week, well,

I'm not sure how I'd manage.' He quickly turned to Mary. 'How we'll manage, I mean.'

Archie piped up. 'Well, my son, you'll have to do the same as I have done. Learn to live a life without money. We're lucky here in Downside Alley.' Archie winked at his son. 'Everything is provided as long as we use our heads.'

'Tell us about the other two cottages then, Mary,' Jane said, and smiled at the young girl. 'I'm longing to know where you're going to live.'

'Well, Mrs Samways, we really like both the other two. One is Seymour Cottage, which has a beautiful, distant view of the sea from most windows.'

'Oh, that'll be where old Sam Vickers lived; he fished from these shores all his life,' Tom said, knowingly.

'That's right, Granddad. And the other one...' Joe looked at Mary. 'Shall I tell them?'

Mary nodded, a wide smile brightening her face. 'Yes, go on, tell them where we're gonna live!'

'Not too far from here, which is brilliant, because we'll be close to both grandparents.' Joe then looked at his own grandparents. 'And great grandparents! We've chosen Honeysuckle Cottage. It's near the dairy and has three bedrooms, so plenty big enough. And it's three shillings a week, which is cheaper than some.'

Mary felt excited just hearing Joe talk about it. 'Yes, and it's lovely and light. Not all of them are.'

Everyone in the room was relieved and congratulations were echoed all round. Jane got up from the table. She was feeling very happy for the young couple. Everyone needs a good start, she thought. 'Can I get anyone another cup of tea?'

'Tea!' Archie retorted. 'Some home brew would be more like it.'

The men all opted for the beer while the ladies stuck with the tea. Draining his glass before putting it down, Archie asked, 'Well, now that the house is sorted, when's the wedding gonna take place?' He turned to Joe. 'I take it you've asked the young lady?' Then he looked at Dan. 'And her father, of course?'

Joe looked slightly flustered. 'Of course I have, and I'm very happy to say both said, yes.' With that the front door clicked and Peter and Ella entered the passageway. 'And I've also asked Peter to be my best man.'

Peter and Ella walked through the parlour door, their faces glowing with happiness.

'Did someone mention my name?' Peter asked.

Archie smiled at the young couple. 'Ah, come on in you two. Joe's just told us that you're gonna be his best man!'

Peter, whose appetite had been sharpened by the euphoric time spent with Ella, helped himself to two scones. 'Sorry, just feeling famished and can't resist mum's scones. Uh, best man? That's right, I am. But the question is when?'

Joe looked round at the family. 'Well, if it's alright with everyone else, we thought Christmas Eve would be good. It's six weeks away yet, so plenty of time to get things arranged. And almost everyone is off the next day, if there should be any sore heads! I'll need to get cover at the dairy, but I'm sure if I work extra hours for one of the others it should be alright. What do you think?'

Everyone agreed it would be a good day to tie the knot. Joe said he would speak to the vicar and see if he would be able to fit the ceremony in with the festive schedule. The cottage needed painting but Mary was willing to do that, and Peter and Ella said they would lend a hand, too.

Before long Florrie and Violet came back in and were told the good news of the wedding. The revelation of the baby would come later. When Mary asked Florrie and Violet if they would like to be bridesmaids, Archie started to scratch his head. This wedding job was going to cost more than he first thought. How could he earn an extra shilling or two? Jane, who could read him like a book, picked up on his concerns and told him she would make the girls' dresses and would ask Hannah Butt, who had become very good friends with Ella, and was known to be good with needle and cotton, if she would make Mary's outfit, if

Mary approved of course. She added that Alice already had a nice dress from when her niece had married two years before, as did she.

Florrie and Violet who were now fourteen were thrilled and ran upstairs talking excitedly about the wedding. Joe, who had just about got used to the idea of being a husband and father, thought Tom had been rather quiet and so turned his attention to him.

'You'll come to the wedding, won't you Granddad?'

'No, my son. I'm very pleased for you and young Mary. But I won't come.'

Jane looked at her father-in-law. 'Of course you're coming, Dad. Won't be the same without you.'

'No. Sorry, Jane, but I won't be going, my dear.'

Peter couldn't believe his ears. 'Come on, Granddad. You can't let Gran go on her own! Besides which, you'll enjoy it!'

Tom began to get anxious. 'No. No. I won't go, and that's it.'

'It's alright, Dad,' Jane said reassuringly. 'Don't upset yourself. But do tell us why?'

'Well, your gran will tell you I've never liked weddings or any large gatherings of people. And I'll tell you for why, 'tis quite simple really.' To emphasis his words, Tom modulated his voice and continued, 'People come to your wedding, eat all your food and drink all your beer. They talk about you all your life, and when you die they say what a nice bastard he was!'

Everyone was stunned by Tom's outburst. Archie laughed and said, 'Well, there's not a lot you can say to that, Dad. And I don't doubt your wisdom. But, well, we shall miss you.'

Mary smiled reassuringly at Tom. 'We will. But you know, Mr Samways, we're not having many to the wedding, just family and a few friends really. So if you change your mind... well, we'd really like you to come.'

Ella touched Tom's shoulder. 'But if you don't go, Mr Samways, I'll be here to keep you company.' She looked at Peter with a brave smile, then continued. 'Due to my father's vehement opposition to my relationship with Peter, I can't really be seen in public with him. So we can toast the happy couple here with a glass of something.'

Tom was touched by Mary and Ella's words and said he would think about it.

In the end Tom was persuaded to go to his grandson's wedding and Alice had his suit cleaned, the one he had worn to his own wedding. Then two weeks before the ceremony, after coming home after an evening in the pub, he sat in the chair and said that he felt unwell. After going very red in the face, he passed away peacefully – the same way his father and grandfather had done before him. The whole family was in a great state of shock. This had been so unexpected.

Alice was brave and thankful that she had Archie and Jane to live with as she felt very vulnerable. Almost the whole village attended Tom's funeral, which was a great comfort to his family. His eulogy, which was both poignant and humorous, paid fine tribute to him, a man of the soil, to his loyalty, kindness and integrity. It also included his penchant for a pint of beer and that he would often frequent pubs in nearby villages for a change of scene and beer, which regularly resulted in the family not knowing his exact whereabouts.

One villager who had been away at the time of Tom's death returned to see the family dressed up outside the church. Having previously heard of the forthcoming wedding, he assumed it was happening that day. Being polite he asked Archie if it was the day of Joe's wedding.

'No,' said Archie, 'we've come to bury the old man.' Even on such a day as this, Archie's humour did not fail him as he added, 'One thing, we shall know where to find him now!'

And so the vicar who led the funeral one week, led Joe and Mary's wedding service the next. The wedding arrangements had fallen into place quite easily, and Hilda Butt said she would be very happy to play the organ. Hannah bravely put aside her feelings for Joe, and said she was happy to make Mary's wedding suit, and was happy to help Ella and Mary paint the cottage, too. Jane said that when she went to town to buy some material for the bridesmaid dresses she would read the adverts in the confectioner's window to see if there was any second-hand furniture for sale.

After the family gathering on that Sunday afternoon, when Joe and Mary had told the family which cottage they were going to live in, Archie had gone to the pub. He went every Sunday to pay into the Slate Club, which was to help any of the farm labourers who fell ill. Farmer Cooper, and all farmers in fact, did not pay any wage at all when someone was sick. Thankfully, Archie had never had to use it, but his brother Fred did a year or so ago when he had the flu very badly and could not get out of bed. The club could only pay a few shillings, a third of the normal wage, but it kept the wolf from the door. Of course, with Fred, Archie and Jane were on hand to help and had sent food round to his family and paid a bit towards his rent. This was the same with all the folk in Downside Alley; they helped each other out, so that, if humanely possible, no one ever went without.

Archie was very pleased to see Joe in the public bar, which was filled exclusively with men, the atmosphere being thick with smoke from their pipes and cigarettes. He quickly ordered a pint for them both, and exchanged banter with a few of the local characters while he waited. Joe knew his father's Sunday night routine and had hoped to catch him there for a chat. Although he was now over Hannah, and very much looking forward to becoming a father, Joe was still concerned about certain matters. Archie could see that his son had something on his mind and encouraged him to open up. 'Now then, Joe, what's on your mind?'

'Nothing really.' Archie gave him a questioning look.

'Well, yes, there is something. I know we spoke about money before and you said I would have to do as you have done and live a life without money. But, Dad, how is that possible in reality?'

'It's possible because it has to be. Now, you get your wage, which is adequate for your basic needs. And for any extras, well, you must do as I have done and live off your wits.'

'Poaching, you mean? That's not right, Father.'

Archie lowered his voice. 'Keep your voice down, son. It may not be right, but without it life would be pretty grim. And besides, it's not the only way to supplement your income. I was just thinking to meself t'other day that if you needed extra money when Mary finishes her school job, as your cottage is near the roadside, perhaps she could sell her homemade cakes and jam outside your cottage. Lots of folk come through Downside Alley now on their way to the Cove. She could earn a good few bob, I reckon. Anyway, what sort of thing are you wishing to buy?'

'Well, Mary is asking for so many things for the house, and... and everything costs so much!'

'Ah. It always did, Joe, always did.'

'When I think of what everything costs, and all the things we need for the house, well, it seems to me that... you have to be rich to be poor today!'

Archie scratched his head. 'Thass pretty deep, my son, and very true. Look, my advice to you is not to worry too much about money. All our wedded life your mother and I have had no money worries because we had no money! See, it's simple. When the need arises, the money will come. Just keep your faith. I mean, look how the house came?'

Joe nodded. 'I guess you're right, Dad. Just wish I had your faith though.'

'Well, I don't go to church very often as you know. But I thinks to meself, any darn fool knows there's a God. I'm not very good with words, son, but I do know that keeping faith in him, well 'tis the only way.'

'Thanks for your advice, Dad.'

'I, er, I don't really believe in giving advice. But if it helps, well then I'm glad.'

'I understand what you're saying, Dad. Thanks a lot.'

'No trouble, son. Anything else on your mind? What with the wedding and all that?'

Joe looked a bit sheepish. 'I, er, thought I knew all about women, and I do love Mary, but I'm just not sure what love is... really. And how do you keep a woman happy?'

Archie had not expected this. 'Thass a big question, Joe. I know you're gonna be a father before long, so you obviously know the joy of a woman's love, but that's not everything. To have a good marriage, what you need to do is keep your missus happy. And I believe this can be achieved in many ways, but one I find works for me is to warm her side of the bed up afore she gets in. She'll appreciate that, and, er...,' Archie grinned widely, 'no doubt she'll show you, my son.'

'That's a good tip, Father.' Joe laughed as he swilled back the last of his beer. 'So love is never having to get into cold sheets?'

'Well, 'tis a good start.'

Feeling relaxed, Joe ordered another pint for them both. 'We've got a lot to celebrate, Dad.'

Archie lifted his pint in agreement. 'Cheers. May this be the worst of our days!'

'I'll drink to that. And, er, thanks again for your help.'

As the two enjoyed their pint, a neighbour, Frank Roper, came to the bar and ordered up a Gold Top. Archie couldn't resist asking Frank why he didn't drink the draught beer.

'Well, Archie, the Gold Top 'ave got a kick in it that the draught beer seems to lack nowadays. Mind you, 'tis a bit dangerous.'

'Dangerous! How can beer be dangerous, Frank?'

'After a few it makes you see double and think you're single!' Joe and Archie laughed at the old chap, who was a comical creature at the best of times. After downing his first Gold Top, Frank took out a photo of a smartly dressed man with a gun in one hand and a coat over the other arm. By his side was a Spaniel. He flashed the photo in front of Archie and Joe.

'Whose that then, Frank,' Archie asked.

'Huh. That's the man who spent all me money.'

Archie turned the photo over and read – *Frank off to the shoot, 1909.* As Archie and Joe laughed at Frank's wry humour, Frank lifted his glass of beer.

'Wish I'd drunk more when it was cheaper!'

'Don't we all, Frank? Don't we all?' Looking down at his fast growing belly, Archie declared, "tis not the cost, 'tis the upkeep!'

All three laughed at the nonsense. Joe looked at the pub clock and downed his beer. 'See you then, Frank.'

Frank lifted up his glass to them both. Archie patted his neighbour on the back and then followed Joe out of the bar. Once outside, Joe told his father that he was off to see Mary and that he would see him later.

As Archie strolled home from the pub that evening, the full moon lit the whole of Downside and he could see for miles. No good for poaching tonight, he mused. As he approached the top end of Downside Alley he could hear the strains of a tuneless song, something he had heard many times before, and recognised its source instantly. The Hicks family, two sisters Miriam and Marnie, and their brother Wilf, lived at number twenty one. The brother was the breadwinner and worked as a hedger and ditcher on the estate and filled in with any odd jobs that needed doing. His sisters, who kept house, were both eccentric, dressing and acting in most unconventional ways. They had lived on the estate for years, their father, now deceased, had been the estate manager for four decades. The sisters did not mix in with the village and rarely showed their faces, but when it was a full moon they both sat on their doorstep, one with an accordion hung over her shoulder, and sang. Their song was dull and repetitive with nonsensical words.

That particular evening Archie paused to see if he could make any sense of their musical entertainment. As they straightened themselves up and smiled confidently at each other, the two ladies began the song once again:

Why does the baby elephant always wear his tail on the front?

And why does the hippopotamus never lay an egg like an ostrich?

Then the accordion player gave a rendering of her own before the song was repeated once more. Archie smiled to himself. Poor souls; like most of the people in Downside Alley, they were harmless.

With it being so light, Archie decided to take a detour via the common. All the animals were settled for the night and all was still. During the summer evenings the place was alive with bird song and the sound of children's voices as they played freely amid the heather. Tonight all he could hear was the call of two owls sending messages to each other. He felt pleased that the Sunday tea had gone well and that Joe and Mary were going to live near them. The herd instinct was strong in his family, something that he valued very much. He had never tired of hearing, and subsequently retelling, the story his grandfather had told him of how the Samways came to live in Downside Alley. They had previously lived on a small farm further along the coast at a place called Hadworth, which was tenanted to the Cooper family. When the latter was offered a much larger farm, one thousand acres in fact, at Downside, they decided to take up the challenge and in 1885, the Samways family moved with them.

The farm and estate belonged to the Harrington family and due to the farm's moribund state the Coopers were able to lease it free for the first year, giving them a chance to get on their feet. Because the land had been fallow for some time, it yielded a most wonderful crop of barleycorn, and the farmer gave strict instructions to his workers to scythe the crop by hand so as not to waste an ear. The gamble paid off and it was the good harvest that put them on their feet. Archie had heard his father say that loyalty was the last core and was proud that his family had been loyal to the farmer for all those years, and of course he in his own way had been loyal to them.

And so as he turned to make his way home, Archie reflected with pride that with another generation on the way, the Samways family chain continued to grow.

CHAPTER SIX

There had been a hard frost the night before Joe and Mary's wedding on Christmas Eve 1938, but the low winter sun had gradually melted most of it away, and the icicles, which had earlier clung tenaciously to the thatched roofs, thawed by the time of the afternoon service.

Jane, Alice and the twins had been hard at work making cakes, sandwiches and jellies for the previous two days and Alice had made the two-tier wedding cake a month before, continually adding more brandy when it was available. It was a real village wedding and a very happy occasion for all the family.

It was thought for a while that the wedding may have to be delayed due to the carpenter having to make some pheasant cages before replacing rotten floorboards and windows in Joe and Mary's cottage. When the estate workers were discussing the matter in the workshop, one of the older workers, being well used to the order of priorities on the estate, commented to Joe, "'tis pheasants before peasants here.' However, as Dan Bowditch was the carpenter and the cottage was for his daughter, he worked extra hours so that the wedding could take place on time. No one, especially Dan, wanted the date put back. Mary was beginning to show, and that would never do.

Any reservations Archie and Jane may have had about their new daughter-in-law being a good wife were quickly dispelled. Mary was always up early. She kept the house spotless and cooked wholesome food for her husband and any family member who happened to call by at meal times. Having qualified as a school teacher, Mary taught the infants in the Church of England school in Downside Alley, but her conditions of service dictated that she had to resign on marriage. So, when the school broke up for Christmas, Mary had to leave her job. Taking her husband's advice to earn some extra money, the following Easter, when Farmer Cooper opened up his camping field once more and visitors were heading for the Cove, Mary began baking cakes and making jam to sell to pay for the extras she needed for the baby. But as the weeks went by and Mary became increasingly tired, Joe tried to persuade her to stop the baking. Still being anxious about money, she resisted until Joe had some good news about his job. Francis Cox, the head dairyman, was retiring, giving Joe the ideal opportunity to take over and earn more money.

'Now that I have the opportunity to rent the cows off the farmer and take all the profits myself, we'll be in clover, my darling.'

'Well, you work very hard, Joe. Whatever

money you earn, my love, you deserve it.' She patted her over-large tummy. 'Me and the little one here are so fortunate to have you, Joe. I love you more each day.'

Joe towered over his petite wife; then, framing her face with his hands, kissed her. 'I love you too, Mary.'

While Joe had been adjusting to married life, Peter had applied to join the RAF, and by January 1939 had been accepted. He was soon on his training. When Peter came home on leave, unless Ella's father was out of the village, they usually met at Mrs Butt's house, with Hannah being their alibi. Because the meetings were clandestine assignations they were all the more romantic. And although their time together was both passionate and heady, somehow they stopped at making love as both wanted to wait until their wedding day. As time went on and the Second World War was upon them, planning their wedding day kept them focused on the future, a future without war and hostility.

One particular morning, having finished breakfast an hour earlier, Godfrey came back into the dining room to collect some notes. There he found Ella reading a letter from Peter. Before she had time to conceal it, her father spoke.

'From the Samways lad, I guess. Well, I'm

glad he joined up, it will do him good. But he's not the one for you, my dear. He'll always be a country bumpkin, it's in his genes.'

Ella was furious. 'How can you judge him without even meeting him? He is a very kind, intelligent man. Only you won't even give him a chance, will you?'

Godfrey tried to assuage his daughter. 'Look, my dear. I'm not saying anything about him other than he is not the man for you. Which reminds me, we have had another invitation from the Harrington family. I do hope you will accept this time.'

'I have no intention of accepting. I don't even like Charles Harrington.'

'But you hardly know him, Ella. He is such a catch for you, my dear. One day soon he will take over the whole of the Downside estate. You'd be a fool to turn away the opportunity of getting to know him better. And besides, he likes you.'

'Father, love has nothing to do with what you own.'

'Love! That's all you young girls think about. You need to wake up, my dear Ella.'

'I promised mother that I would not quarrel with you. But if you persist in this hideous conversation... well, how can I not?' Ella stormed out of the room.

'Silly girl. She'll change her mind yet.'

When they met that evening, Ella told Hannah about the quarrel with her father. And it was then that Hannah suggested to Ella that she should at least consider going to the Harrington's party.

The two girls were so thankful to have each other to share their burdens and happiness with, and although Hannah had accepted the fact that Joe was a married man, whenever she met him her heart leapt; even though she had vowed not to come between him and Mary, she told herself that she couldn't help her feelings.

Ella resolved to pair her friend up with one of Peter's distant cousins. After discussing it with him on his next leave it was decided to arrange a blind date with William. Hannah had known Will all her life, but because he was younger than her she had only ever thought of him as a village lad. In 1939, aged sixteen, he was too young to serve in the war, and had been put in charge of the dairy when Joe and the other dairymen enlisted. He was a good-looking, open-faced, young man with large, heavy-lidded brown eyes and a happy, caring nature. Although Hannah was hesitant at first, she soon realised that he was fully mature, and very attractive. She mused how odd it was that you can know someone for years and never think of them in a romantic way, until you have that close intimate time with them, and then it's like you are meeting them for the first time.

It had to be said that Will was really chuffed that Hannah obviously liked him. He had not had a girlfriend before and was rather shy as to how to approach the whole love thing. Joe and Peter offered him some useful tips and before long he was only happy when he had his arm around Hannah and was looking lovingly into her eyes. Inevitably, though, before too many months had passed, Will received his call-up papers for the Army. Before too long, he was sent to the Far East.

Hannah longed for Will's letters as did Ella for Peter's and the two would swoon over them together in the privacy of Hannah's bedroom.

Through her savings, Mary had been able to buy a decent cot and some bedding. Jane and Alice had been knitting cardigans and jumpers in white and lemon wool. And Mary's mum, not being a knitter, had made a beautiful quilt for the new arrival's cot. The small bedroom was decorated in white distemper and, besides holding the wooden cot, had some tall drawers in which nappies and clothes were stored. These had been brought second-hand from one of Joe's cousins.

As Mary surveyed the finished room on this particular sunny day in June, she felt proud and happy at what she and Joe had achieved. Turning to descend the stairs, she felt her first twinge of labour pains. Calmly and slowly she made her way to her parents' cottage, where her mother made her a cup of tea.

'It'll be a while yet, dear. But while you're resting here I will go and ask your father to fetch the district nurse. I won't be long.'

'Thanks, Mum. I'm just fine.'

Fortunately, Dan's workshop was at the bottom of the garden, having in previous years been a stable for the oxen. He was busy making the coffin for one of the older estate workers, Dave Mowlam. He had been a farm labourer on the estate all his life and had died in the cottage in Downside Alley where he had been born eighty-seven years earlier. Dave had been a sad-looking man, who had a dry sense of humour and, it could be said, a realistic outlook on life. Since the passing of Granfer Higgins in 1936, Dave had been the oldest man in the village and the local boys would often tease him about this, saying, 'You must be proud to be the oldest man in the village, Dave?' To which he replied, 'Huh! there's no future in that!' Visitors would often see him sitting on the bench outside the village blacksmith's shop, and would be curious to glean some knowledge from him about the good old days. Dave would always take out his pipe, which he held firmly in his mouth with his one tooth, and say, 'There's no good old days.' And that would be that. He could not be drawn into any conversations. This was a shame really, for living in the country all his life he had great knowledge of many things, and he was a true countryman, not just someone who lived in the country.

If the truth be known, Dave had witnessed and endured many hardships and like most country folk, did not wish to dwell on them. The only person he had slightly opened up to was Peter after he had told Dave that he was making notes about the old way of life. Dave had smiled weakly, saying, 'It seems to me that you have to live a life to know how to live it, but I will share some memories with you, 'long as you don't print them in my lifetime.' Feeling privileged, Peter assured him he would honour his wish.

Although he shared some stories with Peter, Dave did say that much of the past was best left there. That was just his nature; he was a man of few words who had lived an abstemious life. When Farmer Cooper had suggested Dave should retire when he reached seventy, he had been very upset, telling his boss that he would not have taken the job if he hadn't thought it was for life!

Following news of his death, his family, who were all on farm labourer's wages, wondered how on earth they could afford to pay for his funeral. Someone else who was concerned was Dan Bowditch, who had often made coffins for villagers and never got paid for his work. Even though he knew the dire circumstances of some of the families, this did not stop him from making the coffin. Quite often a distant relative or friend would visit Dan after the funeral and offer to cover the costs involved, and this was how it was with Dave. For when his relatives came to dispose of Dave's meagre contents, Sadie, one of the nosier cousins had delved into Dave's Army coat pocket to find a fistful of white, five pound notes. When they counted up the money they were amazed to find it amounted to over three hundred pounds, a huge amount for a farm worker. And so Dave had a dignified funeral with all costs covered and a nest egg going to each member of his family.

The district nurse, Ann Stevens, lived near Downside Cove in the largest of the coastguard cottages, her husband being the chief coastguard of eight men, who guarded the local coastline. The houses, which were tall and whitewashed, were built when the threat of Napoleon had seemed imminent, and all had a magnificent view of the cove and sea beyond.

Ann had already attended a birth, which had in fact kept her up all night, and by the time Dan Bowditch was knocking at her door, she had been in bed for just two hours. Bleary eyed, she assured Dan that she would be along to Downside Alley within the hour, which she was.

It was a sunny, breezy morning and the

mile-and-a-half walk over to Downside Alley had blown away any tiredness that the nurse had had. She loved her job even though sometimes it could be very distressing when a baby or mother died, or at times, both. But this was a rare occurrence, and mostly her job gave her much pleasure. Not being a local person by birth, she was often amused by the ways and lives of Downside folk, who seemed to view life in a very philosophical way. As she walked over to Mary's house she reflected on Mary and her family. She did not know too much about the Samways clan other than that Archie, Mary's father-in-law, and Fred, his brother, were real characters. She knew that Mary's father was the village carpenter and had met him at times when he had had the sad task of making a coffin for a baby who had died just after birth.

By the time Ann arrived at Honeysuckle Cottage, Mary was in mid labour. After checking her over and satisfying herself that everything was in place for the delivery, the midwife had a refreshing cup of tea made by Agnes, the expectant grandmother. But before Ann could finish her drink, Mary's labour intensified and Ann was soon at the end of the bed, checking how much the young woman had dilated.

For a first labour it was fairly swift and straightforward. With constant encouragement from Ann, Mary remained calm and in control until the last few contractions when the pains were all encompassing and she screamed loudly. But soon the head was visible and because the baby was small, it soon slipped out. Ann lifted up the new born, cut the cord and, after wrapping the baby in a clean piece of towelling, handed the bundle to Mary, telling her, 'You have a beautiful baby boy.'

Mary's face was full of joy and the pain quickly forgotten as she looked at the small pink face peeping out from the towel. Before long, Ann delivered the afterbirth, which Agnes took away to be buried in the garden.

It was mid-afternoon and before attending to the second milking of the day, Joe looked in to see how Mary was. He was over the moon to know that the baby had been safely delivered and that Mary was well. He ran up the cottage stairs in a trice, and his face beamed as his eyes met Mary's.

'We've got a baby son, Joe. Come, see! He's so handsome!'

Joe went over to the cot. As he looked at his perfectly formed son, tears poured down his cheeks. 'It's a miracle, Mary! He is so perfect! How clever you are, my darling girl.' He stroked Mary's hair and kissed her.

'Just look at his black curls! And his dear little fingers!'

Joe turned to Ann. 'Thank you, thank you.'

Ann's face was full of smiles. 'It's my pleasure. Your Mary was a good girl. Didn't give me any trouble.'

Joe looked at Mary. 'Well done, my darling. I'm so proud of you.' Then turning to Ann and pointing at the cot, he said, 'Oh, by the way, this is Thomas.'

Ann smiled at the young Thomas, who was sleeping contentedly. 'Well, Thomas, you're a lucky young chap to have such a caring family.' Having finished her midwifery duties, she packed up her black bag, said goodbye to the proud new parents and made her way home. As she tumbled into her bed later that day she felt happy and relieved that another safe delivery had been accomplished, and was soon in a deep, untroubled sleep.

During the summer of 1940, the south coast of England, being easily accessible to Luftwaffe bombers based in northern France, suffered many raids as the bombers made their way to Bristol. And with fighter command squadrons from RAF Parwell active in the skies over the area, attempting to prevent the bombers getting through, Downside Alley was often under attack.

One of these occasions was when Peter managed to get home for the weekend through a fellow airman covering for him. The secret meeting he had had with Ella, which saw her climbing out of her bedroom window and jumping into his arms, made everything worthwhile, and the following morning as he got ready to return to base, one of the biggest raids ever over Downside Alley took place.

As he pumped the tyres up on his bicycle he could hear the far-off drone of the German bombers, and he looked at Archie, who was trying to comfort the family dog, Bounce.

'There's some planes about, Dad.'

'By the sound of it, my son, there's a lot of planes about.'

'Well, you go in then, Dad. I'll be off in a minute.'

'Go in! No, I feel safer out of doors. An' besides, Bounce won't stop howling 'till they Germans have gone over. Funny how he knows the difference between our planes and the Germans.' He looked up. 'Here they come.'

The two watched as the planes, flying low in the sky and all in perfect formation, pounded overhead. Before long the RAF fighter planes from Parwell were alongside the enemy planes, attacking them. The noise was frightening and powerful. Remembering that he was home without permission, Peter realised he had to catch the train, and with his tyres now fully pumped, said goodbye to his father, mounted his bicycle and headed for Sandham station, only to discover that due to the train line having been bombed further to the west, no more trains were leaving that day.

Having no choice but to return home, he was was stopped in his tracks by a road block, due to a bomb being dropped on the highway. Carrying his bicycle on his shoulder, Peter made a detour over the fields and, much to Archie's surprise, walked through the cottage gate.

When Peter told Joe, who was also home for the weekend, that he would be in trouble for being absent without leave, he suggested that Peter phone the airman who had covered for him and explain why he was delayed. So, after walking to the nearest public phone box, Peter called his colleague, who was covering his job in the postal sorting office, who nonchalantly told him not to worry, it was all covered.

The following morning, Peter was relieved to find that the bomb, which had not exploded, had been removed and he was able catch his train and resume his duties. His bicycle was left at Block's, the ironmonger's, who charged sixpence to store it until Archie walked to Sandham the next day to collect it.

Inevitably, war changes everything and life at Downside Alley was no exception. With its onset, with Joe, Peter and many others away fighting for their country, Hannah and Ella had volunteered to help at Downside Farm. Hannah was released from her shop duties and Ella only helped at the school occasionally, with Mrs Brit, who had retired from her canteen work four years earlier, taking over Ella's lunchtime duties. Many of the old men went back to help on the farm and it seemed to Ella quite an amazing sight to see a wagon load of white-haired, white-bearded old men going off to work in the fields.

When she had time, Ella called to see Mr and Mrs Samways and was always made to feel very welcome. She couldn't help but compare the warm, happy atmosphere in their home with the rather cold one in her own. Her father was kept busy with his medical duties, golf and shooting. And as she was kept occupied herself, the two rarely met, except at meal times, when the conversation was brief but polite.

Much to Godfrey's dismay he had been called to treat a few of the Downside Alley folk, and often wondered how they could afford to pay him, but pay him they did. Mrs Hunt, a middle-aged woman with a large family, was always complaining of pains of some sort and would repeatedly tell him, 'If 'tis not me back, doctor, 'tis me belly. An' if 'tis not me belly, 'tis me back.'

Godfrey found it hard to talk to the locals on their level and was often at a loss as how to reply to their puerile chatter. The most memorable of all his visits came in the middle of the night in September 1940, and concerned Archie and Jane's immediate neighbours, the Cutler family. The head of the family was a widow, Cherry, known to everyone as Gran, who lived with her brother James, her son Billy, daughter Rosa, and Rosa's illegitimate son, Ernest. James, a skilled but timid man, worked for the estate as head shepherd. No one knew the identity of Ernest's father, and as Rosa rarely went out of the village, being a little backward, it was supposed that it must be someone in Downside Alley, but Rosa, like most country folk, was not going to talk about her business, and so it remained a secret.

On this particular night there had been a heavy air raid for some hours. Finally, the all clear had sounded, something they only heard at Downside Alley if the wind was in the right direction, and everyone was at last able to go to bed. The Samways family had not been settled long when a heavy banging was heard at the door. Archie and Jane were shocked into silence for a minute or so. Could it be one of the German air crew, gunned down? Peter, who was at home on leave, took charge of the situation and told his parents not to worry, he would see who it was.

Due to the blackout there were no lights anywhere. Feeling somewhat nervous, Peter took a candle with him as well as a sharp knife in his back pocket as he sought to ascertain what on earth the loud banging was all about. As he gingerly opened the door, to his surprise he found James, his neighbour, standing before him. As he heaved a sigh of relief, Peter murmured, 'Oh, it's you, James!'

Before Peter could ask anything else, James muttered, 'Is Mrs Samways there?'

Peter nodded, then went back into the cottage to get his mother. Feeling concerned, Jane hurriedly pulled on an old coat, and taking the candle from Peter, went down the stairs and along the flagstone hallway to the front door, where James was looking very sheepish.

'What's the matter, James?'

'Rosa,' he replied. Offering no more information, he led Jane into his cottage where he ascended the narrow stairs and gestured her to follow.

There, inside the small, low ceilinged bedroom, was Granny Cutler and Rosa, who was cuddling a new-born baby. After sending James to go and fetch Doctor Harvey, Jane kicked into her midwife role and, taking some scissors from Granny Cutler, clipped the cord. She then washed the baby, a little girl, later named Daisy, in the warm water that Granny had made ready.

After assuring herself that everything was as satisfactory as it could be, she waited for the doctor to come. She knew the afterbirth had still to come away and hoped the doctor would be there soon to see that safely delivered.

Godfrey was not amused at being called out at such an ungodly hour, and when he found the cause, he was furious. Rosa had not told anyone of the impending birth and had had no advice or help during her pregnancy.

'Why didn't you come and see me?' Godfrey fumed. 'You must have known you were pregnant?'

'I didn't know,' Rosa said, almost in tears.

'You *must* have known.'

Godfrey urged Rosa to push the afterbirth out. Once everything was clean and the baby was sucking from her mother's breast, Godfrey picked up his black bag and prepared to leave. As he turned towards Rosa and Gran, he added, 'I will call and see you tomorrow. Goodnight.'

CHAPTER SEVEN

By August 1941, Peter had been posted abroad. After reading the notice board stating that lessons would be given in Russian, the eight young corporals, of which Peter was one, gave a bit of a gasp. Having been all kitted out with brand new uniforms they somehow thought they were off to fly the flag in Canada.

This was not to be, and soon the young men were learning some basic Russian. The notice had come just a few days after they had left Iceland in August 1941, and it was around another two weeks until they disembarked at Archangel. From there their ultimate destination involved a three-day train ride to Murmansk, one-hundred- and-fifty miles into the Arctic Circle. The single train track meant they often had to stop and shunt into a siding to let another train pass.

The small troop of men heard that the reason they were there arose from a plea to Winston Churchill from Stalin for help. Consequently, Churchill sent Hurricane planes in crates to be assembled on the aerodrome at Murmansk. The RAF servicemen instructed the Russians how to assemble and fly them. Peter, who was ground crew, was one of the corporals ordered to guard the operation quarters, where the commanding officer and interpreters were stationed. A NAAFI provided their basic needs and it was there that much of the harmless banter took place. There was always a shortage of cash and change was often given in boxes of matches, which the lads used to throw around the shop.

One of the rules stated that you couldn't go in the cafe with your overcoat on, and another dictated that the men were under curfew and had to be off the street by dark. This gave Peter the chance to write to Ella, which he did every day. Although the letters were censored, Peter was able to give her brief details about some of the happenings in his day-to-day life. One thing, which amused him was when he and the others went for a steam bath. One of the attendants, an older Russian lady, used to pat the men's bottoms as they passed by her. Peter added that the men's comments were not printable! He also conveyed to her the snowy, Arctic landscape around him and how he would often see wounded Russians being taken to hospital on a horse-drawn sledge. Although it was very cold, their time in Murmansk was enjoyable and certainly very useful to the war effort. The Russians were quick to learn and after a few weeks the RAF's mission was complete.

When on parade one day at the quayside, some British sailors were there, and when they spotted the RAF lads, whom they regarded as sissy, chanted, 'Don't worry, girls, we'll get you home.' And they did, just a short while later. The journey home took eight days, much quicker than the voyage out, but the sea was so rough that one of the men had to strap his belt, which was secured round his body, to the stanchion[7], to keep him safe while he was being sick. Another was heard to declare, 'I don't care if I live or die.'

Happily, they were soon home, and Peter could not wait to see his family and Ella. The young couple shared an ecstatically happy leave. They went to the cinema in Sandham to see *Pride and Prejudice*, and stayed on even though a warning was flashed up on the screen stating that an air raid was in progress and if anyone decided to leave to please go quietly and that the film would continue for those who wished to stay. The cinema was virtually full of young couples and those who decided to leave could be seen creeping towards the foyer, the young girls giggling at their uniformed boyfriends who were gallantly trying to look dignified as their own gas masks dangled from their shoulders.

They spent time dancing in the town hall, surrounded by happy, boisterous GIs[8], who, amid much laughter and frivolity, tried to teach the locals the latest dance moves. But their most happiest time was spent in the privacy of Archie and Jane's front room!

After one of those happy evenings sharing intimate moments together, Ella asked, 'Where are you going to be posted now, my love?'

'Somewhere in England, I think. But sadly I can't talk about it.' He looked downcast. 'And it does mean that I will be away for some months without leave.'

Ella's happy expression drained away, and Peter quickly took her in his arms and kissed her. Then breaking away he said, 'But that's not yet. We have two more days together. Let's not spoil them, eh?'

'I wish you were here for Christmas though!'

'I know. It's just how my leave has fallen. You'll be fine. Aren't you going to a party? I thought I heard Hannah talking about it the other day.'

'Huh. That's just to please my father. It won't be a party, more an endurance. And anyway, I've not accepted yet.'

Peter laughed at her troubled expression. 'You go. I'm sure you'll handle it admirably. And anyway, Mum and Dad are having a bit of a knees up, so Mum said. So it's not all gloom.'

Ella replaced her momentary anger with a brave smile. 'I can never be cross for long when you're here.' She put her arms round Peter's shoulders and kissed him gently.

'Good. Wish I could stay. But it won't be long now until this war is over and I can put a ring on that dainty finger.' He kissed her left hand. 'I love you so much. Now, how about we put on that new record I bought you by Frank Sinatra? He's America's newest favourite, by all accounts.'

Ella smiled at Peter's enthusiasm as he wound up the gramophone. Soon the two were dancing to *Night and Day*.

Ella decided to take Hannah and Peter's advice and accept the invitation to the Harrington's Christmas party. She knew that the whole evening must be an act. She had acted before when her mother took her to the local drama school in London. It was easy. You just pretended to be someone else. And as she descended the stairs with her father waiting for her in the hallway, his eyes lit up.

'You look beautiful, my dear, perfect for the Harrington's.'

'Thank you, Father.'

And as Godfrey escorted her out to the waiting car he was brimming with happiness. This would be the night, he thought, that would change their lives.

The party was already in full swing when Ella and her father arrived. They were greeted in the large hallway by the squire, his wife and their two children, Charles and Sophie. The waitress, a young girl from the village whom Ella recognised, held a tray of glasses full of sparkling Champagne before them. As Ella sipped, Sophie asked her if she would like to dance. Remembering her vow to act the part, Ella accepted and was soon in the drawing room, which had been transformed into a ballroom. The John Jarvis band, who fortunately were all on leave over Christmas, and whom Ella had heard on the night she met Peter, were in full swing with *I Got it Bad, and That Ain't Good*. Lots of people were already on the floor and Ella and Sophie blended in seamlessly.

Sophie was a gregarious, vibrant girl and Ella couldn't help but feel that in fact they could be friends. Two unknown men in evening dress came over and asked them to dance. The girls looked at each other, giggled and said 'yes'.

After a few jazz songs, Don Gibbs, the singer, told them that it was time to slow the pace right down and they began to play *Georgia on my Mind*. Suddenly alarm bells rang in Ella's head. This was their song, hers and Peter's! How could she behave in this carefree way when she was unofficially engaged to her wonderful darling, Peter? She ran off the dance floor and made for the first empty room she could find, which had an elaborate dining table and chairs in the middle of it. She sat down and composed herself. As her head cleared she made the decision that she would make her excuses and go home. She was just about to go when someone came into the room. Charles Harrington.

'Ah, there you are, Ella. What on earth are

you doing in here?'

Ella was horrified to see who it was but tried to stay calm. 'I, er, have a headache. So was just taking some time out.'

'Well, don't take too long. I'm longing to dance with the most beautiful girl in the house.'

Dear Lord! She felt decidedly sick. 'Thank you. But I think it best if I go home... it's the only cure, really.'

He walked towards her, thinking, she can't go home. Not yet. With his back to her he poured her a drink and, taking a tablet from his pocket, popped it into the glass. 'Here. Have a drink it will help, I'm sure.'

Not wishing to exasperate things, Ella took the drink and sipped it. She thought it tasted odd, so just pretended to sip some more. She had to think of a way to get out of this room. Then, too late, suddenly his arms were around her.

'You can't go without giving me a Christmas kiss, now can you, Ella?' As he pushed down hard on her mouth, she struggled to break free, but to no avail.

Before she knew what was happening, in a moment he had pushed her down on the table, forced her legs open and was tearing at her briefs. All the time, Ella desperately struggled to push him off, but he was so heavy, it was impossible. Very quickly he penetrated her. She screamed with the pain, but this was deadened by Charles's large, bony hand, which silenced her as he continued to thrust himself further inside her. Still struggling and fighting to be free of the grotesque ordeal, Ella managed to bite his cheek, hard. He immediately withdrew and wiped his bloodied cheek.

'Bitch!'

With that he buttoned up his flies and left the room. He picked up a glass from a passing waitress. Winking at her, he made the girl blush. As he guzzled the Champagne, one of his pals, who he had earlier had a bet with as to how many females he could have sex with that Christmas, walked by.

'Ah, Cedric. You owe me ten pounds!'

Cedric took a note out of his wallet. 'Your first this Christmas?'

'Yes! But not my last!'

Back in the dining room, Ella was beside herself. It had all happened so quickly, it all seemed unreal. Then as she felt some liquid running down her thighs and a throbbing pain in her groin, she knew what had just happened was starkly real. My God! This was her very worst nightmare. Her head was spinning and as she made to get up she could see her briefs hanging from an elaborately carved chair. In an almost zombie-like fashion she pulled them on and, straightening her clothes, made for the door, where she walked into Sophie, who was looking for her.

'There you are, Ella! Are you alright? I've been looking for you. Come on, let's dance some more.'

'I, er, I'm not feeling too good. I must... I must go home.'

'Oh, I'm so sorry to hear that. We had a ball earlier. Are you alright to go home on your own? I'm sure Charles will escort you.'

'No, no! I'm fine. But thanks.'

'Okay, if you're sure, honey.'

The band started to play, *In the Mood,* and a tall, geekish-looking man called out to Sophie, 'Come and dance, Sophie darling.'

Sophie gave Ella a smile of resignation and headed for the dance floor.

After talking to some contemporaries of the squire about the war and awful loss of some of Wren's churches, Godfrey made his way into the ballroom to look for Ella. Having scanned the dimly lit room in depth to no avail he walked over to Charles, who was chatting to a tall, elegant lady who had a rather hideous, horse-like laugh, and asked him if he had seen Ella anywhere. Excusing himself from the lady, Charles put his arm on Godfrey's shoulder. 'The last I saw of her she was in the garden, feeling unwell. As I chatted to her and encouraged her to come back into the house,' he pointed to his cheek, 'a damn piece of holly caught my cheek.'

Godfrey looked at the nasty scratch on his face. 'That was unfortunate. But thank you for helping Ella. Is she still in the garden, do you know?'

'No. She decided to go home. But look. No need for you to worry, she'll be fine I'm sure.'

Godfrey looked a little hesitant.

'Come and have another drink. The night is young yet.' Charles summoned a waitress and, after handing Godfrey a glass of Champagne, introduced him to Cedric, before heading for a slim blonde who he had been eyeing up while talking to the doctor.

Ella ran all the way home, stumbling in places and stifling her cries. She did not want anyone asking about her wellbeing. She need not have worried, Downside Alley was silent. Her hands were shaking as she put the key in the door. Running upstairs, she flung herself on her bed and sobbed uncontrollably.

She felt her life was over. How could she face anyone? How could she face Peter? My God! Her beloved Peter, he would never love her now! She rushed into the bathroom, tore her clothes off, and scrubbed herself all over, as if to remove any trace of that vile man. As she scrubbed away, the effects of the drug that Charles had spiked her drink with suddenly took over and she collapsed on the bathroom floor.

The next morning she was awoken by Mrs Butt tapping on the bathroom door. 'Are you in there, Ella? Are you alright, dear?'

Images of the night before flooded her brain and she struggled to speak. Then, as her head cleared, she thought quickly and muttered, 'I'm alright, Mrs Butt. Thank you. Just got a nasty bug... could be food poisoning.'

'Oh dear. Is there anything I can get you?'

'No thanks. I'll just sip water.'

'Alright, dear. Well, you just rest, and call out if you need me.'

'I will. Thank you, Mrs Butt.' Thinking that she could not face anyone, not even Hannah, she added. 'Best if I don't see anyone for a while. It may be a virus and I wouldn't want to pass it on.'

Mrs Butt seemed satisfied with that, as did her father and Hannah.

The days that followed were a blur for Ella. She retreated deep into herself, almost closing down. Her moods swung wildly from thinking it would be alright, no one need know, to feeling so unworthy and reviled that she wanted to harm herself. But common sense stepped in and prevented her from doing so. One day she leapt up and thumbed quickly through some of her books. Surely there would be a message of hope within the pages of the classics. But as she flicked through the pages of *Tess of the d'Urbervilles* her heart sank once more as she read Hardy's poignant lines:

> *But some might say, where was Tess's guardian angel? Where was the providence of her simple faith? Perhaps, like that other god of whom the ironical Tishbite spoke, he was talking, or he was pursuing, or he was in a journey, or he was sleeping and not to be awaked.*

As she read and reread the prophetic text Ella told herself that, like Tess, she was doomed. Her life seemed to be draining away from her. This was the most hideous of nightmares. If only, if only, she could wake up.

As the New Year began, Ella had to pretend to be recovering and was seen at meal times, although she ate pitifully little. She persuaded her father that her stomach had shrunk because of the virus or poisoning, whatever it was. And he had to agree that lack of appetite was a symptom for some while making recovery.

On a sunny Friday in January, Hannah went

to see Ella, and although it was a strain for Ella, as she hated concealing the truth, the two spent a happy time together, with Hannah doing most of the talking. Brimming over with happiness, she told Ella about Will's proposal.

'Will says that as soon as he knows when he's coming home, I am to book the registry office in Sandham! I know that with hundreds of miles between us, the proposal might not seem so romantic as yours, El. But those words on that piece of paper are all the world to me. Oh, Ella, it's so exciting!'

Ella had hugged her friend and was pleased when Hannah asked her to be a witness. The two girls celebrated the good news with a trip into Sandham to go to the cinema. Although Ella had been reluctant at first, she was glad that she went, and that just for two hours or so, she could forget her own horrific troubles.

The friends went to see *The Wizard of Oz*, and gasped along with the rest of the cinema-goers when the screen turned into glorious colour and Judy Garland walked through the vibrant flowers. They giggled at the Munchkins and the Wicked Witch of the West, and both agreed that they had had a lovely time. Saying goodbye at the end of the evening they hugged each other and said they would meet in a week's time.

So much for making plans; the following day came with the devastating news that Will had been killed. Ella was shattered for her friend and knew, despite her own trauma, that she must do all she could to comfort Hannah.

'How will I cope, El?' Hannah sobbed to her friend shortly after hearing news of the telegram, which had been sent to Will's parents. 'I loved him so much. I just can't believe he's not coming home... the pain inside of me is so unbearable!'

Ella hugged her friend closely. This was so awful. Life really was so bloody unfair.

Will's job in the Far East had been to drive the Colonel round, and when he stood in for another driver on his day off, he was tragically killed in a mine explosion. Letters that were ready to post came through to his parents and Hannah, revealing the filthy conditions he was living in. Will was cheerful enough about it though, saying that he had been given a mongoose, which lived with him all the time, and which killed the rats. Cheerful letters from son to parents, from boyfriend to girlfriend, written to make them smile, and not worry. Sadly, they were to be his last. Another village lad lost in foreign fields.

About three weeks later, after having gone through every conceivable emotion, Hannah was thinking that she would like a change in her work routine, and thought about helping with local children. She knew that more mothers were working as part of the war effort, and as a result there were increasing numbers of children needing care.

Before she had time to think about this too much, due to the fact that she was now over eighteen, a letter arrived informing her that she needed to register for work and subsequently attend an interview. Within a short time she found herself working in one of the children's nurseries in Sandham. Amazingly, her wish to change her circumstances had been granted, and even though it was long hours, she embraced it with enthusiasm. Although she missed her old life, Hannah was just thankful to be busy and to be of help to others, something she had always found therapeutic.

The war raged on, but this meant little to Ella. With her friend gone, her world closed in around her even more. She found it hard to focus on anything and just could not bring herself to pick up her pen and write to Peter. She became very introspect and, what's more, very worryingly, she was late with her period.

CHAPTER EIGHT

In the eighteenth century, coaches used to pass through Downside Alley on their way to Lyme Regis and then on to Exeter. It was reputed that the flint cottage inhabited by Archie, Jane and their family had formerly been the local coaching inn where horses would be changed over or rest for the night before journeying on. This would certainly explain the larger than normal rooms, and the unusual facility of a second floor, which, although dominated by the roof trusses, proved useful as an extra bedroom when the Samways family moved in.

Inlaid on one side of the high-roofed cottage was a large brick with the date 1777 carved into it. The garden was full of fruit trees and bushes and the Seven Sisters Rose, planted many years before, framed the front door. The square entrance hall had an intriguingly small window with very thick glass. This, according to local rumour, was so that the inhabitants of the eighteenth and early nineteenth centuries could look out to see if the press gang[9] was coming to forcibly remove the men and take them to sea to serve their country. Although the garden was packed with vegetables, fruit bushes and trees, it was bereft of any flowers apart from the rose. Archie repeatedly told his family that he did not grow anything that he couldn't eat. So Jane had a few geraniums planted in treacle tins, which brightened the kitchen window sill.

One Sunday afternoon when Peter was on his last weekend's leave before reporting for his new posting, all the family had the luxury of being together. Violet and Florrie had unusually been on the same shift at Downside House, which was now being used as a Red Cross hospital. Now home from work, they were full of chatter. Violet, being the more talkative of the two sisters, began the conversation.

'Phoebe, Mr Wilding's daughter, you know, the baker who delivered the bread and cakes to the house today, she was telling us about her life and how she fills her spare time.' Violet looked disconsolately at her father. 'Seems to me they have it much better than we do!'

Archie did not like this kind of talk. 'I don't know about that. They've got a privy at the end of the garden, same as we 'ave. Only difference is they cut up the *News of the World* to wipe their bottoms, and we cuts up the *Western Gazette*!'

'Well, they won't have to cut up paper soon,' Florrie said knowingly, 'cos she told me as she was unloading the trays of fancy cakes, that her father is going to have a toilet installed inside the house, and that they would be using proper toilet paper!'

'I heard her say that too!' Violet said. 'And guess what? Her whole family go out to eat in a restaurant, ev-er-y week!'

Archie did his usual thing when he was thinking and scratched his head. 'Well, 'tisn't right! To think that folk go out to eat and go to the toilet indoors, well... the world's gone mad!'

'I don't know about mad, but it's certainly changing, Father. In years to come, I think every house will have an inside privy,' Florrie put forward. 'It's bound to happen.'

'Well, it ain't gonna 'appen here! Tain't natural.' Archie shook his head and continued, 'It seems to me that every step forward we humans make, be a step backwards. Mark my words, they'll be taking them all out again one day!'

Jane's clear thinking eased the situation. 'Don't worry, my dear. Squire Harrington will never fork out the money to bring the privies inside, least not in our life-time.'

Jane went to the kitchen, brought in the tea things, and soon all were happily munching her homemade cake and sandwiches. After filling his belly, Archie was much more relaxed. He smiled as he looked round the table, happy to see his family gathered there. Then, as he turned his thoughts to other things, he looked round at the old cottage walls.

'If only walls could talk, eh? They could tell us some rare old tales, you know.'

'And not all good ones, I reckon,' replied Florrie, as she reached for another piece of bread and jam.

'Maybe so, maid. Life's never been easy, thass for sure. But 'twould be good to go back, see how they lived a 'undred years ago, 'specially as this was a coaching inn.'

'Same as we are now, Father,' Peter said as he finished his cup of tea. Then, hearing laughter, he looked out of the cottage window. 'They had their sorrows and their fun. Just like the Cutlers next door. Look at them!'

Everyone turned and looked out of the window to see Granny Cutler sat in the wooden porch laughing as James chased Rosa and Billy round the garden with a bunch of stinging nettles in hand. The Samways family laughed at their bucolic neighbours and their simple entertainment.

'Ah well. Don't cost 'em anything,' Archie said.

Jane smiled. 'No. Such innocent souls really. I'll never forget when Gran's husband, Reuben, died, just after they'd been away for a week's holiday, and I went in to see him in his coffin.'

Peter looked at his mother. 'I remember, Mum. I went with you. First corpse I'd seen!'

Jane laughed. 'That's right. Well, as I looked at his peaceful, suntanned face, I said to Gran that he looked really well. Smiling innocently, the old lady replied, "Yes. I think his week's holiday did him good!"'

When Jane opened the window the following morning shortly before six o'clock, she could hear that Archie was already at work in the wash house. This was the usual Monday morning routine, and Archie had been up since before five to light the fire under the copper, which heated the water, enabling Jane to do the family's washing.

Smoke was already flying up from the wash house chimney and this was a welcome sight. Later, as Jane watched the results of her morning's work fluttering in the breeze on the fifty foot long wire line, she thought it a lovely sight, and was thankful that another wash day was over.

As he wriggled into the clean sheets later that night, Archie cuddled his wife and remarked how lovely and fresh the sheets were, adding, 'What's more, my dear, like everything we enjoy, it costs us nothing 'cept our labour.'

Jane kissed him on his cheek. 'And of course, the best thing of all is, as you so often say, we have no bills!'

Everyone had to play their part in the war, and this included Archie. Although he continued with his game-keeping duties during the day, in the evenings, well some of them, he was one of Downside Alley's Home Guard, the regiment set up by Winston Churchill in 1940 to defend the home front.

The Home Guard consisted of an army of volunteers. Most were men who were too old to serve in the armed forces, or, at the other end of the age scale, those who at seventeen were too young to be called up. Others who also volunteered were those who, due to health problems, were not fit for military service.

At Downside Alley, Farmer Cooper was put forward by Mr White, the estate's manager, to be Captain of the Home Guard, but not having had any military training he instructed his men in a most unorthodox way. Every week the eclectic band of men would assemble for practice in the village hall, an old Army hut from the First World War. On Sundays they would go on exercise outside the village, practising how to capture the enemy.

On their way home they would stop off at the local pub and discuss their manoeuvres, although the Wright brothers, being teetotallers and chapel-goers, would remain in the wagon. After returning from one of the midweek training sessions, Archie relayed the humorous antics of the evening's events to his wife.

'What a performance it were tonight, my dear. The gas capes were issued.'

Jane looked horrified.

'Yea. And all one size too! Size five, whatever that means. Well, when poor old Georgie Trim, you know the little chap from the cove?'

Jane nodded. 'I know. His wife is as tall as he is short.'

'Thass the one. Well, when he got into his cape, it completely covered him from head to toe! An' all Farmer Cooper could do was to laugh at little Georgie, before saying to him, "Good God, Trim, you ain't never gonna get gassed!"'

'Oh my! An' I bet they're heavy, Arch?'

'Ah, they be,' Archie laughed. 'But Georgie 'ad a chance to laugh at him. Cos then we all 'ad to roll the capes up neat and rest 'em on our back packs. An' when old Cooper demonstrated this, his pack was a bit of a mess, and he couldn't get through the door. Course we all started to laugh. And give him his due, he laughed, too.'

Jane smiled at the mental picture of the scene described.

'Why should England tremble, eh, Arch?'

'You'd say that if you were there, m'dear.'

'Paint the picture then, my love.'

'Well, the first job we do is to line up in our uniforms. Then Farmer Cooper orders us to remove cigarettes... which are behind the men's ears of course. Then comes the distributing of the stripes.'

'Stripes?'

'Ah. On Sunday we all had a go at shooting at a target, and during tonight's meeting the red stripes were handed out to the best crack shot.'

'That must be you, Arch, surely!'

'Thass kind, but you know all us men be used to firing at a rabbit or pheasant.'

'Oh, so who has a sharper eye than you then?'

'Well, you know that Farmer Cooper be the Captain?' Jane nodded. 'An', well, he be soft-hearted really, though at times he pretends to be hard.'

'And?'

'The Sergeant of the Home Guard, Bill Strange, asks old Cooper, "Whose gonna get the stripes, sir?" And old Cooper, with his face beaming, says "Give 'em all one."' Archie passed his red stripes to Jane. 'So if you could sew them on the cuff, my dear, that would be good.'

'Course I will. But it don't seem fair that James Cutler has the same status as you, Arch. His eyes are quite bad, poor man.'

'True. I don't believe he's ever carried a gun in his life. Against his principles, he says. But if you'd seen his face when he was presented with them there red stripes... well, you'd be pleased for him.'

'Umm, poor James doesn't have much in life. 'cept his beer and black cat. Was that the end of the evening then?'

'Not quite. When we were walking up to receive our stripes, blow me if Cooper didn't give out the orders for the next day.' Archie laughed. 'Not to me. But some of the farm labourers like Robert Penfold and Doug Miles. Just as they were receiving their stripes from Sergeant Strange,

Cooper would say some it like, "Now Robert, you go and trim out the hedge in Greystones in the morning." And to Doug he says, "You can help the shepherd wi' moving the sheep an' hurdles."'

Jane giggled. 'Well there's a thing. Saved him time in the mornin', I suppose?'

'Thass right. I believe he's got a thing or two on his mind at the moment. What wi' his missus not being well an' his daughter leading him a merry dance.'

'Don't surprise me, Arch. She always was a flighty thing.' Jane smiled at her husband. 'Well, I s'pose we can all sleep easier in our beds wi' you chaps guarding us?'

Archie laughed. 'If you heard what 'appened when old Cooper roused us all in the night 'bout a month ago, you might not think so. When he banged on Jack Burgess's door and shouted, "Come on Jack, an invasion is expected. Bring what weapons you 'ave." Old Jack told him he only had a knobbly stick. And can you believe it? Old Cooper said, "Bring it on Jack, that'll be alright."'

'I must 'ave slept through that one, m'dear. What happened when you assembled?'

'Well, after dragging ourselves out of bed and getting to the hut as quick as we could, Cooper told us that it had been a false alarm, which was good news to us all. But as dawn was breaking by then, Cooper says we may as well start work for the day. No extra pay though.'

'When I think of all the hours you and the others do, seems to I that none of you are ever properly paid for your labours.'

'Thass the way of the world, m'dear. But we must count our blessings, you know. Even in war time, in spite of some heavy air raids, we be sheltered from the ways of the world in Downside Alley.' Archie looked affectionately at Jane. 'An' thass the way I like it.'

It was true that Farmer Cooper did have a few things on his mind at the moment and his usual strict morning routine had gone slightly awry.

The normal procedure of the day was that the workers assembled outside his farmhouse door at six o'clock and received their orders for the day. In the winter months they started an hour later, and although it was pitch dark as they trudged their way up to the farmhouse, by the time they had walked to their allotted field for the day, daylight was breaking. They did not get paid until they started work at seven o'clock, nor did they get paid when they had to go and collect their wages from the farmhouse. This they did in their own time. But this was the time-worn tradition and the labourers accepted it, glad of a job, glad of a home.

Farmer Cooper was a fairly tolerant boss. He avoided sacking men if he could, and only ever did so in the event of a worker being caught stealing. When he had taken over the farm from his father, part of his unwritten lease was that he should take on Colin Price, a farm labourer who only had one arm. In spite of his disability, Colin worked as well as his fellow workers, and never shirked. This was no problem for Farmer Cooper, and, watching Colin working so adeptly, he found he had great respect for him.

Cooper enjoyed his life as a farmer, as had his father and grandfather before him. His family had come to Downside Alley with the Harrington's in the last century and farming was in his blood. Against his family's wishes he had married his cousin, Anita, who, it has to be said, was a rather plain-looking woman, but who had a heart of gold and could somehow, whatever the problem, come up with a solution, and always with a smile. He loved her smile, and he loved her. She always made everything seem right. But this latest problem with their daughter seemed unsolvable, even for Anita, who was already struggling with the various symptoms of the menopause, and the problem with their daughter Juliet was not helping. Juliet, who had always been rather headstrong, had got very friendly with two American ladies who had taken on the lease of Brookside Manor, a large house on the Downside estate. The ladies were very avant-garde and always throwing wild parties.

Cyril and Anita Cooper were wise enough to know that youth must have its fling, and at first turned a blind eye to their daughter's antics, hoping the novelty would soon wear off and she would get fed up with the shallowness of it all. As loving parents they always told her to take care and not stay out too late. But this latest revelation had knocked them sideways and they didn't know how best to respond.

One morning, after being out all night, Juliet breezed into the dining room as her parents were breakfasting. After pouring herself a glass of orange juice she spoke to them in a language that they struggled to understand.

'Mummy, Daddy, I have to tell you something.'

Anita and Cyril looked at each other, wondering what was coming; then smiled expectantly at their daughter, whose face was glowing.

'Go ahead, my dear,' Anita said kindly.

'I know you won't want to hear this. The thing is, I don't fit in at Downside Alley. I'm not one of your country bumpkins and never will be. Things never work out how you think, do they? I mean, you educated me, which I am thankful for. But you can't really expect me to have the knowledge I have and be happy to just spend my life riding horses and fraternising with the yokels!'

'We just thought that...' Anita began.

'I know you just thought. You thought you knew best. But, you see... you don't.' Juliet walked to the French window, then turned to face her parents once more. 'The fact is that I've fallen in love... and I'm going away with her.' She looked at her parents' faces as they tried to absorb their daughter's last word.

'Yes, that's right. I said *her*. Until now my life has been nothing but a yawning. Now I'm fully alive and want to spend the rest of my life with Caprice Fothergill. She is the most amazing, beautiful creature that God ever made. And what's more, she is very rich. We will want for nothing. So surely, Mummy and Daddy, you must be happy for me?' Juliet grinned at her parents, and, seeing their shocked faces, burst into laughter. 'Oh don't worry. No one else need know... although I guess the servants will gossip after finding me in bed with Caprice.'

Like a robot, Anita stood and went to the sideboard. She poured two whiskies and handed one to her husband. They both knocked them back in silence.

'Here, let me get you another,' Juliet replenished their glasses. 'I'm going upstairs to pack. I'll write when we get to Scotland, which is where we will stay until this God damn war is over.' Juliet giggled. 'You see how mad I am on her... even talking like her!' She topped up her glass of juice, spilling some on the white damask tablecloth. 'Where was I? Ah, yes, Scotland.

131

Caprice's father has a castle in the Highlands. So at least I'll be able to put my country pursuits into practice. I will write to you once we are there, although it won't be for a while as we are stopping off in Wales first to visit some distant cousin of Caprice's.'

She hesitated for a moment. 'I'm sorry if I have disappointed you. You have both been good parents, something for which I am grateful.' She bent over and kissed them both on the cheek. 'Goodbye.'

Cyril and Anita sat in silence for some while. Alma, their servant, came in and asked if Miss Juliet wanted a cooked breakfast. Anita managed to smile weakly at Alma, and, waving her hand, told her that Miss Juliet would not be eating with them today.

After some time had passed, Cyril checked his fob watch and, standing up, told his wife that he really should be getting on. But as he began to walk, his legs gave way underneath him and he sat down again. Anita went over to him and placed her arms on his shoulders.

'We will get over this, my dear. We simply have to.'

Cyril turned and smiled at his wife, and, patting her hand, answered, 'Yes, we will.'

Of course, they were both in deep shock and found it hard to come to terms with what had just happened. Since Juliet had been born they had devoted their lives to her, giving her all that was possible within their means. Their world had been turned upside down, and like everyone who had gone through similar heartbreak, it would never be the same again.

As Juliet had surmised, rumours soon went round Downside Alley about the elopement of the farmer's daughter. Most people were saddened for the farmer and his wife. Some gloated on the juicy details, but not for long. Life had to go on and, once recovered from the initial shock, Anita and Cyril resigned themselves to the stark reality that their daughter was a lesbian, and that they would never have their much thought about grandchildren.

When Archie and Jane had heard the news they were shocked and saddened, and Archie summed up the situation by saying, 'Build me four walls wi' no trouble, an' I'll move in.'

Before too long, Cyril and Anita's lives returned to the normal routine. They did receive a missive from Juliet saying that she was well and ecstatically happy, and both agreed that, in spite of things not turning out as they had wished, they were happy for her, and conveyed this in their letters. Cyril put all his energies into the farm once more and Anita continued her work with the Women's Royal Voluntary Service and looking after the women who were drafted into the village to help on the land.

Just like the whole of England, Downside Alley was a different place in the war years. For one thing, although there were fewer men in the vicinity, there were more women. Many workers throughout the country were exempt from military service because of their jobs, which were labelled as work of national importance. This included miners, brewery workers, bakers and farm workers. But with the latter it was up to the boss if a worker was able to join up or not. Some workers wanted to, but if the boss said he wanted them, then they had to stay on the farm. Conversely, if a man wanted to stay on the farm but his boss wanted him to go, he had to go.

Cyril Cooper, being a genial man, let those who wanted to serve their country go. Single, young, fit women were called up to the WRENS or WRAFS, while married women were sent to work on the railway or in factories. And at Downside Farm, with a glut of vacancies, Cyril Cooper had been allocated some Land Girls.

Most were country girls, but some who were from the city adapted to their new way of life and married local men after the war; an innocent invasion, which broke up the centuries' old way of life where local girls married local boys.

The work was hard for those not accustomed to it and the days were long. The girls were billeted in the farmhouse and cottages in Downside Alley. The arrival of Avril Houghton and Sarah Whitefield to the farmhouse, with all their mundane chatter of boys and dances, seemed like a breath of fresh air to the recently beleaguered Cyril and Anita Cooper.

Archie had been asked to help at the dairy and to show the new Land Girl, Topsy, how to milk the cows by hand. He had to admit she picked it up fairly quickly, and as they were both milking, Topsy asked what it was really like to live in Downside Alley. He told her it was not to be despised because they got the butcher three times a week.

'Three times a week!' she exclaimed in her cockney accent. To which Archie told her that the butcher came once with the pig's head and twice for the money! She had seen the funny side of it and, after changing cows, quizzed her tutor about various other aspects of the area.

When Archie, Jane, Alice, Violet and Florrie were eating their meal that night, Violet spoke of her encounter with one of the Land Girls. She laughed as she relayed what had happened.

'When I was pushing out a soldier in his wheelchair this afternoon, I met one of the Land Girls, Topsy, she said her name was. She was wheeling a barrow load of dung up to the farmhouse to go on Farmer Cooper's roses apparently. Anyway, she was quite a bubbly character and couldn't wait to tell me that she was dating Paul Cox, the trainee blacksmith. Well, he can't be no more than sixteen!'

Florrie's eyes lit up. 'I didn't know you'd met

Topsy, Vi. She was the girl I was telling you about who was dating the cockney soldier. You know, he'd been chatting *me* up the week before!'

Archie scratched his head and laughed. 'Well, I'm blowed. Thass the maid who helped out wi' the milkin' s'marning. Picked it up quick she did. And as we were talking she asked me if there were any rich farmers in the area.'

Violet giggled. 'Sounds to me like she's addicted to men!'

Grandma Alice, who had been listening quietly to the chatter, suddenly joined in. 'Well, my dears, this reminds me of something my godmother Olivia-May Goodenough used to say, and I ain't thought of it for years. Olivia was off farming stock, a no nonsense type. Quite eccentric really, but very generous. Anyway, when she heard of women rather like this here Topsy you're talking about, she used to say that if one fella was not enough, then a hundred is not too many!'

Violet and Florrie tried to suppress their giggles. They had never heard their grandmother speak of such things.

Archie was amused. 'I remember Olivia, mother. Did she have any other such gems to brighten our day?'

Alice fell silent, wondering whether to repeat Olivia's observations or not. After a short while she thought, why not?

'Well, she did say, and mind you, I can't relate

to this, cos I had a very happy marriage with your granddad.' Violet and Florrie looked at one another. What was coming? 'Olivia said, and I'll never forget it, that when one of her neighbours told her that her husband was seeing another woman, quite unperturbed Olivia said, 'What *she* do have, we don't have to have!'

Everyone in the room roared with laughter. As Jane wiped the tears from her eyes she said, 'It's a bit sad really, but a fact of life, I s'pose?'

'Well, as I said, Olivia was a no nonsense type of person. And that sums up her outlook on life. She never wanted to make a fuss. So much so that when she died she left her body to medical research.'

As Alice's last words left her mouth the mood tangibly dipped, and so Jane quickly changed the subject. 'Enough of this nonsense. Florrie and Violet, tell us about the soldiers that you care for. Are they all handsome and single?'

Violet spoke first. 'Most are married actually, and a few are handsome, I guess.'

'They're all terrible flirts,' Florrie said, adding, 'Still, after what they've been through, who can blame them?'

'You're telling me! I've never had my bottom pinched so many times!'

Archie's ears pricked up at this. 'You be careful what you're doing, my maid. They're soldiers from far away, and you are there to help 'em. Thass all.'

'Oh you don't need to worry about us, father. Florrie and I have got our heads screwed on.'

Jane felt she had to speak up. 'Yes, you have, thank goodness. But when love does come along, every good intention goes out the window.'

Archie scratched his head. 'Ah, but you must be careful not to confuse love and, er, lust.'

Florrie blushed. And, giggling, Violet spoke up, 'Mother has told us about the facts of life, Father. And as I said, we have got our heads screwed on.'

Jane felt a bit awkward and wanted to close the conversation. 'Your father's right, girls, just you be careful.'

The girls' work at the house was voluntary, but when they were eighteen in May 1942, they each received an envelope marked OHMS. Enclosed were their call-up papers and soon both were enlisting for the WRAFS. After training they found themselves living in a mainly female environment and residing in the recently vacated married quarters near a home-based aerodrome, their male counterparts having been sent to serve abroad.

CHAPTER NINE

When man deceives others to cover up his own sin it is the biggest sham of all. And this was the case when Charles Harrington received sympathy for the deep scratch on his cheek, which supposedly came from the sharp prick of a holly leaf.

Apart from being bloody annoyed at how the Harvey bitch, as he mentally called her, had disfigured his face, he had not given Ella another thought since the night of the party. Among the local men, Mister Charles, as he was referred, had a fierce reputation as a serial seducer and womaniser. The estate workers often laughed amongst themselves about his antics and nicknamed him Cuckoo Harrington, as, like the cuckoo, he slept in anyone's nest. Amusing it may have been for the workers but the heartache for his parents, and many unsuspecting girls, was immense.

No one had thought to warn the new doctor or his daughter about the libertine who was thinly disguised as a gentleman. How could they? To speak ill against their master's son would only bring trouble on themselves.

Where his tyrannical streak came from no one could really say. Both his parents were decent, upright people. His father Hugh

Harrington was a magistrate, serving on the bench at Sandham, and was well known throughout the south. Having a strong sense of leadership, Hugh had formed the local Territorial Army before the Second World War, and had encouraged his son to join. Charles, however, preferred to don an RAF uniform and joined the RAF Volunteer Reserve, wearing the brass badge with VR engraved on it with haughty pride. When war broke out he automatically became an officer, something that boosted his inflated ego even more.

It can only be assumed that the rogue gene which erupted in Charles, giving him a cold, clinical, arrogant view of the world and its people, came from way back. On hearing of Charles' callous nature, Archie had thought to himself that he must be a throwback from his grandfather, Henry Harrington, whom Archie had known in his childhood, but wisely decided to keep his thoughts to himself.

The thought of Mister Charles being in charge of the estate one day filled the villagers with dread. But as has been proved true time and time again, most of the things people worry about never happen...

The carrier bus was packed with villagers going to Sandham market. Even the roof was piled high with baskets of live chickens to be sold. There were vast amounts of various vegetables to be auctioned, and the voices of the travellers reached fever pitch.

Hilda Butt and Jane Samways were both on the morning's transport and chatted freely to each other.

'Another year and the war still rages, Jane.'

'I know, Hilda. It's hard to believe it's 1942 and still no sign of peace. But we must count our blessings. At least we have enough food. What with the veg in the garden and chickens providing eggs, we mustn't grumble, eh?'

'Oh no, Jane, mustn't grumble. It's not so good in the cities, poor souls. And all the bombings they have to endure!'

'My sister Lily has lost everything. Lucky to have survived, she said.'

Hilda shook her head. 'That's awful, Jane. They say the King and Queen 'ave bin to see those bombed out in the East End, such great moral support for them.'

Jane nodded. 'I heard that, too.'

The bus went over a large rut and everyone shrieked. After rescuing her shopping bag, which had fallen to the floor, Hilda turned her thoughts to Ella and decided to voice her concerns to Jane.

'Have you seen Ella lately, Jane?'

'No, not lately. What with working on the farm and everything, I expect she's busy. Is she alright?'

'Well, I have to admit I am rather concerned about her. She's become very withdrawn. Not eating much either.'

Jane turned to face Hilda. 'Oh, that doesn't sound good. I wonder what the problem can be. Peter is still writing, I know, so it can't be that. Shall I have a word with her, do you think?'

'You can if you like. I've tried, but to no avail.' Hilda paused, then with a more resolute voice said, 'I think I will try again though.'

They came to a halt outside the market. Not realising the severity of Ella's symptoms, Jane was happy to leave matters in Hilda's hands.

'Hilda, do tell Ella to call round and see us. We do miss seeing her. Such a lovely girl.'

'I will, Jane. Thanks then. I'll see you later.'

While serving dinner, Hilda quietly asked Ella if she would call and see her at her house later that evening. After picking at her food, Ella had nodded her agreement but said nothing.

Hilda had the kettle on in readiness for Ella, and soon had a cup of tea and a piece of cake in front of her guest.

'I've asked you to come, Ella, as I'm very concerned about you. You're not the same girl you were a few weeks ago. Please let me know what the problem is. Whatever it is, no one else need know... I just want to help you, dear.'

Ella remained motionless. How could she ever explain the savagery she had endured? How could she ever become properly alive again?

Not put off by Ella's silence, Hilda realised that there must be a severe problem and, whatever its awfulness, it had to come out. She went down on her knees in front of Ella and placed her hands into the young girl's.

'Please, dear. Just tell me. I promise you I can help.'

Ella looked directly into Hilda's face where she saw a smiling, gentle lady, pleading silently for a response.

'Please, dear. It can't be that bad. Nothing is.' Those last words triggered an explosion of emotion inside Ella. And she knew she must speak out for the injustice that was brimming over inside of her. She composed herself and cleared her throat.

'I, I... I was raped... it happened at the Christmas party.'

Hilda had not known what to expect, but it was not this. Before she had a chance to reply, Ella continued, amid her sobs.

'Oh, Mrs Butt. It was terrible! He was just like a savage animal. And as for me, well, all I know is... my life is....' She looked down at the floor and whispered, 'It's over!'

'Now, now, my dear Ella, although this is a terrible thing to have happened to you, and it certainly is, it will be alright. Together we can overcome this dark period for you and brighter days will come again. You'll see.'

Ella stared blankly at Mrs Butt. If only she were right. But, no, things could never, ever come right now.

'I know you mean well, Mrs Butt. And you are so very kind, but that's not all.'

'Tell me, dear. Tell me please. I need to know all before I can help.'

Ella twisted her handkerchief in her hands. How could she even say it! Yet, she knew she must. It had been hidden inside her head for too long.

'I'm late for my period.' She held her head in her hands. 'I'm frightened, Mrs Butt, so very frightened.'

This was the worst possible scenario. Hilda stood up and asked Ella to do the same. She hugged Ella for some minutes, using the time not only to console, but to think.

When Ella sat down again, Hilda poured her a fresh cup of tea, the other being untouched.

'You sip this, Ella. It will help. Thank you for telling me your problems, dear. As you have probably guessed, it looks as if you are having a baby.'

Ella's deepest fears were confirmed. She had tried so hard to push those thoughts away. But now, here was this trusted, kindly lady telling her that in a few months, she, Ella, was, in all probability, going to have a baby.

'Dear God! What will I tell my father? And, oh... Peter, my darling Peter. He won't want anything to do with me now!'

'Let's take one day and one problem at a time, eh? I've been thinking. My sister, Amy Trent, who lives in Cranmoor St Michael, has recently been widowed. You could go and live with her, as a companion. Well, that's what we'll say, just until the baby is born. Then after the birth, the baby can be adopted and you can return to Downside Alley. No one needs to know the truth. You will then be free to carry on with your life.'

To Ella it seemed she had just been thrown a huge life line.

'Oh, Mrs Butt, you are so kind. You've given me hope.'

'There's always hope, my dear; even in the darkest of situations. A door never closes without a window opening. Things will look brighter soon, Ella. You'll see.'

'But... I just can't see how.'

'Keep your faith and trust in God. Things will come right. They always do in the end.'

'I don't know... I can't see anything at the moment, just... pain.' She stared blankly at the floor, before continuing, 'I hope Father won't make too much of a fuss about me going away.'

'Leave him to me. He'll be alright. I'll make him understand that my sister is in great need.'

'I hope you're right.' Ella gave Hilda a weak smile, then suddenly remembered her work.

'But what about my job on the farm? You can't just leave in war time, and Farmer Cooper will be....' Before she had time to finish her sentence, Hilda put her hand up.

'Don't go worrying about Farmer Cooper. After I've spoken to your father I'll go and see him, and explain that you're too ill to work at the moment. That will buy us time until you've gone away.'

Ella was still unconvinced. 'But what will happen then? I'll have the authorities after me for not working!'

Hilda smiled kindly at the young girl. 'No one will be after you, Ella. Once you are at Amy's house, I will call and see Cyril Cooper again and explain the problem. I've known him and his wife for years, and I'm sure he will understand the complexity of the situation as long as I tell him that after the birth you will return to the farm.'

Hilda's words managed to placate the distressed Ella and she agreed with all that the older lady had said.

And so, within two weeks everything was arranged. Godfrey was surprisingly understanding, and waved Ella off quite cheerfully. His life was changing, too. To meet the ever-demanding medical needs in London, after Ella had left, he decided to help out with the Red Cross there. And knowing it was only temporary, the squire supported this move and said, in Godfrey's absence, he would use the doctor from Woodleigh for his medical needs.

Life had changed for the squire, too. His house had been commandeered and he and his family were now living in North Lodge, on the estate.

Cyril Cooper had listened to Hilda's news about Ella with a sad heart. He reasoned that babies often came when least expected and said that, as she was pregnant, her duties on the farm would be too heavy for her anyway, but looked forward to seeing her as soon as she could. He also assured Hilda, whom he counted as a good friend, that as far as he was concerned, Ella had just moved away.

The following month, when Hilda met Jane on the carrier, she was able to explain that Ella was now over her bug and had gone to be a companion to her recently widowed sister and that she had been released by Farmer Cooper, who said he had a glut of Land Girls anyway. Fortunately, Jane was not au fait with the rules of women working during the war, and so did not realise that women could only be released from their duties if they were pregnant.

'Oh, I am pleased she is better and able to be of help to your sister. Will she be away long, do you think?'

'Well, as long as Amy needs her really. A few months, I would think.'

'We all look forward to seeing her in the

autumn then. I expect Farmer Cooper will need her at harvest time.'

'All being well, I should think Amy will be on her feet by then. It was all so unexpected, you see, her husband passing like that. And she has a weak heart as it is... left over from when she had diphtheria, you know. So Ella's help and company will really help, I'm sure.'

When Jane got home that day there were two letters waiting for her, one from Peter and one from Joe. Reading them, she realised anew how much she missed them both.

Joe had joined the Army one month after his baby son was born. Naturally, Mary was upset with him going away, especially as they had a new baby. But back then in 1939, Joe could see that war was looming and if he didn't join a regiment of his own choosing he would soon be conscripted and would have to go where he was sent

Jane remembered the day that Joe had sent his papers off. He often teased his gran and on that particular day he breezed in when they were all having lunch, and, with his face full of smiles, declared, 'I've done it, Gran.'

'What's that, my son?'

'I've joined the Army.'

'Whatever have you done that for?' Gran

asked questioningly.

'I'm fed up with looking up cows' backsides!'

Everyone laughed including Gran.

'Any advice for me then, Gran?'

Alice certainly had. 'Yes, Joe. Don't let anything above your shoulders get too big.'

Joe laughed. 'Of course I won't, Gran. I'll always remember the colour of my roots.'

'So you should, my son. You be proud of them. They go deep in Downside Alley.'

As they all gathered round the table the following Sunday, Mary, who had by then understood Joe's reasons for joining, told everyone that she was very proud of her husband, and that they must come and visit her and baby Thomas whenever they wished to.

'Try and keep us away!' Jane had said. 'And I know you have your parents near, but if there is anything you need, don't be too proud to ask.'

'Jane's right. We're here to help wherever we can,' Archie had added, smiling brightly at his daughter-in-law. 'Having young Thomas round us, well, it reminds us of when our boys were small.'

Now, in 1942, as Jane washed up after dinner she couldn't help but think of those happy days when her two young men were small boys. Both were always so helpful, and not only just to the family. She remembered them doing jobs for Mrs Pike, an elderly widow, one of which they did on their way to school. Every day Mrs Pike filled two large buckets of water from a spring in the lane for her daily needs. And if boys saw that the first bucket was full, they would swap them over for her and, if they had time, would carry them into her cottage. No one ever asked them to, they just did it.

The girls were equally as thoughtful and would often run into the kitchen with a bunch of wildflowers for her, and always made her a pretty handmade card for her birthday. Jane reflected how quickly those years had gone, and remembered her mother saying that the happiest times were when the children were small. How right she was.

As she looked up from her daydreaming, she noticed Mabel White go by the window and knock on Alice's door. She was just about to go and see what on earth Mabel could want with Alice, when Mary called out from the sitting room. 'Are you ready, Mum?' In her reverie, Jane had forgotten her promise to go for a walk with Mary and Thomas. Quickly taking off her apron, she answered, 'Yes, just coming.'

After sharing Sunday dinner with the family, Alice had felt tired, and after excusing herself had gone into her little cottage and made herself a cup of tea. Settling herself in her favourite chair by the fire, it wasn't long before she dozed off to sleep.

Fifteen minutes later a loud rap came to the door, instantly waking Alice from her deep sleep where she had been dreaming about when she had first gone out with Tom. As Alice staggered to her feet, she wondered who on earth it could be. Archie and Jane had the main door to the cottage, and it was unusual for anyone to come to the small side entrance.

As she opened the narrow door, Alice was surprised to see Mabel White standing there. Mabel was married to the estate's manager, a friendly, though mealy mouthed sort of man who cow-towed to his boss's needs. However he came to marry Mabel though was a mystery to all who knew him, and they guessed quite rightly that Mabel had married him. Mabel was a gossipy, sarcastic type of woman who was always right. Alice was polite to her, but neither she or her family had much to do with Mabel if they could help it.

'Good afternoon, Mabel. How can I help?' Alice asked.

'Can I come in for a few minutes, Mrs Samways?' Alice was reluctant, but what else could she do but to say of course. Mabel took a seat without being offered it and looked all round the cosy room.

'Oh, how nice you have it! Amazing for a stable, isn't it?'

'Yes. Amazing,' Alice agreed. This was Mabel

151

at her best and bitchiest. 'How can I help?'

'It's more like how I can help you, Alice.'

'Oh?'

'Yes. I believe that your grandson, Peter, who has been away fighting in this awful war for some time now, has been seeing the doctor's daughter?'

'That's right. Ella. She's a lovely girl.'

'Really? Well, you might not think so when I tell you what has happened.'

Alice stiffened. Whatever was coming now? 'Which is what, Mabel?'

'Ella is pregnant!'

Alice knew she must remain calm in the face of this awful revelation.

'And how do *you* know this?'

'Well, my dear, I just do. And I thought you were probably unaware of the news, and would wish to warn Peter... and your family of course. She's a bad lot, of that there's no doubt.'

'Thank you for telling me, Mabel.' Alice stood up and gestured Mabel to do the same. Then pointing to the door, Alice said, 'There is my door, and I would be happy if you would pass through it.'

'Well, there's no need to get funny with me.'

'I'm not. I just wish you to leave.'

'Mark my words, it's true. And don't forget where you heard it first.'

Alice closed the door firmly behind her unwanted visitor. In shock, she slowly made her way to the nearest chair and sat down. This was concerning news. Although, considering its source, not necessarily true. She gathered her thoughts. They had not seen Ella for a few weeks, which was unusual and Alice recalled that Jane had told her just recently that Ella had gone to Canford St Michael to help Hilda Butt's sister. She thought of Peter and how this would affect him. She thought of Ella, and knew in her heart that she was a lovely young girl. Weighing everything up, Alice knew what she must do, and was thankful that she could do it without involving anyone else.

Following her meeting with Hilda, Ella soon found herself in a different world, and as she settled into her bed on the first night at Amy Trent's cottage, in spite of her dire situation, she was thankful to have the kindness and support of Hilda and her sister, without whom she knew she would be totally lost. She quickly got into the routine of helping Amy with household duties, and taking an afternoon stroll with her through the lanes of Cranmoor St Michael.

Amy had been asked by her sister to keep a close eye on Ella, and had been left strict instructions that if she noticed Ella's anxieties building up, she was to phone Hilda and Hilda would then try to calm her down as much as she could on the end of the telephone. Hilda's kind voice certainly seemed to lift the young girl's mood, and Hilda was so thankful that her sister had had the telephone recently installed, a real life line in this precarious situation.

The unusual decision to have the telephone connected was made after Amy's husband had passed away so that she could easily contact Hilda, who, being the doctor's housekeeper, was in the fortunate position to have the use of his telephone. Amy was an observant lady and sometimes if she noticed Ella becoming withdrawn and uncommunicative, she would suggest a trip into town on the local bus, where they would have a cup of tea and cake in the newly opened tearooms.

It was on one of those earlier outings that the malicious Mabel White had seen Ella coming out of the doctor's surgery and then witnessed her being sick in a side street. Mabel had quickly come to the conclusion that the young, single girl was pregnant.

Ella had not been away from Downside Alley long when Hilda told her that her father had gone away to London to help with the Red Cross. He had said that he would like Hilda to continue to keep the house in order, as once the war was over he would be returning and would be in need of her full services again. Ella was greatly relieved to hear this news, and in the letter which he had left for her, he explained that with her away and there being a great need for doctors in the capital, it seemed the logical thing to do.

With her father gone she felt happier phoning Hilda, which she did more and more, knowing that Godfrey was not around to pick up the telephone.

Amazingly the days and weeks sped by, and soon she felt the baby moving inside of her.

It had been early one morning and at first she thought it was trapped wind, then, as the kick was felt again, she realised that this was the movement of a human life inside of her. As she lay there wrestling with her thoughts and emotions, imagining various scenarios, she realised that giving up the baby, her baby, was going to be very difficult. Dressing quickly, she went downstairs and phoned Hilda, telling her of her decision to keep it. Hilda had listened patiently to Ella's change of mind, and said that she was coming over to see her and Amy later, and they would discuss the options then.

That afternoon, after having a cup of tea, Amy, Hilda and Ella had a long discussion about possible options following the baby's birth, which, taking in the young girl's circumstances, were limited. Amy told Ella that although she was most happy to help her during her pregnancy, due to her weak heart she felt unable to have a young baby living with her.

'I understand that, Mrs Trent,' Ella had replied. 'And I'm just so thankful to have your help at this crucial time.' As Ella looked at Hilda for some sort of answer, Hilda felt she had to be realistic.

'My dear, I understand how you must feel at this time. Feeling your baby move inside you is a very poignant moment for any mother. But, Ella, where would you live? I would willingly help, but my home is in Downside Alley, where everyone knows you, and where your father will be returning to.'

Ella's heart sunk. Up to that point Hilda had always given her a solution to her problems: but not this time. Her mind was in such a quandary as her true feelings burst out.

'This baby has ruined my life! And yet it's all I have in the world. And even if I do have the baby adopted, Peter won't want to know me when he hears what's happened, and he *will* hear, that's for sure! Surely there is somewhere I can go and start again with my own flesh and blood!'

Hilda went over to Ella and cuddled her in her arms. 'My dear girl, I wish I had the answer.'

'But you said it would all be alright, didn't you?'

'I did. And it will be perfectly alright if you have the baby adopted. He or she will go to a good home, perhaps to a couple who can't have children of their own. and will be cherished.'

Ella began to get hysterical. 'But *I* want to cherish it!'

Amy, who had been listening in silence,

came up with another option. 'The only other possibility is that you get a job as a nanny or housekeeper, where the family don't mind you having a baby. But I have to say that, sadly, those types of people are rare. However, Hilda and I can start to make enquiries about that possibility. If that's what you want?'

Ella was over the moon and hugged Amy as she said, 'I want that more than anything. Thank you.' She turned to Hilda. 'Thank you both.'

And so that was how it was left. Hilda and Amy answered all sorts of advertisements in the local newspapers and magazines, but unfortunately to no avail. No one was willing to take on a baby.

As the birth drew near, Trudy, the district nurse, who was going to deliver the baby, told Ella that she would need to decide by the time her baby was a month old, if she was having it adopted or not. And that she had a list of people who would be very suitable parents if the baby was put up for adoption. In her heart, Ella still clung on to the belief that an answer would come, and that she would be able to keep her baby. It was this thought that kept her going through the following weeks. The baby was due at the end of September, but it was two weeks late, and after having a long, painful labour, Ella's baby was born on October 15, 1942.

CHAPTER TEN

November 1942

As Peter stared disbelievingly at the barbed wire and large sign, a soldier, who was fully armed, walked over to him.

'Sorry, mate, you can't go any further. The village has been taken over by the War Office.'

'But, but, you don't understand. I live here. I've just come home on leave to see my family.'

'No one lives here now. Sorry, but you'll have to go back.'

'But... where is everybody? Where are my family? I, I don't understand.'

'Bin away in the war 'ave you, mate? Nobody told you about the evacuation?'

'Evacuation! But, but... where've they all gone?'

'Couldn't tell you, mate. Your best bet is Farmer Cooper. He's auctioning his cows and machinery in the barn just back there. Maybe he can 'elp.'

Still reeling with the shock, Peter nodded his thanks to the soldier and made his way to the ancient tithe barn. Inside, the auction was well under way, although most of the folk were onlookers rather than bidders. Peter spotted Cyril Cooper slumped over a threshing machine in the corner, watching his life-time's work go under the hammer, and made his way over to him. Unsure of what to say, Peter could only guess at the older man's thoughts.

'It's a terrible sight, sir.'

The farmer, his eyes bleak with despair, nodded at the young man.

'Everything's fetching next to nothing. All so sudden, you see. Three week's notice is all we 'ad. Devastating 'tis.'

The magnitude of it all suddenly hit Peter full on. 'Where is everyone? Where's my family?'

Some cows were heard lowing in the background as they were rounded up for the auction, and Farmer Cooper dropped a tear. He wiped it away with a dirty hand.

'Some 'ave gone to Sandham, some to the outlying villages. Some 'ave gone to their graves, poor souls. The shock, you see.'

'Dear God! But *my* family, where are they? Please help me, Mr Cooper.' The farmer was distracted by the auctioneer's bidding. 'I must find them. I've been away, you see, fighting in the war... and I've come home... to, to surprise them....' His voice trailed off.

The farmer turned his thoughts away from the horror around him and looked at Peter, remembering when he used to gather his cows from the common for him when he was just a boy.

'Gone to your Uncle Ron's, I believe. 'Tis

vacant, with him being away in the war.'

Peter gave a huge sigh of relief. 'Thank you. Thank you so much.' The farmer nodded his head, then turned his attention back to the auction.

Peter's thought were all over the place as he made his way to his Uncle Ron's house, which was about three miles away. He knew obviously that there was a war on and that people had to make sacrifices, but evacuating a whole village at such short notice seemed so cruel.

By the time he reached his uncle's house he had calmed down a little, thankful that at least his family had a home.

The kitchen door was ajar and as he pushed it carefully open he saw his mother busily rolling out some pastry on the kitchen table. Hearing the door, she looked up. Peter rushed towards her and the two embraced.

'Oh, Mum!'

After shedding some tears of relief at seeing her son, Jane composed herself. 'Sorry we couldn't let you know, Peter. We, we had no chance, you see.'

'It's alright, Mum. I've seen Farmer Cooper and he told me about the evacuation... I'm so sorry.' Peter glanced around the room. 'Where's Gran?'

Jane looked crestfallen. 'I'm sorry, son. She... she passed away.' Her voice lowered to a whisper. 'The shock of it all.'

Peter hugged his mother tightly. 'Oh, Mum. I'm so sorry.'

Jane nodded her head. 'She's at peace now at least. She really went downhill after receiving the letter. Well, it was torture for us all. Poor soul.'

'Letter? Who from?'

'The War Office. The village was wanted for target practice. Some said they saw Churchill here weeks before the news came.'

'Dear Gran.'

Jane fought back the tears. 'We laid her to rest last week in the cemetery at Downside Alley. Alongside Granddad and all her family.'

As he comforted his mother, Peter suddenly thought of Ella. 'My God! What am I thinking about? Ella. Mum, where's Ella?'

Jane's face momentarily dropped. But she quickly composed herself. 'She's gone to be a companion to Mrs Butt's sister, Amy, who has just lost her husband.'

Peter was in no mood for the ins and outs of other people's lives. 'Where, Mother? Where is she?'

'Why don't you wait until the war is over, Peter. Everything will be different then.'

Peter tried to reason with his mother. 'Look, I've been away for almost a year and have not heard from Ella for almost as long. I must see her, Mother. Don't you understand?'

'Of course I understand, son. Please at least

wait until your father comes home. He's been anxious to see you too, you know.'

'Just tell me where she is, please Mum. Of course I'll come back and see you and Dad later. But please, please, just give me the address.'

'It's a few miles away and...'

'Please Mum, the address.'

Jane sighed and reluctantly gave in. 'All I know is the name of the village.'

'Where? Just tell me where?'

'Cranmoor St Michael. It's north of Sandham... only I wish you wouldn't go... I mean, how will you get there?'

Nothing was going to stop Peter. 'Did Joe's motorbike make it here?'

'Yes, it's in the shed. But...'

'I know, I know, it's his pride and joy. I'll take care of it.'

Jane's head was in a whirl. 'Only I wish you'd...'

But Peter was gone. Jane slumped back onto the kitchen chair and half whispered, 'Poor Peter. Poor Ella.'

Peter wasted no time and was soon speeding along the country lanes towards Sandham. Fortunately, he noticed a small decrepit sign in the hedge pointing to Cranmoor St Michael, and was soon approaching the village. He stopped by the village green and looked around for a clue. There was a lone man leaning on a cottage gate. As he approached him, the old chap grinned and nodded at him.

'You be lost, I s'pose?'

'I, er, well yes, I am in a way.' Peter racked his brains trying to remember what his mother had told him. 'I'm looking for a young woman who is lodging with a recently widowed lady.'

The man lifted his cap, scratched his head and thought for what seemed to Peter an eternity. 'Ah, you be looking for Mrs Trent, I reckon. She do live in Rose Cottage. 'Tis just over there wi' the green gate.' The man pointed to a detached cottage just a few yards away. Peter could have kissed him. He was within minutes of seeing his darling Ella.

'Thank you so much.'

Two minutes later Peter was knocking determinedly on the green, half-cut door. It was opened by an elderly lady with grey hair tied up in a bun. She smiled pleasantly at him.

'Are you Mrs Butt's sister?'

'Yes. Is she alright? No trouble I hope?'

'Oh no, she's fine. Just checking I was at the right house. I believe Miss Harvey is lodging here?'

The elderly lady stiffened, took a deep breath and slightly closed the door. 'She is here, but is unable to see anyone at present.'

'Oh but I'm her boyfriend. I've been away in

the war, and I'm desperate to see her.'

'As I said, she can't see anyone at this time.'

Peter was beginning to boil up inside. Ella was in this cottage and he meant to get to her. 'Look, Mrs Trent, I don't mean to be rude, but you don't understand.'

'I understand perfectly, young man.' She went to shut the door. 'Now if you'll excuse me.'

Peter, who was normally very polite and well mannered, barged past the elderly lady and found himself in a small cottage parlour. The sight that met his eyes turned his whole world upside down. He stared coldly at the scene as if frozen. Ella was sat on a low soft chair and beside her was a baby's cot. Ella looked up, her pale face etched in pain.

Looking at the cot, in a staccato voice Peter asked, 'Is there a baby in there?'

'Yes.'

'Is it your baby?'

'Yes.' Ella made to get up. 'I, I was...'

Oblivious to what Ella was trying to say, Peter had already turned and was going back through the front door.

Before he knew it Peter was driving furiously through the country lanes, his mind in meltdown. After dipping down into the valley he soon found himself by the barbed wire and armed patrol, which had prevented him getting to Downside Alley some hours before. And in spite of the protesting soldiers Peter drove at speed through the barricade. He passed all the abandoned cottages, continuing on until he reached the sea. Moments later he was standing on the cliff edge, with the noise of the pounding waves and screeching seagulls filling his head.

A lone, clear voice somehow broke through the cacophony and cut through Peter's fog.

'That looks bloody dangerous, Samways!'

Peter turned round to see Edward Spencer just a few yards from him. He stared blankly as the figure walked towards him.

'How did you... what are you doing here?'

The Sergeant held out his hand, which Peter grasped, and then put his arm firmly around him. 'That's it, old boy.' They were now safely away from the cliff edge. 'Let's go and sit in my car. I've got a tot of whisky in the glove compartment. Never know when you're going to need it, eh?'

The two men sat in the Morris Cowley, and Peter was soon sipping from Edward's hip flask. After a few swigs he handed it back. 'Thank you, Sergeant.'

'No problem. But, er, do call me Edward... how are you feeling now?'

'Better, Ser, er, Edward, just totally and utterly shattered. My whole life has collapsed in a most horrendous way.'

'I'm really sorry to hear that, Samways. Look, can I take you to see someone? Your parents maybe?' He looked at Peter and gave him an encouraging smile. 'Umm?'

Peter, still wrestling with flashbacks of Ella and the baby, managed a weak 'yes'. He looked up at the Sergeant. 'But how on earth...?'

'...Did I get here? Well, when I arrived at Woodleigh House, I could see lots of Army trucks in the drive, which started to ring alarm bells. Then before I had reached the door an American officer came out to ask who I was. I told him my name and explained that I was the rightful owner of the property and asked what the hell he and his men were doing there! Slapping me on the back, he told me that the house had been commandeered by the Army at the beginning of the war, and then recently given over to the Americans. He then went on to say that he understood the owner of the house had gone to live in another property on the estate. So then I apprised him with the news of my father's death and that I was now the owner. In his dulcet tones he said that he was real sorry about that, and that the house would be returned to me after the war was over.

'Bit of a bloody shock that was! So anyway, after he'd gone back in the house, I poked around some sheds which had caught my eye while I was talking to the yank, and lo and behold one of them had this fine motor in, and even had the keys in the ignition! After checking that this baby started, I sent the taxi man on his way, and, being on my own, something which I've never liked, and with nothing to do, I thought I'd take a trip to see you.'

'But... what about the barbed wire?'

'I was flagged down, of course, and while conversing with the soldiers heard about some young terror who had rammed through the barricade. Realising the shock you must have had on finding the village a no go area, I took a calculated guess that it was you, and asked if I could go through and find out. They waved me on and here I am.'

The reality of what he had been about to do on the cliff top smacked Peter full on, and he quietly said, 'You saved my life.'

'Just returning the favour, old chap, and thankful that, by a quirk of fate, I came.' Edward started the car. 'Now, let's go and see your family, eh?'

Before long Peter and Edward were sat at the kitchen table with Jane, who poured them all a cup of tea. Now the whisky had worn off, Peter was in a dark space once more, and, for a while, uncharacteristically let the circumstances get the better of him. Jane tried to reason with her son as he rambled on. Edward sat in silence, deeply saddened by what he heard.

'Mother! Ella has a baby! A baby! My God, how could she?'

'What about poor Ella? It's hard for her, too.'

'Hard for *her*! What about me? My life has been ruined.'

'So has her life, Peter.'

'No! What she did was of her own making. And I'm supposed to just get on with it?'

Jane gave a huge sigh. This was so very difficult, delicate and heart-breaking. 'I understand your sheer frustration, Peter. But what you must realise is that... is that...' Jane paused.

'Yes, yes, what is it Mother? What I must realise is what?!'

Jane searched for the right words. 'Is that Ella, your dear Ella, is a victim.'

Peter looked hard at his mother, questioning her expression. What was she inferring?

'Victim! You mean...'

Feeling stronger, Jane realised the whole truth must come out. 'Yes, Ella was savagely raped.'

Jane went over to Peter, knelt down and cuddled him. After a few minutes, Peter looked up at his mother and the Sergeant. Thinking of his earlier reaction and behaviour, he was stunned and lost for words. Edward smiled kindly at him as Jane got up and went back to her chair.

'I'm so sorry, old boy.'

Peter shook his head, struggling to take in the immensity of it all.

Jane put her hand in her apron pocket. 'Oh, I had meant to give you this earlier.' She handed Peter an envelope marked with his name. 'It's from Gran. She wrote it not long before she died.'

Still shaking, Peter took the envelope and smiled weakly. 'Thank you.' He read the letter silently, then looked up. 'My goodness! Listen to this.'

My Dear Peter,

I may not see the end of the war but I pray you do. Having lived through the First World War, I know that war changes everything, and when you return, nothing will be quite the same. Nothing, that is, except the love you have from your family, which is constant and true.

In life, things are rarely as they seem. I don't say this in a negative way, for there is much genuine love and kindness in human nature. But I say this as someone who has lived her life without blinkers, and I wish you to do the same. Life is now, Peter, and right now, surrounded by family love, you have everything.

I wish to tell you something that not even your mother knows. The man who brought me up was not my real father. No, my real father abandoned my mother when he heard she was pregnant. But the man she later married was a most wonderful man, so kind, loving and caring. I could not have wished for a kinder father and I treasure the many happy hours we shared together. I feel blest, and I know my mother did as well, to have known such unselfish, genuine love.

Love, true love, is so precious. If you find it, Peter, hold on to it and cherish it. For armed with true love you can overcome whatever trials life may throw at you.

Thank you for every kindness you have ever shown me. God bless.

My love as always.
Gran xx

As Jane wiped her eyes, Edward, who was visibly moved, cleared his throat. 'What an incredible woman. I wished I'd known her.'

Peter was really choked. His emotions were all over the place, as he answered, 'Yes, she was.'

Jane blew her nose and asked, 'Has the letter helped, son?'

'Yes, Mum.' Peter looked down, deep in thought. Then looking up at his mother said, 'Thanks to Gran, my mind has cleared, and, well, I know what I must do.'

Edward was relieved that the situation was beginning to resolve itself, and addressed Peter. 'Can I help? I mean, is there anywhere I can take you?'

'Can you take me to see Ella, please?'

'My pleasure. Show me the way.'

Peter hugged his mother and followed Edward to the car. Half an hour later, for the second time that day, Peter was walking up the path to Rose Cottage. This time though, it was Edward Spencer who knocked at the door. He explained to Mrs Trent that Peter now knew all about Ella's predicament and wanted to apologise for his earlier rudeness. Mrs Trent went to speak with Ella, and then, after a few nerve-racking minutes, told Peter that he could 'Go on through'.

For Peter it was like a take two as he walked into the room. For everything seemed just the same as his earlier visit. Ella was sat on a chair with the cot next to her. She looked up as he entered the room, her face full of nervous anxiety and uncertainty. However, her fears were unfounded for Peter walked straight over to her and got down on his knees.

'Can you forgive my awful behaviour of this morning, my darling?'

As Ella took his hand, tears of relief fell silently down her face and the pain visibly evaporated. 'There is nothing to forgive, my love. You had a terrible shock.'

Peter looked lovingly into Ella's face. The face that was so familiar to him. The face he had longed to see for so long. He realised that she was just the same person and he knew what he had to do. Still on his knees, he took both of her hands in his.

'My darling, wonderful Ella, would you do me the great honour of becoming my wife?'

Ella could hardly believe what she had just heard. Those few short words had taken her from the darkest, bleakest situation to the highest heights of happiness. Feeling indescribably overjoyed, she answered, 'Yes. Oh, yes, my darling Peter.'

With his face bursting with happiness, Peter stood and gently pulled Ella up beside him, then removing a small box from his pocket, took out a solitaire diamond ring and slipped it onto Ella's finger. Tears of joy slipped down Ella's cheeks as she fell into Peter's arms. After a few moments, Peter tilted her face towards him and kissed her gently, then, feeling Ella respond warmly, passionately. As they broke apart moments later, Peter turned towards the cot.

'When will the baby wake up?'

Ella giggled. 'She should be awake soon.' As the two watched the tiny babe, she stirred and opened her eyes.

'May I hold her, please?'

'Yes. Yes, of course you can.' Ella bent down and gently lifted up the pretty dark-haired baby.

She passed her to Peter and said, 'This is Georgia.'

Georgia looked up at him, her face a picture of contentment. As Peter looked lovingly into her small, cherub-like face, he said, 'Hello, Georgia, I'm your father. I've been away for a while, but I'm here to stay now.'

CHAPTER ELEVEN

1942

Notice of the evacuation had come from Tim, the postman, who had the unenviable task of delivering the official paper to each household. Before he even placed the envelope into their hands, the villagers of Downside Alley and the whole Downside estate knew that it was bad news by Tim's emotionally drained face, which was etched in sadness.

Incredibly, alternative housing had been arranged for each family, scattering them within a twenty-mile radius of their homes. The whole of the estate was shrouded in shock and disbelief at the harsh reality this cruel blow had brought to all of their lives. But with only a few short weeks' notice, everyone had to take control of the situation and prepare for the move as best they could.

For some of the locals this proved impossible and not long after the fatal letter had been delivered, an urgent knocking came to Jane and Archie's door. Jane opened it to see Miriam Hicks, with three hats on. Miriam was one of the two sisters who were affected by the moon, and everyone in Downside Alley knew they were slightly eccentric. Before Jane had time to offer a word of greeting, Miriam unleashed her verbose spiel.

'Have ee got the letter, missus? 'Tis the devil's work, that's for sure. An' we must fight the devil wi' all our might. What do ee say?'

Trying hard not to laugh at the poor soul's ridiculously perched hats, the top one of which had a bunch of fake cherries balancing precariously on it, Jane spoke gently to her neighbour. 'Oh, Miriam! I know it's very distressing. But you know, we must do all we can to help our country.'

'Fine words, lady. But 'tis too late for that. You'll see, too late.'

'No, not too late, Miriam. We have the letter as proof of our return.'

'Hah. Nothin' is as it seems, missus. Nothin'.' With that, shaking her head, she scuttled down the path and was soon knocking on Gran Cutler's door, repeating her wild message.

Whether her words were prophetic or not, who can say? But before too many days had passed, the two sisters were taken to the local asylum on the outskirts of Sandham, where both died within the month.

For once in his life Archie was dumbfounded. He struggled to cope with the fact that this savage blow of fate had dictated that the whole village be moved, without any thought for the irrevocable distress it would cause its inhabitants. He was especially grieved about the loss of his home and garden, which was full of sustaining food for the winter ahead. But as always, in a dire situation, Jane composed herself enough to think clearly and comforted her husband.

'I know 'tis a terrible shock, my dear. But we must remember that in the letter it did assure us that after the war is over, we will be able to return.'

'Ah, I know it did. But I've not forgotten what Ella told us that first night she ate with us and you asked her what her hobbies were. She was so enthusiastic about old Tom Hardy and gave us some quotes from his books. Remember?'

Jane nodded her head, and looked at her husband in amazement. She was surprised that he had listened so intently. 'And which one struck a chord with you, my dear?

Archie scratched his head. 'The one where it said that, words be wind. An' I believe thass true, cos I've had assurances before which 'ave come to nothin'!' By now, Archie had worked himself up and started to go red in the face.

'Do calm down, my dear. It won't do you any good. I was speaking to the vicar earlier and he felt sure that we would be back one day. He said that one of the politicians had more or less said so.'

Archie was in the sort of mood that every assurance was a further aggravation.

'Hah, Father used to say, and I believe the old man wasn't far wrong, when he said that you can't trust parsons or politicians. Cos both of 'em tell a good tale!' With that Archie got up and thundered through the door. Jane gave a huge sigh. She knew that after a good walk up the garden he would simmer down, and she realised that the news had been a massive shock to her husband. Downside Alley was his refuge, unshakeable, as he thought. And now, well, who knows? You could only take each day as it came, especially in war time.

The thought had suddenly occurred to her that although they could contact their daughters and Joe fairly easily, they had no way of contacting Peter. Before she had the time to dwell on that daunting thought, an awful moan was heard and Jane quickly made her way to Alice's bedroom where her mother-in-law was struggling to breathe. Jane was soon at her side and, taking her hand, she smiled at the old lady, who was desperately trying to say something.

'It's alright, Mum. Try and relax and take some deep breaths. Can I get you some water?'

Alice had managed to lift her hand and give a dismissive gesture. Witnessing Alice gasping for breath and her desire to communicate something, Jane realised the severity of the situation and put her ear to Alice's mouth. 'What is it, dear?' she asked kindly.

'Letter for Peter,' the old lady whispered as she pointed vaguely at the chest of drawers.

'Letter for Peter,' Jane repeated. 'Okay. I'll make sure he gets it, Mum. Don't worry.' Jane smiled lovingly at Alice whose face suddenly took on a glow of serenity as she closed her eyes and breathed her last.

After his walk round the garden, surveying his winter cabbages and sprouts, Archie went back into his cottage. Taking off his cap, he began talking to Jane with his back to her.

'Sorry I got a bit high handed, my dear, but...' His voice trailed off as he turned to see the shock on his wife's face. 'What is it, Jane? What's 'appened?'

'It's your Mum, Arch. She, she's...' Jane looked into her husband's face. 'She's gone. I'm so sorry, my dear.'

Archie slumped onto the couch. 'Gone? What, you mean...?'

'Yes, my love. She's passed away.'

Archie sat silent for a minute or so. 'How can it be? I mean, I know she's 'ad the flu, but she was getting over that... well, I thought she was.' Jane sat next to her husband and took his hand.

'I think it was the shock, Arch. You know, the shock of the evacuation. And then getting the flu, well the poor soul didn't have the strength to fight it.'

As he struggled to take in the reality of what had happened, Archie fought back the tears. 'You could be right, my dear. I mean, look how 'tis affected us? Poor Mum, she's lived in Downside Alley all her life. She must have felt it much more than she let on.'

'Didn't want to worry us, bless her.'

'That was Mum. Always thinking of others before herself.'

'A lovely epitaph, that.'

'So 'tis.' Archie stood, and paced up and down for a while. 'I s'pose we'd better get the doctor. Then let the vicar know.'

'Would that be the vicar you were talking about earlier?' Jane said in a mildly teasing voice as she tried to lighten the situation.

'Ah. That'll be the one. Perhaps I shouldn't 'ave been so critical.' His mind lapsed for a moment. 'A sober thought, my dear, but you never know when you're gonna need that chap wi' his collar on backwards!' Archie felt humbled. 'I think I'll just go and see Mum, while it's quiet.'

'I'll go along to the shop and ask them if they'd ring the doctor, then.'

'Alright, my dear.'

And so the following week, just a few days before they moved out of Downside Alley, Archie and his family buried Alice alongside her beloved husband, Tom.

By the time Peter arrived unexpectedly at his uncle's cottage, Jane had learnt the tragic news about Ella. It was not through gossip but quite innocently, through Ann, the district nurse. Ann had been on the carrier to Sandham on the same day as Jane, who at the last minute had decided to go to town and buy herself some material to make a black skirt for Alice's funeral the following day. Which was providential as it turned out, for as soon as Ann got sight of Jane she went and sat next to her, and, with her face beaming, said, 'You must be very proud of your new granddaughter, Mrs Samways? Just a few days old, I believe?' At first Jane had thought Ann had mistaken her for someone else, then, quick as lightning, everything fell into place, and she realised that Ella had been away to conceal her pregnancy.

Her minor delay in replying went unnoticed by Ann, who continued, 'Course, I didn't deliver her, but Trudy, the district nurse, who covers the north of the area, told me the news this morning when we met at the hospital. Beautiful babe, she said, with lots of dark hair. Although, as I'm sure you know, the poor girl had a bad time with her labour.' Ann's chatter had given Jane time to revert to her normal, sangfroid self.

'Oh, yes. It's wonderful news.'

'Have you seen her yet?'

'No, not yet. But we will as soon as we've moved. Sadly, my mother-in-law has just passed away... it's her funeral tomorrow, and, well, everything's happened at once.'

'Oh, I am so sorry to hear that. You poor things. Still, you know what they say, each day gives and each day takes. Good job you've got the little babe, eh?'

'Yes. A good job, as you say.' Jane concealed her shock by changing the conversation. 'Where are you going to live, Ann?'

'Well, what with the coastline covered in mines and barbed wire, there are no other coastguard duties for my husband. We've been given a cottage on the nearby estate of Woodleigh, and my husband has been given a job working in the munitions factory in Sandham. Not ideal, but we've got to count our blessings. I mean, the news of the evacuation was horrific, but like everyone else in the country, we just have to do our best until life returns to normal. Well, that is, if it ever does.'

'I'm sure it will. We must be positive, Ann.'

'Got no choice, have we?'

Relieved that the carrier was approaching its destination at Sandham, Jane stood up, and after saying goodbye to her fellow passenger made her way to the high street. Digesting the full impact of Ann's news, she realised that the imminent evacuation had a positive side. Of course, she did not know what Ella's plans were, nor her real situation. But knowing Ella as she did she could only surmise that something sinister and beyond the young girl's control had taken place.

With the villagers of Downside Alley and the whole estate being scattered in every direction, Jane thought that the evacuation would give Ella, Peter, Archie and herself clear thinking time to do the right thing by everyone and put proper plans into place.

And although this reprieve might not be permanent, it would give them enough breathing space to make key decisions without the interference of the neighbours' saccharine comments.

CHAPTER TWELVE

Peter and Ella had a lot of catching up to do and a lot of arrangements to make for their wedding. It was all very exciting. The only depressing moment came when Peter brought up the subject of Georgia's father. He only did so after much thought and thinking he was doing the best thing for Ella.

'I think he should be made to pay for his horrific cruelty to you, darling. And for all the pain and trauma he has inflicted upon you.'

Ella had thought this question might arise and had given it a great deal of consideration. 'I know you mean well, my love. But if we let him into our lives now, we will never be rid of him. He is a vile man who has nothing in his life, nor will he ever have. He is too evil to ever find happiness. I'm not sure he even wants it. But we, my darling, have Georgia and each other... we have everything! Let's not invite him in to spoil it, please.'

Peter was silent for a while. He hated injustice, but as he thought over Ella's words he knew that she was right, and he vowed there and then not to think of the scoundrel ever again. He looked into Ella's beautiful face, then, as he took her hands in his, said, 'I should have known that's what you would say. Your spontaneous thoughts are always seminal and I am in awe of you, my darling. You're right of course. That odious libertine is not worth a moment's thought.' Peter kissed her. 'Thank you for being you... I love you so much.'

After sharing some tender moments, Peter broke away. 'Of course, the other person we have to deal with is your father.'

Ella pulled him back towards her. 'With all this blissful happiness, I forgot to tell you that he is in London. I received a letter from him some time ago telling me he had volunteered to help with the Red Cross there.'

'He must have put that plan into action when he heard of the evacuation, I guess.'

'No, before then, he left not long after I did. I have corresponded with him, but haven't seen him since February.'

'Fancy that! So, he's doing something good then?'

'Yea. Bit of a shock, I know.'

Peter looked concerned. 'I just worry that he will try and stop the wedding.'

'He can't! I'll be twenty-one in January.' Ella kissed Peter. 'And then, my darling, I will be free to do as I wish.'

Peter smiled at Ella's delighted face. Then, remembering that Godfrey was her only relative, said, 'I suppose we could invite him?'

'What! I'd rather not take that risk, thank you. I'll let him know about us when the war is over and he comes back to Downside Alley. That'll be fine.'

'You sound quite unperturbed.'

'I am! Remember how he tried to keep us apart? And to throw me in the arms of you know who?'

Peter smiled at Ella's momentary feistiness. He took her in his arms. 'Of course I do. You win. He won't be invited. Now, Miss Harvey, enough of this. I think we'd better start making out our wedding list!'

Peter's parents and close relatives were thrilled with the wonderful news of the forthcoming wedding. Although Peter had vowed not to speak of Charles Harrington again, he felt he ought to tell his parents, so that they were fully aware of the facts in case of any future altercation.

Archie and Jane had been shocked at the awful ordeal Ella had endured. Both spoke of it in bed, which was where they often had a heart to heart, on the night that they had heard the news, and concluded their conversation on a positive note.

'We must make the best of it, my love,' Jane said with a voice full of love.

'Of course, my dear! And we must welcome the poor little stranger.'

The wedding date was set for mid-January 1943 when Ella was beyond the age of consent, which also tied in with Joe's next leave. Peter's brother was to be best man, and his nephew, Thomas, a page boy. Ella had written to Hannah, asking her to be her maid of honour, which she was thrilled about. And someone else who was beside herself with happiness was Hilda Butt. When Ella told her that Peter was going to be Georgia's father and that they were to be wed, the two had hugged each other tightly, and both had cried with joy and emotion.

There being hardly anything to spend your money on in the war, Peter had saved much of his wages and was able to pay for a small reception in Sandham's town hall. With the war still raging, clothes could only be bought with clothing coupons. And so everyone in the family pooled them, which was enough to buy a smart outfit for Ella, complete with a jaunty hat and elegant gloves.

Hannah, who for the past few months had immersed herself in her job, was thrilled at being in touch with Ella and her family once again. She offered to make a dress for herself and Jane. Since being sent to work in the nursery she had moved back in with her mother, Hilda, who, when she received news of the evacuation was told that she had been assigned a flat above the grocery shop in Sandham.

It had been a very happy day when Ella and Hannah met for the first time since Georgia's birth. Ella was full of the joys of motherhood and wedding plans. Hannah was in good spirits too, amusing her friend with tales she had heard at the nursery from Margaret, the lady in charge. Margaret's sister Jess worked at Sandham's laundry.

'You should read the notes that the soldiers put inside their laundry, El! Very flirtatious, and quite rude some of them!' Blushing, Hannah giggled. 'But, like Jess said, harmless really... cos she'll never meet them. And let's face it, some will never return.'

Until they could find a vacant house, which was not easy in the current climate, Peter and Ella went to live with Archie and Jane at Brook House. Although their bedroom was quite small, there was a tiny box room, which was big enough to take Georgia's cot and chest of drawers. Jane made them as comfortable as she could, and said that she felt sure they would have their own place once the war was over.

Snow had fallen the night before the wedding and as Archie struggled to get some coal for the range, he muttered to himself that maybe the next wedding would be in the summertime. However, before long, Joe, who was living in a flat with his family in the next hamlet to his parents, appeared at their door and offered to clear the paths of snow.

The wedding was at three o' clock and by the time Ella arrived at St Andrew's Church in Sandham the welcome sunshine had melted the worst of the snow away. Whether it was because of the special circumstances of the situation, or whether everyone was just very happy to have something good to celebrate, was unclear, but everyone had smiling faces throughout the day and absolutely everything went like clockwork. Peter's speech was very touching, while Joe's was very humorous. Jane was in charge of Georgia, who looked gorgeous in a newly knitted pink outfit, and she only cried once. Everyone loved the little girl, and the local vicar, who had been very supportive of the young couple, said he would be delighted to Christen her. Ella and Peter thanked him and said that when they returned from their short honeymoon they would go and see him.

Beer was often in short supply during the war, with pubs running out from time to time, but Archie made sure this was not going to happen by bringing along his home brew, and wine for the toast. When they had to leave their home in Downside Alley his brewery equipment was one of the things that Archie was adamant should go with them, and he was often thankful that he had insisted. The pub kindly lent them some glasses, and the food that Wilding's, the local baker supplied was delicious. A three-piece band, consisting of older men from Sandham, provided the music and gave those who wished to, the opportunity to dance.

Everything was in full swing when Peter noticed a stranger standing by the door. He was speaking to Fred, Archie's brother. And after catching his nephew's eye, Fred beckoned Peter over.

As Ella watched her husband speaking to the stranger, she suddenly felt uneasy. And although she wanted to go over to Peter, she resisted, and waited patiently for him to finish his conversation.

After about ten minutes Peter returned and Ella was able to ascertain who the stranger was. 'What is it, darling? Who was that man?'

Peter smiled at Ella as he put his arm around her. 'It's alright. I've just had a bit of a shock.' Before Ella could say anything, he added, 'But a very nice one.' Peter led Ella through some doors to a side lobby where it was quieter. The two of them sat down.

'The man who appeared at the door is Edward Spencer's solicitor.' He paused, trying to take it all in.

'Edward Spencer! But that's the man who was so kind the day when...'

'Yes. The day I came to my senses.'

'But why is his solicitor here? I... I don't

understand.'

Peter took Ella's hands in his. 'Well, the reason he came was to tell me that Edward passed away two weeks ago.'

'Oh, that's so sad, my love. I am sorry.'

'Yes, it is sad, very sad. Apparently, he knew he would not live that long. All the male side of his family have died fairly young with a heart attack, which is sudden and final.'

'Golly. What a burden to carry around.'

'I know. But that's not all. I... I can hardly believe what has happened myself.'

'What?' 'What is it, darling? Tell me.'

Peter gave a huge sigh. 'He has left me everything in his will.'

As Ella took a sharp intake of breath, she whispered, 'That is so kind of him, Peter.'

'It certainly is.' He looked into Ella's face. 'When I say everything, I mean everything. The entire Woodleigh estate... and a huge amount of money too! And what's more, Mr Cousins told me that Edward had made his latest will soon after he rescued me from the cliff edge!'

Ella opened her mouth to speak, but no words would come. Peter handed her an envelope, which contained a handwritten letter from Edward. Ella took the envelope and was just about to read it when Peter said, 'Please read it aloud, darling. My mind was in a bit of a whirl when I read it just now with the solicitor looking on.'

'Okay, here goes.' Ella looked down at the short missive. 'It's quite brief.'

Dear Peter,

By now you will have met Mr Cousins, my solicitor, and will know the news of my will.

I hope you're not too baffled by it. It's just that you are the most decent chap I know, and there is no one else I would rather leave the old place to than you.

To be honest this is nothing compared to what you have, your gorgeous soon-to-be wife, your loyal and steadfast family, and your beautiful little girl. But it is my sincerest hope that the old country pile will bring you all every happiness, which you richly deserve. With regards the money, well, you will need a fair portion of it for the upkeep of the estate. As for the rest, all I ask is that you enjoy it.

Albeit a little late, as regards my term here on earth, I learnt a lot from you, Peter, and feel privileged to have met you and your family, all extraordinary people.

With every good wish,
Edward Spencer

Peter and Ella stood and hugged each other.

Tears flowed down their cheeks. They were shell shocked but very happy. Edward's death was tragic; his generous legacy almost beyond belief.

The doors to the main hall opened and strains of *Night and Day* could be heard. Jane appeared, looking worried. 'Are you alright? Everyone is asking for you.'

'Sorry, Mum. We're fine. Absolutely fine. Just had a bit of a shock, but the nicest one you could have.'

Ella took her mother-in-law's hand. 'It's good news, Mum. We'll tell you all about it later, when all the guests have gone.'

Jane looked from one to the other and, seeing their happy faces, was satisfied that all was well. 'Well, that's a relief. Come back in and have a dance.'

As the newlyweds took to the floor they were joined by Mary and Joe, who had requested *The Bells Are Ringing for Me and my Girl*, followed by *The Way You Look Tonight.* Archie's beer and wine were taking effect and soon half the guests were up and dancing. Everyone was relaxed and happy, the horrors of war being put aside, at least for a while.

When their perfect wedding day was over the young couple made their way to the Red Lion Hotel in Sandham, which Joe had paid for as a wedding present. Leaving all the excitement of the day downstairs, the two climbed the Rococo$_{10}$ stairway to their well laid out bedroom. Hannah, who had been watching over Georgia, smiled at her friends as they entered the room and whispered, 'She's fast asleep.'

Ella's face was radiant as she answered her friend. 'Thanks so much, Hannah.'

As Hannah made for the door, she turned back to look at the joyful faces of the newlyweds. 'No problem. See you tomorrow. Night, night.'

Peter went to the door to see her out. 'Goodnight, Hannah. Thanks again.'

Peter and Ella went over to the wooden cot and gazed at Georgia. As they both looked lovingly at the dear little face of their daughter tucked up in the lemon and white bedding, they felt blessed. They had told Archie and Jane that they would have a good talk with them the next day. The news of Edward's legacy was still sinking in, and as it was their honeymoon night they thought it best to talk about it in the morning. Or, as Peter said, 'We'll be up all night discussing it and floating round the room.'

As Peter undressed Ella, all inhibitions flew away. This was the night they had both dreamt about for such a long time. As her clothes slipped to the floor, Peter kissed her all over. When she was completely naked he carried her over to the bed and undressed himself before lying down beside her. They kissed each other on the lips, gently at first and then, as the passion took over, harder. With his confident touch he awakened her to a heightened pleasure, which she had not known before. When both were fully satisfied by their passionate lovemaking, Peter lay down beside her once more, and the two held each other, kissing tenderly and crying at the sheer joy of loving each other, which was the fulfilment of their most treasured dreams.

The next day, as the whole family sat round the table tucking into Jane's rabbit stew and bread and butter pudding, it was plain for everyone to see that Peter and Ella were glowing with joy and happiness. Violet and Florrie were only home for two days, but this was long enough to hear of Edward's largesse to Peter.

Hearing that some good news was about to be broken, Archie found some rhubarb wine, which he had been keeping for a special occasion, and, by all accounts, this was it.

Peter was unsure of where to start and hesitated at first.

'Just spit it out, son,' Archie said.

'Right. Well, at the reception yesterday, which was wonderful, and I thank you all.' He looked at Ella. 'We both do. For everything you did to make our day so special. We will never forget it.'

'Carry on, darling,' Ella urged, smiling at her husband.

'Of course. The good news... extraordinary news, in fact, is that Edward Spencer, my former Sergeant, who I know you met, Mum and Dad, having very sadly passed away recently, has... has left me his entire estate and money!'

There was a stunned silence. Peter and Ella looked at each other. Ella felt she must speak. 'Isn't it wonderful news?'

'Would that be the Woodleigh estate, son?' Archie asked.

'Yes! That's right, Dad.'

Jane stood up and went to Peter and gave him a hug. With tears running down her cheeks she said, 'It's a miracle. After everything that's happened, it's a miracle.' Unsure of the correct protocol, she blurted out, 'Let's toast Edward.'

They all raised their glasses, and after the toast all began talking at once. Joe went over to his brother and patted him on the back. 'That's amazing news, Pete. Good for you.'

But somehow the atmosphere was not right to Peter, and standing up he declared, 'This is not just for me and Ella, but for all of you. There is no one else I would rather share my good fortune with than you, my family. Ella and I have a great deal of talking and planning to do, but if anyone is in need of anything, please, just ask. My only sadness is that dear Gran is not here to see this day.'

Peter was thoughtful for a few seconds. 'In his letter to me, Edward told me that I have everything, because I have a loyal, steadfast family, and he is quite right. He said his legacy is nothing to what I already have. And that applies to us all. We are all so fortunate to have had the guidance and wisdom of Gran and Mum and Dad. Nothing can take that away. With this inheritance, if we use it wisely, we can build on what we already have and can make a difference to all our lives... and, hopefully, others too.'

Archie, who has been listening intently to his son's speech, stood up. 'Thank you, my son, for sharing your good news with us. And it is good news. And if Gran were here she would remind you of the days when you used to empty her and Granddad's bucket in the garden, when she would tell you that although she couldn't reward you, you would be rewarded, my son. Now, with this 'ere news today, that day has arrived and I couldn't be happier. And I tell you what, when you go to your new estate I'd love to come with you and trap a few rabbits. Our garden at Brook House is like a postage stamp, and what's more, we 'ad to buy the rabbit we had for dinner today!'

Everyone laughed. Amid the lively chatter that followed, Jane, Ella and Mary began to clear the plates. Just then Georgia awoke and began to cry. Peter picked her up and cuddled her.

'Edward is right. Nothing is more precious

than the things we already have. By his kindness we can build a better life for this little one.' Sniffing the air and wrinkling up his nose, he added, 'But for right now, young lady, I think you need a nappy change!' He handed her to Ella. 'And so it's over to you, Mummy.'

CHAPTER THIRTEEN

With so much to be done, it was a blessing that Peter had been granted two weeks' marriage leave. After their brief two-day honeymoon, and before going back, Ella suggested to Peter that when she had time she could perhaps write a letter to all their tenants, introducing themselves as the new owners and saying that they looked forward to meeting them all in good time. Peter thought it a very good idea and put his thoughts to Ella about other estate matters.

'I think we ought to introduce ourselves personally to the vicar, farmer and publican. What say you?'

'Good idea, my love, but when were you thinking of doing it?'

'Well, it can only be this morning or tomorrow, as we have the appointment with Mr Cousins this afternoon. Thinking about it, this morning would be preferable, cos if Mr Cousins shows us a suitable house today we could maybe move in tomorrow. Then the following day I'm off to Wales, as you know.' Peter kissed Ella tenderly. 'But, my darling, I will let you decide.'

Ella smiled brightly. 'Right, there's no time like the present. Or do you think we should make an appointment?'

'Well, manners suggest that we should. But

the publican will be at his bar, the farmer should be on his farm, and, well, the vicar should be in the vicarage. Let's take a chance, eh? We should see at least one of them.'

Twenty minutes later, having left Georgia with Jane, Peter and Ella were sat in the vicarage with the Reverend Simon Morley, sipping a freshly made cup of tea, served by his rather gauche wife. Fortunately, as they walked up the drive, he was coming back from the church, having just had a choir rehearsal.

After introducing themselves to Reverend Morley they were invited into the study where Peter explained that he and Ella were the new owners of the Woodleigh estate and just about to move in. Ella added that they would like to be involved with any fundraising events for the church. Reverend Morley's previously stern face lit up as he replied, 'That is so kind of you, and very much appreciated. The previous owner, Brigadier Spencer, was rather reclusive, taking no interest in the village at all apart from attending the odd cricket match.'

Not wishing to discredit Edward's father, Peter said, 'Well, *we* hope to become more involved as time passes and peace is restored.'

'Yes, quite. Thank you. Well, it would be nice to see you at the Sunday services,' he looked at Peter, 'though I realise you are away most of the time at present.' Then, looking at Ella, he added, 'You are most welcome any time, Mrs Samways.'

'Thank you, Reverend Morley. Do you have a Sunday school for the children?'

The Reverend looked slightly flustered. 'No. We don't at this time. It's very hard to find the right leader, you know. The last one we had turned out to be a, er, a sex offender.' He paused and noted Peter and Ella's look of horror. 'Yes, very unfortunate.'

Peter and Ella voiced their concern. 'That's awful. How was he caught?'

A wry smile slithered across the Reverend's face. 'Yes, everyone assumed it was a man. But, no, this was a woman.' He noted a further look of disbelief on the faces of his guests. 'She came highly recommended too, and, I have to say, I rather liked her. But, the poor unfortunate boy whom she abused ran home immediately after Sunday school and told his mother that the teacher had, er, hum, touched his private parts as he was putting away the hymn books in the vestry.'

Peter was silent, while Ella exclaimed, 'Oh, my goodness!'

'Yes, rather disturbing, isn't it? But it was soon forgotten. The woman concerned left as soon as she was confronted with the accusation, and the boy, well, he just got on with it, I suppose. His family didn't stay too long at Woodleigh after the incident. The father said to me that a fresh start was needed. And that was that.'

'Was that long ago?' Ella asked.

'Must be three years now. And no Sunday school since. So if you or anyone you know would like to take on the role, well, that would be marvellous.'

'I'm afraid I couldn't at the moment, Reverend, but in the future we may be able to help.'

'Any support you can give will be most welcome.'

Peter and Ella finished their tea, thanked Reverend Morley for seeing them, and made their way to the front door. Shaking their hands, he said, 'It's been a great pleasure to meet you both. I wish you all the best with the running of the estate, and look forward to seeing you soon. God bless.' With that he closed the door, and Peter and Ella walked arm in arm down the drive.

Ella smiled at her husband. 'One down, two to go.'

'Well, for all Dad says about the clergy, I think it's good to get to know your vicar, whoever you are. And he seems a decent enough bloke.'

'Yes. What a tale about the Sunday school teacher though!'

'I know. Bit grim that, wasn't it? Just goes to show, you have to be alert all the time, especially round children, no matter how plausible people seem.'

'Funny how things come back to you, isn't it? This incident reminds me of something I heard on a film, which went along the lines of – we are all governed by our sexuality. And, you know just thinking of what we've experienced and know about in our lives, I think it's true, don't you?'

'Maybe.' Peter was conscious that the conversation was getting a bit heavy. 'Anyway, back to what we were saying; did you mean it... you know, what you said about helping with a Sunday school?'

'In the future, perhaps. I do think it's important for the children to be introduced early to the Bible stories and the teachings of Jesus. I must give that some thought.'

'Well, I certainly enjoyed my time at Sunday school. But you do need a good teacher.'

'Same as in your teenage years, you need a good mentor.'

'And who was yours, my darling?'

Ella smiled in remembrance. 'My wonderful Mother! Who was yours?'

'Mum, Dad and Gran. All incredible people. So wise, so unreservedly loving, and so very astute. I can only aspire to emulate them.' By now the two were walking into the pub, which had not long opened. Landlord, Bill Bradley, welcomed them with a massive smile as they entered the long bar. 'Welcome, folks. What can I get you?'

Peter smiled at the tall, imposing landlord. 'A pint of best bitter, please.' He turned to Ella, who said, 'A lemonade for me, thanks.'

'Coming up, sir. I don't think we've had the

pleasure of seeing you here before. So, what brings you here to Woodleigh today?'

'No. We've not been in your pub before. But we are just about to move here, and wanted to introduce ourselves.'

'Well, that's real gentlemanly of you, sir. Found a house to rent, have you? The estate's got a new owner, but I've not met him yet.'

Ella sipped her drink, trying to conceal her giggles. Peter beamed at the landlord. 'But you have now.' He extended his hand across the bar. 'I'm Peter Samways, and this is my wife, Ella. We are the new owners of the Woodleigh estate.'

Bill looked at the young couple, stroked his bristly beard and laughed heartily. 'Well, I'll be blowed! Fancy you coming in here!' His eyes sparkled as he poured them a whisky each. 'Have this on me. It's real nice to meet you both.' Ella tried to stop him from pouring the drink, but it was too late.

'That won't do you any harm, my dear. I reckon you'll need it, with all the work you've got to do.' He stroked his beard again. 'It's quite incredible, you're the first estate owner to set foot in here. And my family have had the pub for over a hundred years.'

Putting down his glass, Peter exclaimed, 'Over a hundred years! That's amazing. I guess you know a lot of local tales then?'

'Oh yes. Not much goes on here that I don't know about. Mind you, I've only served here for ten years. I had to come home from America when the old man took bad. Humped too many of the barrels, I reckon.'

Ella joined in the conversation. 'Are your family from America then?'

'No, not originally. My uncle and father went out there in 1901 to start a new life. But my grandfather, who was running this pub at the time, got took bad, and so me father came back to help. History repeating itself, with me doing the same for me father a few years later.' Bill reached behind him, picked up a packet of woodbines and, taking a cigarette out, lit it up.

'What made you decide to go to America, Bill?'

Puffing clouds of smoke into the air, Bill answered with the cigarette still in his mouth. 'Well, I'd had a good education and prospects were not good here in the 1920s, so as a sixteen-year-old boy, just left school I had, father thought it would give me a better chance in life.'

'Goodness!' Ella said in surprise. 'That was a long journey for a sixteen year old.'

'It was really, cos I was on me own, you see, and the boat was crammed full of people.'

Peter was fascinated. 'That was some undertaking, Bill. And what happened when you got there? I mean to say, how did your uncle find you amidst the sea of faces?'

Bill took a final draw on the cigarette, and although it was only half smoked, stubbed it out, then looked at his newest customers with a knowing grin. 'That was all worked out by Father and Uncle before I left. When we sailed into the harbour, I put on my bright red school cap, the one I wore at Sandham Grammar, and it did the trick. Soon as I walked off the gang plank, Uncle Robert was there with open arms to greet me.'

'What an adventure it must have been,' Ella said, smiling at Bill.

'You could say that, my dear. I worked for Uncle Robert, first in his bookshop, which was alright. But wanting to set up in business on my own, Uncle financed a hat shop for me, and I became known as Bill Hat.' He nodded to himself. 'Yes, they were good days.'

'It must have been a shock for you having to come home, though?'

'No, not a shock, Peter, quite a blessing in a way. I was starting to drink too much and the business was going downhill. So it gave me a bit of a jolt, which I needed. Anyway, that's enough about me, folks. As I said before, it's real nice to see you here. I really appreciate you coming, just as long as you're not going to tell me that you're going to put up the rent!'

Peter laughed. 'No. The thought hadn't even occurred to us.' Peter looked at Ella with a twinkle in his eye. 'But now that you mention it... no, only kidding. Just pleased to know that you have a good business here, Bill. And if you have any concerns, just let us know.'

A group of soldiers entered the bar, and Bill looked towards them. 'Be with you in a minute, lads.' Peter and Ella stood up and said their goodbyes. 'Thanks for calling now. Do come again... oh, and, er, good luck with the estate.'

Once outside, Peter and Ella linked arms and made their way towards the lane. Peter looked at his watch. 'Do you know, it's almost twelve o'clock? I think we'll leave Farmer Hudson for another day, if that's okay with you?'

Ella nodded her head. 'Absolutely! Anyway, I don't know about you, my darling, but I'm starving! Must have been the whisky, sharpened my appetite. Still, a good morning, I'd say. Nice to have met Reverend Morley and Bill. It really feels as if we are part of the village now!' Peter gave her a squeeze. 'Yes, it really does!'

After an enjoyable lunch, Peter and Ella relaxed by the fire before getting ready to meet Edward's solicitor, who was coming to their house at two o'clock. Mr Cousins arrived promptly and was shown into the study where, after shaking hands with Peter and Ella and exchanging pleasantries, the official paperwork was read and signed, and various bunches of keys handed over. Following the formalities, Mr Cousins drove the young couple to look around the estate, but sadly they only glimpsed Woodleigh House as it had been commandeered by the American Army. It was only when Mr Cousins was telling the couple this that Peter recalled Edward telling him of the Army's occupation of his father's house.

As the house was away from the rest of the village and had a separate drive, leading directly to the main road, the Army did not interfere with the villagers of Woodleigh, and, in fact, once the Samways family had moved in, they did not know their military neighbours were there. Ella had felt disappointed that Woodleigh House was not available for them. However, Mr Cousins soon told them about another house, which had always been occupied by the estate manager and which was empty. He suggested that maybe that would be suitable for them to move into. He went on to tell them that it was L-shaped and only marginally smaller than Woodleigh House; adding that it had been built in the eighteenth century for the then owner, who had found favour with the royal family. Peter and Ella were fascinated and, feeling excited by the prospect of living in such an architecturally interesting house, asked if they could view it.

From the outside, the walls were rather plain looking, with grey paint covering the exterior. But once inside the whole feeling of the property changed; the windows were diamond leaded with chamfered mullions and the rooms were spacious, the kitchen being of a good size and well equipped with cupboards going from floor to ceiling on one wall. It was called Rylands, and as they looked round the elegant drawing room,

Peter and Ella hugged each other in excitement, saying that it would be perfect for them until Woodleigh House became available.

Regarding the other cottages on the estate, Mr Cousins explained that some had been empty before the war, the estate having been somewhat neglected by the Brigadier, whose failing health mentally and physically had left him rather remote and uninterested in his business affairs. Combined with the fact that his only son was virtually estranged from him, a predicament which, when he had days upon days to reflect on, he concluded was largely his own fault, this had left him a very sad and lonely old man. Following the evacuation of the Downside estate, two of the dwellings had been allocated on a temporary basis to people who had been made homeless. He added that there were still four further empty cottages which, with some minor decoration, could be lived in.

And so, with help from Joe and Mary, Peter and Ella moved into Rylands the next day. Although there was a good deal of painting to do, Ella said she would do this a bit at a time. Like Peter, she was so thrilled and excited to have a home to call their own. One of their neighbours was Ann, the district nurse, whom Ella soon made friends with and was always kept up-to-date with the latest births and their various dramas whenever they met. Thankfully, the carrier came by Woodleigh once a week and

Ella could meet up with Jane, Mary and Hannah from time to time. Hannah had decided to learn to drive, and this gave Ella the idea of employing her as a chauffeur and home help once the war was over and she was free to leave the nursery. Hannah was over the moon at the thought of working with her friends, but just disappointed that she had to wait.

When Peter had reluctantly left his family the day after moving into Rylands, he travelled to Pembrokeshire where he had been posted to serve at a radar station at St David's Head, and where he was in charge of forty men. The headquarters was in a farmyard, and the large number of WAAFS$_{11}$ who were serving at the station were billeted in the farmhouse, while he and his fellow airmen slept at the radar station. A small Army camp was nearby at Castle Martin, and quite amazingly it had a modern cinema come theatre. It was there, in 1943, that Peter and some friends spent an enjoyable evening listening to Henry Hall's$_{12}$ band playing.

The whole area was teeming with rabbits and Peter was amused that one of the RAF lads would trap and send some of them in the post to his wife who lived in Newcastle. The rabbits, which were just tied with string and the address attached on a label, always got there safely, with the postman only once complaining that, 'It's a bit high today, missus!'

He enjoyed his eighteen months there and

counted it a blest posting for he didn't work at night, and best of all he was able to take a long weekend's leave every six weeks. This was sheer luxury, as leave began after duty at nine o'clock on Friday morning, leaving him free until duty at midnight the following Monday.

It was arranged that Georgia would be christened twelve weeks after the wedding when Peter had one of those glorious long weekends. It being spring-time the church was beautifully decorated with daffodils, primroses and bluebells, their scent pervading the whole of the ancient building.

Hannah and Mary were thrilled to be asked to be Georgia's Godmothers and Joe was asked to be her Godfather, but sadly he could not get leave. And so Archie stood in for Joe and voiced his vows to care for his granddaughter with pride. Afterwards they all celebrated with a high tea at Rylands, the latter having been swiftly spruced up by Ella and Hannah.

As they enjoyed their tea, which included Jane's homemade scones and jam, Mary got up from the table and hurriedly left the room. Ella followed quickly, to find Mary being sick in the kitchen sink. Looking up at Ella, her face ghostly white, she remarked, 'It looks like I'm pregnant again, Ella. I think it was on your wedding day.

We had such fun and, well, you know.' She giggled. 'Heavens! That's better now I've been sick. I hate that initial feeling, don't you?'

Ella nodded in agreement. 'Well that's lovely news, Mary. Does Joe know?'

'No. No one knows yet. But we can tell the family if you like, cos I'll be writing to Joe tonight.'

'Well, at least Thomas is three now, a nice age gap.'

'That's just what I was thinking.'

Ella and Mary went back into the dining room where Mary broke the news. 'More good news! Joe and I are expecting a baby in October. Mind you, he don't know it yet.' Mary's face was lit up with elation as Jane gave her a hug and Archie raised his cup of tea in a toast.

'Thass lovely news, my dear. Here's to you! And make sure you look after yerself, won't you?'

'Course I will,' Mary said cheerfully.

Although Archie was sad that he had temporarily lost Downside Alley, he felt proud that his family was flourishing.

CHAPTER FOURTEEN

Over the next six months there were many changes in the Samways household. Archie and Jane moved into Myrtle Cottage on the Woodleigh estate, and so were able to see Ella and Georgia every day. Having acres of land around him once more meant that Archie was in his element. Archie's job on the Downside estate had been considered one of national importance, and so in spite of the war, his life continued much as normal. But soon after the evacuation the authorities spoke of giving him a job at the local ironmongers in Sandham, which was not too far from his temporary accommodation. Although the job would have been alien to his work as a gamekeeper, Archie had remarked that he would not feel too lost, for some of the shop's multifarious stock included rabbit wires and bull rings.

But this new position never materialised because, once all the estate paperwork was completed and Peter was the official owner of the Woodleigh estate, Peter appointed his father gamekeeper and temporary manager. The authorities were happy with that and, due to his age being forty five at the outbreak of war, had not considered him for the services.

With Joe away, Mary had been delighted

when Peter and Ella offered her and Joe, Rose Cottage on the Woodleigh estate. Although in the absence of Joe, Mary, Ella and Jane had done most of the moving. Jane and Archie were pleased to have their growing family near them, and Archie was even beginning to think of Woodleigh as home, but deep in his heart he missed Downside Alley, which he knew would always be his spiritual home, and he looked forward to the day when he could move back there.

Thomas loved his new home and surroundings, and once he had found his way round he would often run from his home to Rylands and Myrtle Cottage. Mary was keen for him to play with children of his own age, and once a week she took him to the nearby farmhouse where the youngest boy, Max Hudson, was the same age as Thomas. Max had four older brothers who were all at school in Sandham. The joy of a big family is beyond compare, the one snag being that when one is ill, the virus quickly gets passed to the other siblings. And this is what happened to the Hudson children.

Unfortunately, the older boy, Brian, caught whooping cough from his school mates and soon passed it to his brothers. Not knowing this, Mary had taken little Thomas as arranged to the farmhouse to play. When she heard Max coughing, she asked Mrs Hudson if he was alright. The latter, whose nature erred on the sloppy side, casually replied, 'Oh gawd, our Brian's had the whooping cough, so I 'spect that's what Max has got.' Before the last few words were out of Mrs Hudson's mouth, Mary had grabbed Thomas and left.

That night Thomas began whooping, and Mary was beside herself. It was a potentially fatal disease. She called for the doctor in Sandham who said there was no treatment, just keep him isolated from other children and make sure he was propped up in bed with a bowl at his side to be sick in. It was the wretched, continuous cough that caused the poor boy to be sick, and the dear lad would cry every time he was. Mary slept in the same room as him and was up most of the night, making sure he did not choke on his vomit.

Just a few days after Thomas' first bout of coughing, Georgia began to cough. Ella called the doctor immediately who said, because of her age, she must go to hospital where she should stay in isolation. Ella was distraught as she watched her little girl being taken away in the ambulance. She was not allowed to go with her, nor to visit her. It was a horrendous time for all the family. Peter came home at the weekend but could do no more than pace up and down, and to comfort Ella as much as he could.

The only way Peter and Ella could find out how Georgia was doing was to buy the local evening paper. Every child in the isolation ward had been given a number, and every evening the numbers were printed in the local paper, each with an identification code indicating how they were. Thankfully, Georgia never had the seriously ill code, and more often than not it was the stable code. Then suddenly, as quick as it had ascended among them, Thomas and Georgia's cough vastly improved. By the time Georgia came home she had been hospitalised for six long weeks. But the ordeal was not quite over, for when they undressed their little girl on her first night at home they were horrified to see that she was covered in scabs, nasty scabs on the skin caused by dirty linen and blankets. As Peter and Ella held her in their arms, they cried. They cried because their lovely daughter was home and over the worst, and they cried because they were angry at her neglect. As Peter wiped the tears from his eyes and then from Ella's, he said, 'Let's be thankful, darling. She's home with us.'

'I know, but the scabs are simply awful.'

'Of course they are, my love. But they won't kill her! With the right treatment the scabs will heal soon and we'll forget she ever had them.'

With Thomas and Georgia on the mend the whole family thanked the Lord for his great mercies. They knew from the number system in the paper that many children had died, and were dying every week.

Thomas and Georgia's cough, in a milder and ever diminishing form, lasted for weeks. Jane had said, once she knew her two grandchildren were on the mend, that an old wives' tale from Gran was that, whatever time of the year you contracted whooping cough, you would keep it until the following May. And this was certainly true of Thomas and Georgia.

During late September, on a fresh, bright morning, with four weeks to go before her due date, Mary went into labour. Fortunately, district nurse Ann was living a few doors away and was soon beside Mary, examining her. Ann quickly realised that something was not right and had Mary transferred to Sandham hospital.

Jane sent a telegram to Joe, hoping he would be able to get compassionate leave. Jane and Archie offered to look after Thomas and Georgia, while Ella went to the hospital to be at Mary's side. Although Ella had wanted to find Mary's parents, she was not sure of their whereabouts since the evacuation, and, in the given circumstances, did not have time to find out. By the time the doctors came to examine Mary she was in a lot of pain, and Ella was told to wait outside.

This was an anxious time for them all. A time when everyone felt totally helpless. After drinking an insipid cup of tea, Ella went into the hospital chapel and said some prayers for Mary and the unborn baby. In the peace of the chapel she couldn't help but think how powerless was Man, and that without God in their lives, humans were constantly floundering. As she continued in her prayers she was aware of a figure by her side. It was the ward sister, a rather stern-looking woman with an abrupt manner, who asked who was the next of kin.

'Mary's husband, Joe. He's away in the war. Our mother-in-law has sent a telegram.' Ella was beginning to feel uneasy.

'Mrs Samways is very poorly, I'm afraid. The doctors are doing all they can, and hope to get the baby out as soon as possible. But I have to tell you that the mother has a life-threatening problem. I'm sorry.'

'What can I do to help?' Ella asked.

'Nothing really. In these situations we are totally in the doctor's hands... and God's of course. I'll let you know when there is any more news.'

'Thank you.'

The sister walked away and quietly closed the door. Ella was in shock and wished she had someone to talk to. She thought about going home and maybe asking Jane to come in to the hospital. But that would not be fair on Archie. He couldn't look after the little ones on his own. There was nothing to do but wait.

An hour or so later the sister appeared once more. Ella knew it was bad news by the way she approached her. 'I'm sorry to tell you that your sister-in-law has passed away... but the baby, a little girl, has been safely delivered and is healthy and well.' As the sister put an arm around Ella's shoulder, Ella burst into tears. After a few moments the sister asked, 'Would you like to see the baby?'

Numb with the news, Ella nodded her head in the affirmative. A few minutes later Ella was holding the baby in her arms, the baby Mary should have been holding. She was perfect, with a mop of black hair, just like her mother's, she thought. 'What will happen now?' Ella asked.

'The baby will stay here for two weeks, but after that it would be good if the father or his family could take her home.'

'Thank you for your help, Sister. May I see Mary now, please?'

'I think it best if you come back later, or tomorrow. She is not ready yet.'

'I understand, thank you. I hope to come back later with some of my family.'

'Of course. Now if you'll excuse me, I need to carry on with checks on the baby.' Feeling she has been dismissed, Ella handed over the baby to the sister and left the ward.

As the need to get home quickly was imperative, Ella decided to take a taxi, and was soon opening the door at Rylands. Georgia could be heard crying, and as Ella entered the sitting room, Jane came through from the kitchen with her granddaughter in her arms.

'It's her teeth, I think. Poor love.' Jane handed Georgia to Ella, who sat down on the low soft chair and began to feed her. Not knowing how long she would be gone, Ella had left a bottle of powdered milk just in case, but knew that Georgia preferred her own milk the best. As Georgia suckled nicely, Jane asked if there was any news. She had been anxious all morning, but had not wished to pounce on Ella as soon as she walked through the door.

'Oh, Mum. It's so terribly sad. Mary has passed away.' Ella began to cry.

Jane had feared as much and went to console Ella. 'And the baby, too?'

Ella looked up and smiled. It was almost as if she had forgotten the one piece of brightness. 'No. The baby was safely delivered and is a healthy, beautiful little girl.'

Jane hugged Ella as best she could with Georgia sucking away. Just then car tyres were heard on the gravel. The two looked at each other and simultaneously said, 'Joe'. Jane went to the door to meet her son, who looked pale and anxious. After a silent hug, Jane asked him to go into the kitchen, and a few moments later Ella joined them, Georgia having finished feeding.

Joe had looked at both the women's faces, trying to read them. Seeing only sadness, he could bear it no longer. 'Will someone please tell me what's going on?'

Jane spoke in a whispered tone. 'Mary went into labour early, Joe... there were complications and she was taken to the hospital in Sandham.'

'Dear God! It's bad news, isn't it?'

Ella walked over to her brother-in-law. 'She's gone, Joe. Mary's gone.' She put her arms round him and held him tightly as he sobbed into her shoulder. Suddenly he broke away.

'The baby? Did it die, too?'

'No, Joe. Thanks to the skill of the surgeons who had to perform an emergency Caesarean, you have a beautiful baby daughter.' Jane spoke softly, really not knowing what his reaction would be. Joe sat down on a nearby chair, deep in thought for a few minutes.

'So you're telling me that Mary has died giving birth?'

'Mary had complications, Joe. The doctors did all they could. There was nothing else anyone could do.'

'I must see her. I must see her.' As the two women were both wondering whether he was referring to Mary or the baby, he muttered, 'I must see my Mary.'

'Of course. But can I get you a cup of tea first, Joe?'

Joe waved his arms at Ella. 'No. I just want to see my Mary.'

And so the taxi was ordered and an hour later Joe was allowed in to the mortuary to see his wife. She looked as if she was asleep, he thought.

Not a blemish on her face, just as beautiful as she always was. He bent down to kiss her, and was alarmed at how cold she felt. He pushed her hair from her face, as he had so often done. Then, getting onto his knees, he whispered to her, 'My dearest Mary, my darling wife, I'm so sorry I was not there with you, my love. Thank you for giving me a beautiful daughter. I haven't seen her yet. But I'm sure she's just like you. I will tell her all about you as she grows up.' He paused and kissed her hand. As he looked at Mary again, the stark reality hit him. She really was dead. She wouldn't ever call his name again or laugh with him at some silly joke. As he gazed at her, tears fell down his cheeks and onto her face. 'I love you, my darling Mary. God bless.'

Outside the mortuary, Jane was concerned that Joe had been so long. Then he appeared in the doorway and fell into his mother's arms. 'She looks beautiful, Mum. But now I'd like to go and meet Merrily. That's the name we chose for our daughter.'

A few minutes later Joe was cuddling his baby daughter and smiling into her dear little face. 'Just look at her black hair, Mum. That's Mary's hair! Isn't she the most beautiful baby you've ever seen?'

Jane smiled at her son. 'She certainly is. I've been speaking to the Sister, and she must stay in hospital for two weeks, but then we can take her home.'

'Of course. That's where she should be.'

Understandably, Joe's emotions were all over the place. His family helped him as best they could over the following days, which were the hardest time of all. Mary's parents had to be found before funeral arrangements could be made. And in order to find Dan and Agnes, Archie took himself into Sandham, to the town hall. The receptionist was unsure of how to find out details of who had gone where after the evacuation, but fortunately a local councillor, who was au fait with the evacuees' details, passed through the lobby and took Archie into his office. After about fifteen minutes it was found that Mary's parents had been moved to Holywell, a village about half an hour away from Sandham.

Archie decided he had better get a taxi to Holywell, something he had never done before and which was really against his principles. But desperate times called for desperate measures, he told himself, and he thanked God that Peter had had the good fortune to be left some money so that the family could more easily help each other in these trying times.

As he found himself looking out of the taxi window he thought of Joe's words some years earlier when he had said that it was a changing world, Dad, and we must embrace it. Archie found this hard to do but realised that the world he had known was no longer there, certainly not at the moment. He just prayed that life would return to normal after the war and he could get into his old routine of catching his donkey for transport, getting his hands dirty with Downside Alley soil and drinking at the local pub once again.

Thankfully, Dan and Agnes were at home when Archie arrived, and as soon as they saw his face they knew it was bad news. Agnes broke down and collapsed into her husband's arms, while Dan went as white as a sheet, and after firmly placing his wife onto a chair, dashed out to the garden to be sick.

Like Joe, they wanted to see Mary and their baby granddaughter. It was thought it would be best to do this the next day, and, in the meantime, Archie told Dan and Agnes that they were welcome to stay at Rylands, where Joe would be near and they could visit the hospital together. This kind gesture was appreciated and without hesitation the couple decided to take up the offer.

Within an hour, Archie, Dan and Agnes arrived at Rylands, where Ella was waiting with a cup of tea and some supper. Delicious as it was, everyone just picked at their food. The vicar called a bit later and, after saying prayers for Mary, asked Joe and Mary's parents to give some thought to which hymns and readings they would like at Mary's funeral, adding that he would call back in two days' time to finalise the order.

Everyone was completely shell shocked at the day's happenings and tumbled into bed that night with a sense of unreality and numbness.

How they got through the next few days no one really knew. If Gran had been there she would have said that it was through love and love alone, and no one would have argued with her. Everyone did their bit and all were grateful to have the family so close.

Mary's funeral was a simple, poignant affair. 'Just as she would have wished for,' Joe whispered as he scattered some wildflowers - gathered from the undulating hills where they used to walk together - over Mary's coffin.

It had been arranged that, due to Merrily feeding well and putting on weight, she would come home the day after the funeral. Ella had spoken to Peter on the telephone, and the two had agreed that if Agnes and Dan did not feel able to care for Thomas and Merrily, they would offer to look after them until the war was over and Joe returned home. Mary's parents, still in deep shock, had smiled kindly at Joe when he spoke about the immediate care of the children, but after some consideration told him that they felt they were unable to cope with a toddler and a baby. And so, very gratefully, Joe accepted Peter and Ella's kind offer.

Thomas had taken his mother's death badly. Of course, at his tender age he did not understand when his dad told him that his mummy had gone to sleep. His worst time of day was bedtime, when he was used to Mary reading to him. He would cry his heart out as he shouted, 'I want Mummy.' However, after a few short weeks he became accustomed to playing with Georgia and helping Ella to look after Merrily and he calmed right down, reverting to his former, happy self.

After two weeks' compassionate leave Joe had to rejoin his regiment. Before he went, Ella had a chat with him one night about the possibility of him becoming manager of the Woodleigh estate once the war was over. For the first time in a long while his face lit up, and without hesitation, he quietly said, 'Yes. I'd like that.'

With Archie's help, Ella managed the estate as well as she could and was forming some plans for a way forward after the war. The five-hundred-acre estate included a farm, which was currently leased to Mr Hudson. He had the farm for another five years and, as he told Ella, hoped to renew after that. So at least that part of it was being taken care of, Ella thought as she looked at some of the paperwork.

In truth, what with Georgia, Thomas and baby Merrily, Ella had little time for anything else. Not that she minded at all. Looking after the children brought her great joy, and having Jane and Archie on hand was a lifeline at times.

Although official driving lessons were suspended during the war years, Hilda knew that it was Hannah's dearest wish to learn to drive. And so in early November, as a surprise for her daughter's twenty-first birthday, Hilda bought Hannah an Austin 7.

Hilda had been as excited as Hannah was when she asked her daughter to open her bedroom curtains on the morning of her birthday. There, parked by the front door, was a shiny black car. As the two of them peeped through the window, Hilda put her arm around her daughter, gave her the car keys and said, 'Happy birthday, my love.'

Hannah was over the moon and had no idea her mother was going to do this for her. A car of her very own! Well, that was something very special. She gave her mother a huge hug and told her that for no particular reason she would call it Trixie.

Although petrol was strictly rationed, Hilda somehow managed to fill the tank before giving it to her daughter. And so, after reading the manual and basic instructions about how to drive, on her day off from the nursery, Hannah drove over to see Ella and the children.

The journey had been a bit hair-raising at first, but, after a few gear crunches, Hannah was thrilled to bits that she had mastered Trixie. Driving over, Hannah reflected on the news, some weeks ago now, of Mary's passing, which she had been very sad about. She had wanted to comfort Joe, but because of their past, brief encounter, thought it best to stay away. She had sent him a letter conveying her condolences and had left it at that.

As the weather was unusually warm for the time of year, Ella and Hannah decided to make the most of it and have a picnic. An hour or so later, watching Hannah play with the children, Ella smiled at her friend. 'What a different world for you, Han, now that you can drive!'

Hannah, who was tickling Thomas, looked up. 'Sure is. And the world will be even more different once the war is over. Cos then I can join you all at Woodleigh.' She flashed a mischievous grin at Ella. 'That's if the offer is still there?'

Ella laughed. 'Well, let's put it this way, I'm not advertising for anyone else!'

Hannah mopped her brow in fake relief. 'Phew. Thank the Lord for that. Anyway, something I was going to say was, if you can get your hands on some petrol, I'll be only too happy to drive you wherever, on my days off or in the evenings.'

'Thanks, Hannah. We'd love that, but with rationing it's unlikely at the moment.' Ella took out an envelope from her bag and passed it to her friend. 'I know I can't compete with your Mum's present, but I've bought you a little something for your birthday.'

Hannah squealed with delight as she took a photograph of a pristine Royal Enfield bicycle out of the envelope.

Giggling at her friend's delight, Ella said, 'So no excuse for not coming over to see us now, petrol or no petrol.'

Hannah gave Ella a huge hug. 'Oh thanks, Ella. That's really brilliant. I shall call this one Pixie. Just can't wait to ride her!'

Ella was so pleased that Hannah was happy. 'Well, Pixie will fill in until Trixie can be fully unleashed, eh? And until petrol is off of rationing, well, we'll just have to be sensible.'

Hannah shot a questioning look regarding Ella's sobriety. 'Sensible? You and me, El? Not sure about that.' Ella threw a plum at Hannah, and the two laughed at their silliness.

Hannah, who had been keeping her eye on Thomas, suddenly leapt up. 'Whoops! Better go and get Thomas, he's off foraging again.' She laughed as she chased young Thomas out of the ferns and guided him back to the others. 'It's lovely to be able to get out in the fresh air after the stuffy nursery and to have a chase round with these little ones.'

'Well, we are really glad that you can join us. Aren't we, Thomas?'

Thomas, who was now sitting on Ella's knee and munching a sandwich, nodded his head. Merrily, who was in her pram, began to cry.

'I'll get her,' Hannah said, picking up the little bundle. 'Where's her bottle? I'll feed her if you like.' Ella handed Hannah the bottle and, as Merrily began to suck on the teat, peace was restored once more. Georgia, who was now over a year old, was walking rather shakily on the tartan rug. Ella helped her negotiate the uneven ground and rewarded her with some homemade biscuit. As she fell down on her bottom she turned to see a figure approaching. 'Da, Da,' she gurgled.

As far as Ella knew, Peter was miles away. Then as both she and Hannah turned they soon realised that it was Joe that Georgia had spotted, who was running towards them, grinning at the happy scene. 'I was told you were here. It's lovely to see you all.'

'Oh, Joe! What a wonderful surprise. We weren't expecting you 'til tomorrow.' Ella stood up and gave him a hug.

'I managed to get an earlier train.' He ruffled Thomas's hair and smiled at Hannah, who had just taken the bottle from Merrily's mouth. 'Shall I take her?'

Hannah felt a little bashful, but duly handed

over Joe's baby daughter to him. 'Sure. You can change her nappy if you like!'

Joe laughed. 'No. That's one job I leave for you women, that is... if you don't mind?'

Ella smiled broadly at her brother-in-law. 'No, we don't mind, do we Hannah?'

'Not at all. But we won't mind either if you change your mind later on,' Hannah said teasingly.

'Me! Change my mind? Never!' Joe laughed and both Ella and Hannah were happy to see him in brighter spirits. Ella had her theory why...

CHAPTER FIFTEEN

Hannah had been really pleased with Ella's birthday present, and would often ride over to Woodleigh on her day off. Being able to share their friendship more easily was a real fillip for them both and, although Ella knew that Hannah was still tied to her nursery job, she had decided to make her another offer the next time she cycled over.

'I've been thinking, Han, if you would like to, we could spruce up Woodleigh Cottage for you to live in. What do you say?'

'Oh, Ella! I'd love it! How come it's empty though?'

'It's only recently become vacant actually. Mr and Mrs Dolby have just handed back the keys. I expect you know them, they're the couple who have just given up their lease on the Swan Hotel in Sandham?'

Hannah nodded. She had been there once with her aunt and mother for a special birthday meal, and was enchanted by the fourteenth century bar with its original wooden panels, which the eighteenth century hotel had been added on to.

'Well, never wanting to live full-time on the hotel premises, they rented the cottage for years, a sort of retreat it was for them, but they're now emigrating to America.'

'America?'

'Yes, their daughter Beryl has fallen in love with and married a GI. At the moment the newlyweds are living in married quarters here. But when the war is over they will move to California to live near his family.'

'How come her parents are moving now?'

'They're moving to Cornwall first to spend some time with Mrs Dolby's elderly mother, and will emigrate with Beryl and her husband when the war is over. Apparently they have often thought about having a new start and now, with Beryl going to America and with their lease being up on the hotel, they thought it provided them with the ideal opportunity.'

'Blimey! Bit of a story that.'

'Umm. Like all war stories. Fate has taken people to places they would never otherwise have gone. Anyway, they moved out last week. So if you fancy it, my dear Hannah, it's all yours.'

Hannah grinned from ear to ear. 'Wow! Yes please.' She hesitated for a moment before asking, 'What about Mother? Can she come too? She hates living in that damp flat above the shop.'

'Of course she can! It would be lovely to have her here. Is she still working on the railway?'

'Yes, worse luck. Quite long hours for her, poor Mum.'

Ella's face suddenly lit up. 'I've got it! Why didn't I think of it before? She can come and work at Rylands as our cook. That's if she would like to?'

'Oh, my! She'd love it. But she can't just leave.'

Ella sighed. 'Course not, the war, the damn war has stopped so much of normal life.'

Hannah was not going to let the war dampen her enthusiasm, and gave a satisfied grin. 'But she has been told that when the war is over she will be made redundant as her boss is legally bound to give Reggie House his job back, once he returns from the war.'

'Well, do tell her that we'd love to have her with us here.' Ella suddenly looked down at her hands. 'She was so very kind to me, you know?'

Not wanting to dwell on the negative, Hannah replied, 'And she is very fond of you. She'll be just so thrilled to know that in time she can leave the smelly flat and has the offer of a job for the future.'

Ella felt pleased. 'Good. Well, that's settled then. Hopefully petrol will be more freely available after the war, so you'll be able to drop her to work and pick her up, won't you?'

'Course I can... as long as my boss gives me the time off to do it!'

Ella threw a cushion at her friend, who threw it quickly back.

'Peter will be so thrilled when he hears you are coming to live and work here.'

Hannah pinched herself. 'Ouch. It is real then?'

The May evening was quite warm and Hannah took off her cardigan as she watched Ella pour some coffee from the percolator.

'Seeing you do that reminds me of when I was on a longer shift a month or so ago, and during my break I popped into Kathy's Cafe for a reviver. It was quite busy and there were a few GIs there, from the aerodrome at Parwell, I guess. Anyway, one came over and asked if I minded if he sat at my table.'

'Uh, oh. The standard chat-up line.'

'Sort of. There is a twist to this one though. He introduced himself as Slim Ingles, and was charming... and, well, rather attractive actually.'

'Aren't they all? I've seen them in Sandham. So immaculately dressed with impeccable manners. Funnily enough Mr Dolby was just telling me when he returned the keys that he had been to check that the cleaners had done a good job in the hotel, and had felt quite choked as he looked at the low ceiling of the bar in the oldest part of the hotel, which was absolutely crammed full of the GIs' signatures.'

Nostalgia swept over Hannah as she remembered being in the bar one night with a workmate and had watched a boisterous group of GIs writing their names on the ceiling. As she smiled in remembrance, she exclaimed, 'I've seen it, El! One night I was there with Heather, one of the girls from the nursery. The bar was packed and, in jostling his way through the crowd, one of the GIs spilt some beer on my blouse. With a lascivious grin on his face, he apologised and offered to buy me a new one. With those sexy blue eyes piercing right through me, I can tell you, El, I felt very flustered indeed; but managed to say that it was fine, and nothing to worry about.'

'God, Han, you did well to keep your cool. What happened then?'

'I didn't feel cool, I can tell you... Anyway, in his soft American drawl he said, and do forgive my accent, El, "You know, honey, signing this ceiling is gonna be a part of history. To make up for my clumsiness why don't you sign my name for me?"'

Ella's eyes sparkled. 'And did you?'

'Yea, and before I knew what was happening, I found I was being lifted up by this gorgeous GI, who told me his name was Kirk White, and, with all his mates cheering and laughing, my head was in a real spin, as you might imagine.'

'I bet... I'm feeling flushed just thinking about it! What happened then?'

'Well, I managed to write his signature amid all the hundreds of others, and after gently, and I have to say, very slowly, lowering me to the floor, he said it was a great privilege to have me sign for him.' Hannah looked at Ella, her face aglow. 'I can tell you, El, when I touched the ground I felt as weak as a kitten. But before I had time to think, Heather said we'd better go as a skirmish was breaking out further down the bar, and so, after telling Kirk that we were going to the lavatory, we left.'

Ella laughed. 'Phew! What a tale that is, Han! So we nearly lost you to another GI! What a dark horse you are! Anyway, let's hear what happened to, what was his name? Oh, yea, Slim.'

Hannah giggled. 'All I was going to say was, as I sipped my coffee, he, Slim, told me in his attractive accent that the one downfall of you English is that you can't make a decent cup of coffee!'

'The cheeky devil!'

'Well, he was pulling my leg really.'

'Huh, well, I hope you pulled his too, Han.'

'Yea, I did actually. I politely apologised, and told him that I would start a coffee-making class right away.'

'Good for you. What did he say to that?'

'He just laughed and offered me a cigarette. And when I declined he was amazed, and told me that I was the first lady that had ever refused him.'

Ella smiled. 'Bit of a lead in, there?'

'Maybe! Then, in his most seductive voice, he asked me my name. And before I could say it, Betty Richards appeared by his side. Glaring at me she said, "I thought we were going to the cinema, Slim?"'

'Betty Richards? There's one not to tangle with! So, how did Slim get out of that?'

'Well, completely unflustered and giving me a broad smile, he turned to Betty and said, "Of course we are, my sweet."'

Giggling, Ella said. 'Sweet! That's the last thing Miss Betty Richards is.'

'I know. Anyway, standing up, he gestured Betty to go first, then as they approached the door he turned back, gave me a sexy wink and was gone.'

Ella was intrigued and curious. 'Would you have gone out with him, if he'd asked?'

'Well, with his charm, anyone could be tempted. But let's face it, spinning those seductive lines is second nature to him. I don't think so, El. Only lead to more heartache. Anyway, they'll all be off soon, I reckon. Then where would I be?'

'Umm, interesting. You're right there, Hannah. They will be off soon.'

'Ooh, had a tip-off have you?'

'No. Not a tip-off. But you know our dairy farm is split by the main road running through it?'

'Yea.'

'Well, Mr Hudson, who farms here at Woodleigh, told me today that he had been visited by a dispatch rider instructing him that a convoy would be coming through early in the morning, next week in fact, at twenty minutes to six on the dot on June 6, and that they would not stop for anything. So just to make sure the cows were not crossing at that time or for the following few hours.'

'Sounds important! Let's hope this is the beginning of the end, eh?'

'God, yea. To have the war over, and it will be one day, will be a sort of rebirth for us all. One thing for sure, we'll have a huge party to celebrate.'

'Can't wait! And just think how good it will feel to have our freedom back again.' Hannah looked at her watch. 'Huh! It's a quarter to ten! I lose track of time with these light evenings. Better go and give Mum the wonderful news.'

The two stood and hugged each other. Ella walked to the door with her friend. 'Lovely to see you, Han, thanks for coming over. Come again as soon as you can and we can go and look at the cottage.'

Hannah gave Ella a peck on the cheek. 'Thanks, El. It's soooo exciting!' As she pedalled down the drive, Hannah looked into her bicycle mirror to see Ella waving her off from the doorstep. Waving back she thought to herself that in spite of the war and all its disruptions, life was pretty good.

The following week on June 6, 1944 came a pivotal point in the war. It was D-Day and thousands of men took part in the huge operation to free France from the grip of the Germans. Although sadly many men lost their lives, it was a success and, as was later recorded, the beginning of the end of the war in Europe.

Three weeks after Ella's offer of Woodleigh Cottage, Hannah had moved in and was so thrilled to have her own place and space, as she put it. Hilda shed a tear of happiness when her daughter told her of the offer from Ella, and said the thought of it would keep her going through the long days at work. Owing to the fact that she worked in Sandham, she decided, very reluctantly, to stay on in the flat until the war was over, but had helped her daughter move into the cottage and had immediately fallen in love with it and the beautiful estate where it was positioned. That night she thanked God for answering her prayers for Ella, and was in awe at how everything had miraculously worked out.

Hannah, who helped her friends on her two days off, had taken Thomas to school while Peter, who was on one of his long weekends off, and Ella were sifting through some paperwork as Georgia and Merrily played close by.

'I think we are finally up-to-date with the outstanding bills, darling,' Peter said, as he looked up from the desk and smiled.

'Well done, my love. I guess Edward had

the property for such a short time that he was oblivious of them.'

'For sure. When you think about it, he was away when he inherited the estate, and after he came home within a matter of weeks the poor man was dead.'

'I still have to pinch myself to think that we own this beautiful estate. Don't you?'

'I certainly do! And now the GIs have left Woodleigh House, we can make plans for its refurbishment. Course, it will take a while though; as you saw, it's in a bad state. But nothing the local builder can't fix. So when you weigh it all up, my love, the best is yet to come!'

Ella put her arms round her husband's neck and looked into his smiling face. 'Do you mean things are getter even better?'

Peter bent down and kissed her. 'Umm. Better and better. Not before the war is over though. But things are at last looking more hopeful. The D-Day landings were a great success, took the Germans by surprise alright. Now that the Allies have a foothold in Europe, and the second front has been opened, well maybe we're on the last hurdle.'

'Then we can really start to live our new life!'

Not wishing to spend the precious time he had with his family on talk of his latest posting, Peter had kept news of his move until his last day at home. Ella had got so used to him coming home so often that she thought it would just continue that way until the war was over. But this was not to be, and after telling his wife that he was to be posted to Macmerry in Scotland, she had burst into tears.

Peter put his arms round her and lifted her face towards his own, saying, 'It could be much worse, my darling. At least I'm not abroad like so many of my friends. I will get some leave, and now we have the telephone, we can speak once a week.' He smiled at her anxious face. 'So you see, it's not that bad, eh?'

'I know, my love. We are so fortunate compared with lots of other couples. It's just that... well, I'll miss you so.'

Peter gently put his fingers across her delicate cheek. 'And I'll miss you, my darling. But it's not for ever. You'll soon have me here every day, and then you'll get fed up with me!'

Ella's eyes flashed. 'Never! I can never have enough of you!'

Georgia, who was playing with her toys on a blanket on the oak floor, suddenly got fed up and started to cry. Peter lifted her up. 'What is it young lady?'

Now in her father's arms, she smiled happily at him. 'Da Da, play with me.'

'Of course I will, Georgia. What's it to be?' He got down on the floor with his daughter and started to build a tower with some wooden bricks. Georgia laughed as she knocked them down, begging Peter to, 'Do it again, Da Da.'

Ella smiled at the happy scene and checked on Merrily, who was asleep in her pram. As she watched father and daughter playing, Ella felt so fortunate that Georgia and Thomas had made such a good recovery, and that both were now back to their former selves, having regained the weight they lost during their bout of whooping cough.

The sound of the front door opening brought Ella back to the present.

'I'm back,' came Hannah's cheerful voice, followed by her lithe figure as she entered the room. 'What's to do this morning?' Surprised to see all the family there, she exclaimed, 'Sorry, I didn't know you were all in here.'

Peter looked up from his brick building. 'No need to be sorry. Come and help us build the Tower of London!'

Hannah laughed. 'Not much good at building, but not bad at making a cup of tea. Any takers?' Both Ella and Peter declined but told Hannah to go ahead and make herself one.

'How was Thomas? Did he go in alright today?' asked Ella.

'Yes. He was just fine. Now he has Sam for a friend, he's as happy as a sandboy$_{13}$.'

'That's good news. Now, to answer your question, I thought today if you don't mind getting on with painting the back bedroom, that would be great. As it's Peter's last day, we thought we'd pack a picnic and take the children for a walk.'

'Course I don't,' replied Hannah. 'And I'll pick Thomas up at three then, shall I?'

'That would be great. Thanks, Han. Tomorrow though, when you've dropped Thomas off to school, if you've got enough petrol, would you mind taking Peter to the station for nine thirty?'

'No problem. And because we've been so good, Trixie still has some of Mum's original petrol in her tank. I should be back just before nine, so plenty of time. Can I help with the picnic?'

Ella smiled at Hannah. 'Thanks, but it's all done. We were up early with Merrily this morning. Little monkey has got into the routine of waking up at five thirty on the dot.'

'Blimey! I don't know how you cope with all those early mornings. I'd need matchsticks to keep my eyes open, I reckon.'

Peter laughed. 'Oh, you'll get used to it, when your time comes!'

'Me? Not so sure about that!' Hannah flashed her eyes at her laughing friends. Ella had told Hannah recently that although they were her employers, first and foremost they were her friends, adding that if she was unhappy about any aspect of her job or worried at all, she was to tell them. Hugging Ella, Hannah had thanked her for her lovely thoughts, adding that she loved her job and her bosses, too!

'Well, have a nice time. I'll get on with the painting. See you later.'

After saying goodbye to Hannah, Ella went into the kitchen to collect the food hamper, and Peter put Georgia in her pram. Five minutes later the happy couple, each pushing a pram, could be seen walking along Woodleigh Lane, then crossing over into the leafy woods where there was an abundance of sunny glades to choose from to enjoy their picnic. As the ancient wood was alive with butterflies, bees and various other insects, once they had chosen their spot to picnic in, Ella put a fine gauze over Merrily's pram to protect her. Georgia played contentedly on the rug as the family ate their way through the delicious fare. And as he supped some of Archie's home brew, Peter felt completely relaxed, the first time for some while. With his eyes half shut through drowsiness, he told Ella that once in Scotland he would be training in the Grampians in readiness to go to Norway.

Ella had been shocked to hear that Peter was to go abroad, but after some reassurance from him that it was a relatively safe place to be, she too relaxed. Surrounded by the sounds of wildlife, the young couple soon began to unwind, and being totally alone with each other and the children, talked candidly about their hopes and plans for Woodleigh. It had taken some while to register the enormity of Peter's inheritance, and only now could they truly assess its magnitude and the part they had to play in the successful running of the estate.

There were twenty-four cottages, eighteen of which were for the farm workers, a Church of England village school, a shop and post office, the Church of St Michael's, a village pub, the farm, a small garage and workshop and a blacksmith's forge. Thankfully, the farm, garage, forge and the rented cottages ran themselves. And when Ella had taken on the job of collecting the rent every month from the cottages and every quarter from the businesses, she had thought to herself that it was like stepping into the role of Bathsheba in *Far from the Madding Crowd*. This made her smile.

'I have been giving a great deal of thought as to my hopes for the estate, darling. But I'd like to know what you've been thinking before I reveal mine,' Peter said with a teasing look as he finished off his beer.

As Merrily began to cry, Ella took her from the pram and began to feed her with a bottle of cow's milk. Peace restored once more, Ella turned her thoughts back to her husband's question.

'I've given it a lot of thought too, and for sure we do have a great responsibility here. Sometimes I feel your inheritance is almost too much, and the only way I can come to terms with it is to share it with those less fortunate than ourselves. Besides which, it's a way of repaying Edward's amazing kindness to us.'

'Ah, my darling girl, I should have known your philanthropic nature would be thinking along those lines.'

Ella smiled modestly. 'And you, my love. What have you been thinking?'

'Pretty much on the same lines, actually. I've been looking at the financial aspect of the legacy, and the interest our money brings in far exceeds our outgoings for the running of the estate and our personal needs. And of course this will grow year on year. Being put in this privileged position, like you, I would very much like to do something worthy for those in need. Any thoughts?'

Ella had indeed been thinking long and hard about this. Jane had recently heard from her sister, Lily who was very upset that her daughter Mavis was a victim of domestic abuse from her husband. So much so that the baby she had been expecting was lost when Mavis went into labour early, after her husband had punched her badly and pushed her down the stairs. The police had been informed and had given the husband a warning, but this only exasperated the situation and now poor Mavis lived in terror of her life, too frightened to speak to any authorities.

Coincidentally, Hannah had come in to work one morning in quite an agitated state. After a cup of coffee and some gentle words from Ella, Hannah told her that Natalie, one of the girls from the nursery, had burst into tears at work the day before and confided in her that she was pregnant by a soldier. And that in between her sobbing, Natalie said that she had told the father-to-be about the baby, who quite casually informed her that he was already married and couldn't help. Once the girl's parents found out about the baby through witnessing her morning sickness, after beating her with his belt, the father threw her out, leaving her homeless and destitute. She told Hannah that she was living in a friend's shed, but would need to get out soon.

Ella had been very distressed by the horror of the two situations and thought to herself, these were only two of which she knew. How many more were there also in need of help? She had wanted to talk to Peter about this as soon as he got home, but realised that this would have been very unfair. He had lots on his mind, and as their time together was most precious, Ella decided to wait until they could take a walk together and discuss their innermost thoughts openly. Now, taking Peter's hand, Ella told him quietly and calmly about the two incidents. Peter listened intently, deeply saddened and shocked by what he was hearing.

'So, in answer to your question, my love, I was wondering if we could give the two girls a home in one of the empty cottages?'

Peter smiled at his wife's expression, which was anxiously searching his face. He took her hand. 'Of course we can. It's the very least we can do. I will have to leave it all to you, though, that's the only snag at the moment.'

Ella squeezed his hand. 'That's no problem. Hannah is here to help on her days off. And she's a real brick. A wonderful support in every way... she will be so pleased when she hears this news.'

'I'm so glad that she's back, even if it is only part- time. It's wonderful for me to know you are not alone. I mean, I know you have Mum and Dad, and they are a massive support, but with Hannah you have someone your own age to share concerns with.'

'And have a laugh, too!'

Peter grinned. 'Ah, that's very important. Okay, I'll leave that in your hands, my darling. But, what really are your long-term plans?'

Ella looked down and ruffled the grass, then, looking into Peter's face, said, 'Well, you may think I'm mad.'

'No. I'd never think that. What is it you're thinking, my darling?'

'I would love to set up a refuge for women in need. Not just those who are suffering abuse or find themselves homeless... but also,' Ella's voice dropped to a whisper, 'those poor souls who have been raped and left pregnant and alone.'

Peter stood up, pulled her up beside him and held her firmly in his arms. 'That is so brave of you, my angel.' Peter's kind words affected her deeply and she burst into tears. Since recovering from the horrific rape, she had been so encompassed with love and kindness, which had helped to block out her ordeal, that she had not since revisited it. But now, just talking about the plight of others had reopened that wound.

Having embraced in silence for a few moments, Peter continued, 'You have coped with everything so wonderfully, my darling. I'm so very proud of you. We all are. And now this truly inspiring idea you have for a refuge is phenomenal. And it will happen, not until the war is over though, but it will. I promise.'

Ella, who had dried her eyes, looked up and smiled. 'And you know what a promise means?'

Peter laughed. 'How could I forget?'

'Then you don't think I'm crazy?'

'Never! Thanks to Edward and his legacy we can make a difference to lots of people's lives.'

Ella threw her arms round her husband's neck. 'Oh, Peter. This is such fantastic news. We will have to think where the refuge can be, and, oh there are lots of things to think of.'

Peter laughed at Ella's excited face, thrilled to see her joyful once more.

'There are. And my guess is that we would need to build something new, which is purpose built. That is, if you are thinking of having more than three or four ladies at a time?'

'Oh, yes, lots more than that... if it's possible. We will need lots of rooms, because there will be the babies and children, too!'

'Well, this is something we can look at after

the war. That is, if you don't mind waiting?'

'No. I don't mind waiting.'

'Good. Well then, in the meantime, if you look after my cousin and Hannah's friend, that would be an amazing start. Now, enough of all this talk of others, I need some prime time with my wife!'

As they lay down on the blanket, Georgia began to climb all over them. On seeing their laughing faces, Georgia began to laugh too, then, just as the three of them embraced in a family hug, Merrily began to cry.

Later, as they made their way home to Rylands, Peter and Ella were elated that at last they had begun to form their ideas for the future of the estate and their new life.

CHAPTER SIXTEEN

Archie was in good spirits; he had just been to see his brother Fred, who since the evacuation was living on a small-holding at Netherway. He had caught the carrier to Sandham and then another to Netherway.

The two had visited the local pub and reminisced about the old times and how they had earned some extra money when they were young by swishing a dead rat in the river and telling various householders that they had caught it on their land. They had asked whether they wanted them to get rid of it. Of course everyone did, and most gave them a penny to do so.

'Ah, that were a good un, Arch. The missus were real pleased wi' the extra money. Mind you, I never did tell her 'ow I got it.'

'No need to, Fred. As the old man used to say, never let your left hand know what your right hand is doing. From the Good Book of course, an' 'tis true enough.'

Fred burped and said, 'Well, I don't know too much about the Good Book, Arch, but when I thinks of the things we got up to I reckon we never strayed too far from the straight an' narrow.'

'No, I don't reckon we did, Fred.' Grinning

widely at his brother, he added, 'But we had a few nasty skids!'

As the two men supped their beer, the conversation got round to more current affairs, and Archie brought his brother up-to-date with the latest happenings in his family. Fred was taken aback by the news of Peter's inheritance and wondered how he would cope with it. Archie, who had always shunned the thought of having lots of money, had come round to the idea of his son's wealth, and knew that, as a modest man, Peter would cope well and not brag or boast about his new-found status. In short, he was very proud of him.

'The boy 'oull be alright, Fred. He was brought up to respect others whatever their rank in life. An' apparently 'twas those qualities what made his Sergeant leave everything to 'im. He'll handle his peers alright, as well as those working for him. After all, he be off farming stock an' do know all about living on an estate.'

'You're right there, Arch. He always was a nice boy.'

'Ah, so he was,' replied Archie as he swigged down the last of his pint. 'Anyway, tell me about your new neighbours. Are they any good?'

Fred puffed away on his pipe, then taking it out of his mouth said, 'Our grandmother used to say that you want to see the smoke coming out of chimney for twelve months afore you speak to any newcomers, but this evacuation has turned that reasoning on its head.' After taking another puff on his pipe, he continued with a wide grin spreading over his face. 'I did wonder if my nearest neighbour, Sid Dove, was a relation. He gets up to some high jinks, like we used to.'

'Thass good then, Fred, life's too brutal not to have a laugh, says I.'

'Ah, an' you be right. Anyway, I'd been to this pub on a Sunday lunch time, like I always do, an' was sleeping it off under the apple tree in the garden. When I woke up I had a real shock, cos I couldn't move me legs. Blimey, thinks I, I must 'ave 'ad a stroke. Then, as I tried to get up I looked down at me feet to see that me laces from both boots 'ad been tied up together. 'Twas that monkey, Sid, he played a good prank there, eh? I likes 'im, an' we always 'ave a good laugh together.'

'Thass the best medicine, Fred. No doubt about it. Some folks take life too serious, an' it don't get 'em anywhere.' Archie scratched his chin then put his finger up to the barman to signal another pint for him and Fred, who hurriedly drained the last dregs from his glass.

'True enough. What wi' this war still raging, we gotta keep laughing, else we'd go mad. They do say 'tis almost over, then we can go back to our homes in Downside Alley. Now won't that be good, Arch?'

'Ah, 'tis ours by birth right, Fred, an' thass where I want me bones to rest. Long wi' Mother and Father, an' all the rest of 'em.'

'Ah, so do I. An' I miss the smell of the sea in me nostrils. An' lying in bed on a stormy night, listening to they waves as they crash over the rocks and beach.'

The barman brought the two pints of beer and Archie paid him. 'Cheers, mate, 'ave one yerself.' The barman took the extra money and thanked Archie.

'You got plenty of money then, Arch?'

'Not plenty. But enough.'

Fred nodded and wiped the beer off his moustache. 'You still shooting rabbits, Arch?

'When I get a chance. Funnily enough, just the other week one of the farm workers on Peter's estate said he'd heard I was a good shot, an' would I be able to put his dog down, who was in considerable pain. Said he couldn't afford the vet's fees... well, who can?'

'Did ee do it for 'im then, Arch?'

'Course I did. Tied 'im to the tree, an', well, 'twas over very quickly. Like you, I hate to see an animal in pain, just thankful that I could 'elp.'

'Well, the old man taught us to do it in the most humane way. But I thought everyone did.'

'Not everyone had the childhood we 'ad, Fred.'

'No. When you come to think of it, Arch, we were very fortunate. We learnt how to be self-sufficient, not relying on anyone else. An' there's a lot to be said for that.'

'Ah. I'm not sure this generation 'ave quite grasped it like we did. But there, 'tisn't all their fault, this damn war 'ave taken away their youth, same as the First World War took away ours, eh Fred?'

'Ah, an' I know like me you don't dwell on those hellish days, but I couldn't help but think of them t'other day when someone was saying that thankfully no one be gettin' gassed, like they did in the First War. Remember how we 'ad to invent our own gas masks, Arch?'

'Course I do! You mean when we 'ad to pee on our hankies an' put it over our noses to keep the gas away?'

'Thass right. When you think of it, what we 'ad to do to survive in those rat-infested trenches... well, how anyone came out of it alive, I'll never know.'

Both men fell silent as grim images flashed through their minds. Then, relighting his pipe, Fred continued, 'Life's never bin easy, thass for sure. An' we must, all of us, young and old, make the best of it. Now, what say you to a whisky chaser afore we go, Arch?'

Twenty four hours after the picnic, Peter was on his way to Scotland. And as usual the steam train was packed with servicemen and all their kit. Fortunately, he managed to find a seat and spent much of the journey reflecting on his in-depth conversation with Ella about the estate. He knew their plans for a refuge would take a huge amount of organising, but, like all worthy causes that required a vast amount of time and effort, he knew the end result would be a fine achievement and rewarding for everyone involved.

Back at Rylands, Ella was telling Hannah the good news that her friend from the nursery could come and stay at Vine Cottage. Hannah's face lit up with happiness as she rushed over to Ella and hugged her. 'Oh, that is so kind of you and Peter. Natalie will be over the moon. Can't wait to tell her, poor girl. She doesn't even have anywhere to sleep, well, just a battered old chair. Oh, she's gonna be so excited and thankful.'

Ella smiled at Hannah's glowing face. 'She will be sharing with Mavis, Peter's cousin. I hope that's alright?'

'That's no problem. She will be just so thrilled that she has a room of her own and a place where she is safe.'

'That's settled then. You can ride over now and tell Natalie if you like. No need for her to be living in anxiety any longer than needed.'

Hannah almost skipped out of the door, and when she had gone Ella sat down to write to Aunt Lily to let her know that Mavis would be very welcome to come and live with them at Woodleigh. Jane was ecstatic with the news of help for her niece, and offered to look after Georgia and Merrily while Ella and Hannah began cleaning out Vine Cottage for its new inhabitants.

Both Archie and Jane came to babysit the following Monday evening when Ella and Hannah took a trip into Sandham to view the furniture coming up for auction the following day. After noting the items she wanted to purchase, Ella left the details with Archie, who said he was happy to bid for them. Actually, he was quite chuffed about it; he had not been to an auction in years, and looked forward to the entertainment.

Part of the requirement of any auctioneer was to have a great sense of humour and the ability to laugh at himself. This spinning of yarns and making up nonsense created a happy atmosphere, which encouraged people to bid higher, before the gavel banged down in the time-worn way, and the auctioneer shouted, 'All done.'

At the auction the following day, Archie went earlier than he needed, to observe the livestock auction. As he went in Mr Squibb was auctioning some rams and was in the middle of his spiel.

'Now come on you farmers, get your bids in. These are the best rams in the area, apart from the Sandham bus drivers that is.' A titter echoed round the hall as the bidding got underway and the aforementioned rams went under the hammer.

After having a weak cup of tea in the market's leaking tea room, Archie made his way to the farm sale where the small items were being auctioned off first. Mr Ball was taking this auction. He was as equally entertaining as old Squibb and Archie looked forward to some laughs. This time it was a load of dung being auctioned off and it was going to be hard to whip up enthusiasm.

'Now ladies and gentlemen, what am I bid for this load of dung?' Looking round at a sea of blank faces, he knew he was going to have to tell a good yarn to get things moving. 'I'll tell you a true story about a friend of mine who went into the woods with his mistress to have a bit of fun, shall we say. Well, when he came out of the woods, his wife was waiting for him. Glaring at him she asked, "What have you been doing in those woods?" He told her that he got took short and had to go in there to go to the toilet. "I don't believe you," his wife replied. "Show me the evidence." Now gentlemen, my friend would have given any amount of money for that much dung.' He held his fingers about three inches apart. 'Come on then, gentlemen, whose gonna give me the first bid?'

As the hoots of laughter subsided, keen bidding was soon under way. Checking his pocket watch, Archie decided it was time to leave and made his way to the furniture sale room. One of the first items to be sold was a chest-expanding apparatus, and Mr Stone, the auctioneer, was soon in full swing.

'Now come on ladies and gentlemen, whose gonna start me off on these rather splendid chest expanders? The previous owner became very fit after using them...' Mr Ball stopped as his assistant whispered something in his ear. Mr Stone, unusually, looked a little abashed as he continued, 'I'm sorry, gentlemen, I've just been told that the previous owner is dead.' This rather killed the bidding and the expander went for almost nothing.

Archie had a very enjoyable day and when it came to the furniture auction he focused on his instructions and managed to buy all that he had been asked to. Ella and Hannah were thrilled with his day's work and Ella gave Archie some money to have a pint or two in the local pub as a thank you for his help.

A month later, Mavis and Natalie moved into Vine Cottage. Mavis had the larger bedroom while Natalie had the smaller, which led through to a dressing area that she thought would be good for the baby when it arrived. Both had cried when they were told of Peter and Ella's offer of a house. They thought it a miracle and told Ella so when they first met at Rylands when Ella handed them each a key to their new home.

Both ladies said that they would be very happy to help with any chore that needed doing. Ella had been thinking about this, and, realising that neither had an income, guessed that they would want to do something in return for the rent. After giving it some thought, Ella asked Mavis if she would be able to help with the cleaning at Rylands. Mavis was thrilled to be able to help and said yes immediately. Natalie was four months pregnant and so Ella asked if she would be happy to help with the lighter household duties until she was in her last few weeks. Like Mavis, Natalie was only too pleased to help and said that before the war and being sent to work in the nursery, she had been training to be a cook, and if Ella needed help in the kitchen she would be very happy to assist. Ella was delighted with this news and said that her help with the cooking would be most welcome.

And so Ella's dream of helping women who had fallen on difficult times began to take shape. She looked forward to the day when the refuge would be built, but in the meantime with Peter away and the war still raging she had enough to be getting on with.

CHAPTER SEVENTEEN

With Christmas fast approaching everyone was busy preparing for a large family gathering. Peter, Joe, Violet and Florrie had all managed to get some leave over the holiday, the first for many years. Natalie's baby was due during the first week in January and although Ella had banned her from doing anything but light duties, Natalie insisted on helping.

'I'm fine, really, Miss Ella,' which was the name she liked to call her employer by. 'Seems I'm one of the lucky ones who just sails through their pregnancy.' It was true that she carried well, with only a medium-sized bump to show she was in her last trimester.

'Well, if you're sure. I don't want you overdoing things.' Ella smiled kindly at Natalie, who was in the middle of feeding Merrily.

'Course I'm sure. I likes to help.' She looked down at little Merrily. 'Anyway, it's good to get in the swing of what's to come, ain't it?'

Ella smiled. She liked Natalie's cheerful cockney voice and outlook. And after speaking to her not long after she arrived, it was clear that Natalie would like to keep the baby if possible.

'Now me Mum an' Dad 'ave washed their hands of me... well, the babe's all I've got.' Natalie's last words reminded Ella of the day she had uttered the self-same words to Hilda and Amy, and she gave a silent prayer for the countless blessings that had followed. Smiling at Natalie, Ella assured her that she would be able to keep the baby, that she was not alone, and that she was part of the Samways family now.

Natalie had been thrilled to hear this and her beaming face reflected her feelings. 'Awh, thanks, Miss Ella. Now, after I put this bundle of mischief down, shall I start making the Christmas puddin'?'

Ella nodded, saying, 'Yes, thanks, Natalie. That would be good. But let us all do some of the stirring... and make a wish!'

'Course. Meant to be lucky for lots of folk to stir it, ain't it? An' we mustn't forget to put in the thre'penny bits... an' a nice bit of brandy, if there's some to spare?'

Ella smiled at Natalie's expression. 'Yes. There is. I asked Archie just the other day if he could bring me some from the pub. And pooling our rations helps our menu no end. Mind you, we're fortunate to have so much food from the garden.'

Natalie's face lit up as she thought of the rabbits, pheasants and partridges hanging in the shed. 'Yea. An' what wiv Archie's haul from the recent shoot, well, we'll 'ave some lovely meals this Christmas!'

Mavis's scars were receding and with every week that passed she became stronger in herself.

She thanked her lucky stars every day that her cousin and his wife had taken her into their hearts and given her a home. She was a hard-working woman, and since her ordeal with her husband, Sefton, was quite shy with strangers.

Sefton had been so kind to her when they first met on the tram. After alighting, Sefton could see she was struggling with some shopping and had offered to carry the bags to her house. His face was open and friendly, betraying nothing of the selfish bully, which was to emerge later, after they had wed.

Less than a week after their marriage he had shown his true colours and she often had a black eye and swollen lips. Every time the abuse occurred, Sefton somehow managed to make Mavis feel that it was all her fault. This manipulation eroded away her confidence and her very core. In her innocence she didn't realise that bullies never really change. They like to control and they will whatever the consequences. Working in Rylands and surrounded by kindness and support, she felt she had stepped onto another planet, and Natalie, whom she shared Vine Cottage with, was a chirpy soul and easy to live with. Now with family and friends round her, she was looking forward to Christmas for the first time in many years.

Christmas day 1944 was a memorable occasion for all the family. The food, which was washed down with Archie's home-brewed blackberry wine, was delicious and plentiful. Due to rationing, presents were minimal, but everyone agreed as they toasted the family that being together and sharing a wonderful meal was all they needed, and more.

Ella had been buying small presents for the children since the summer, and they were all delighted with their toys, playing happily in front of the fire as the adults played charades and blind man's bluff. When Joe had caught Hannah in the latter and had taken off his blind, it was obvious to everyone that the two still liked each other by the way their eyes lit up as they laughed together, and as they kissed each other for just a little longer than you normally would under the mistletoe. The kiss had reignited the explosive chemistry between them and neither wanted to say goodnight.

Later when Hannah was in the kitchen making a cup of coffee, Ella came in. Neither said a word as they hugged each other tightly. Breaking away, Hannah said, 'God, Ella. It's still there. I'm crazy for him, and... and I think he feels the same.'

Ella smiled kindly at her friend. 'If you really love each other, and I believe you do – cos, boy the vibes between you were hitting us all out there! – Then tell him how you feel, honestly.'

That old enemy, doubt, crept in. 'What if I'm reading him wrong? Maybe he's still mourning for Mary, and just trying to get into the spirit of Christmas.'

'Of course he won't ever forget Mary. And that's something you must accept. But knowing Joe, as I do, I believe his feelings for you are genuine, and that the two of you were made for each other.' She hugged Hannah. 'As far as I can see, dear Han, it was just a matter of time.' Ella's words confirmed what Hannah had been secretly thinking but was almost too scared to believe. Before she had a chance to tell Ella of her thoughts, Joe appeared.

'Where's that coffee, Hannah?' On seeing Ella he went over to her and gave her a peck on the cheek. 'Thanks again for the delicious Christmas dinner, and a wonderful day, Ella. It couldn't have been better in a five-star hotel.' He turned to Hannah. 'And thanks for your help with Thomas and Merrily, Hannah. They really adore you.'

Before Hannah had time to answer, Ella seized the opportunity and said. 'We all do, don't we?' She gave Joe a sparkling smile and left the room.

Joe was immediately at Hannah's side. He put his arms round her waist and pulled her close to him. 'We sure do.' Bending down he kissed her gently, then, feeling her warm response, kissed her more intensely. After a few moments he broke away and whispered, 'I love you, Hannah, so very much.'

Feeling euphoric, Hannah replied, 'I love you

too, Joe... I always have.'

The war, the war that killed thousands of our men every hour of every day, gave an urgency to everything, especially unrequited love, and later that night, without preface, Hannah led Joe to her bedroom where their long-awaited lovemaking was so beautiful and fulfilling that it made them both cry with sheer joy and happiness.

About one o'clock in the morning, Hannah was awoken by a knock at the door and an indistinct voice calling her name. As she quickly pulled on her skirt and jumper she looked back at Joe who was peacefully asleep. How handsome he looked, she thought as her eyes lingered on his naked body, which was only partially covered by the blanket. She could hardly believe what had happened a few hours earlier and was just reliving the ecstasy of it all in her mind when the knocking came again, this time more urgent. She quickly descended the stairs and opened the door to find Ella on her doorstep, shivering and smiling.

'Sorry to wake you up, Han. It's just that Natalie has gone into labour and I wonder if you could come and help Ann, the district nurse? I have knocked her up, and she said she will be over soon.'

The cold night air hit Hannah sharply in the face, and she was now fully awake as the two began to walk down the lane.

'Of course I don't mind. I told Natalie I'd be there for her when the time came.'

Ella gave Hannah a hug. Although she had thought that Hannah and Joe had gone off somewhere to be alone, Ella had no idea that he was in Hannah's bed right now. If she had known, she would never have disturbed her.

'Thanks, my love. But I'll be there if you should need back-up.'

By now the two were at the door of Vine Cottage. 'Thanks for getting me, El. See you in the morning.'

Ella suddenly felt guilty about going home. 'I could stay for a while.'

'No need. Now off you go to bed before Peter misses you.' Hannah could see a figure approaching. 'Look! Ann is here now.'

As Ann reached the door, Ella thanked them both and then headed towards Rylands, as Ann and Hannah entered the dimly lit cottage. Mavis was in the small, warm kitchen making a cup of tea. Although she didn't mind helping, she had told Natalie that she'd be no good to assist in the labour as she couldn't stand the sight of blood. She heaved a sigh of relief as the two ladies appeared at the kitchen door, and looked at Ann.

'She's in quite a bit of pain now. Can I get you both a cup of tea?'

'Thanks, Mavis. Not now, perhaps later.' Ann turned to Hannah. 'Could you bring me some hot water up please, Hannah?'

'Sure.'

Ann pressed the latch on the narrow stair door and made her way up to Natalie's bedroom, where the young girl was pacing up and down. Ann soon took charge of the situation and within a few minutes Natalie was lying on her bed while Ann examined her to see how far dilated she was. When Hannah appeared round the bedroom door Natalie's face broke into a huge smile. Having a friend with you in your hour of need is priceless, Natalie thought.

'Thanks for coming, Hannah. What a time to go into labour though!' She winced as another pain gripped her, and took some deep breaths as Ann had instructed her to when the pain increased. As the pain diminished, she looked at her midwife. 'Lordy. That was a bit of a corker.'

Ann smiled at Natalie's turn of phrase. 'Well, you are about half way through your labour, Natalie, and you're doing very well. The baby is in the right position, and you're dilating beautifully.'

'That's good news then,' Natalie chirped.

Ann put a rubber sheet under the young girl's bottom. 'It is. Now just relax in between the pains, it will help you later on.'

As the night went on and the pains increased, Hannah held Natalie's hand and mopped her brow. And as the dawn broke on that Boxing Day morning, Natalie was in the last stages of labour, and in spite of what she had previously said about not screaming, she screamed.

Ann and Hannah gave constant reassurance that all was well and that the baby would soon be here. The last hour of labour was difficult and Ann had to ask Natalie to stop pushing at one point as the cord was round the baby's neck. Thankfully, Ann was a skilled midwife, and a potential tragedy was avoided. Just when Natalie was thinking that she couldn't do this any more, Ann urged her to give a huge push and, not long after nine o'clock, Natalie gave birth to a bouncing baby boy. As she cradled him in her arms soon afterwards she told Hannah and Ann that as it was St Stephen's Day, she would call him Stephen.

Just as Hannah was making everyone a cup of tea, Ella came to the cottage to see how Natalie was doing.

'All done,' beamed Hannah. 'She had a gorgeous baby boy... oh, about half an hour ago.'

'That is wonderful news! Can I go and see them, do you think?'

'Sure, El. Ann was just delivering the afterbirth when I came down. But I guess it's all done now.'

Ella was moved to tears when she saw the perfect little baby. 'I'm so happy for you, Natalie.

Well done; a relatively short labour, too.'

'And one of the easier ones,' Ann chimed.

'Easier!' Natalie exclaimed. 'Blimey, I don't want one no harder than that, thanks very much.'

The three of them laughed. Ann completed her cleaning routine and then left the happy scene, saying she would come back later in the day to check on Mother and baby.

Before too long Natalie had little Stephen latched on to her breast. Although he did not feed for long, Ann had said this may be the case and not to worry, and that he would feed when he was hungry. And so he did. By the time of Ann's return visit that evening, Stephen had fed twice and was sleeping peacefully in Merrily's cot, which had previously been Georgia's.

Everyone who wasn't already staying at Rylands, had been invited for a late breakfast at ten o'clock, and Hannah had popped home first to have a quick wash and change. Her heart was beating fast as she ran up the stairs, thinking of the ruggedly handsome man in her bed. To her dismay the bed was empty and her spirits sank as she imagined what Joe would have thought when he awoke to find her gone. But she need not have worried. Joe had gone to Rylands an hour before where Peter told him about Natalie going into labour and that Hannah was there by her side.

Hannah was the last to arrive, and as she entered the dining room, breakfast was in full swing. On seeing her, Joe stood up and greeted her with a kiss. 'You must be exhausted after being up all night. So glad of the good news though.'

Hannah smiled. Her head was in a whirl. Did last night mean anything? Or was he just being his normal friendly self? Before she could try to gauge the situation, Jane said, 'You must be starving, my dear. Do sit down and have some breakfast.'

'Thank you.' Feeling a little more relaxed, Hannah realised that she was indeed famished. She looked round at the familiar faces. Everyone was enjoying their breakfast. As her eyes met Joe's, he gave her a warm smile and winked mischievously. Blushing, her heart skipped a beat, and as images from the previous night flashed through her mind, she felt elated.

Under strict instructions from Ann and Ella, Natalie rested for two weeks after the birth of Stephen. Normally she hated to be idle but decided to make the most of that special time to bond with her son, who, like his mother, had fair, wavy hair, and a round, dolly-like face. As Natalie cradled him in her arms and gazed at his little face, she said, 'Cor! He's real 'andsome, ain't he?'

When, in mid January, she did get up, she felt very well and ready to help with the cooking again. Ella agreed, but only for two hours in the morning while Stephen had a sleep. Stephen was a very placid baby, and by the time he was four months old, Natalie was working for half a day in the kitchen, leaving Stephen in his pram while he either slept or played with his toys. If he did cry, and it was very rare, Mavis or Ella would take him for a walk round the garden or amuse him in the study, which they were using as a makeshift nursery.

The day after Hannah and Joe had consummated their love so passionately, the day that had been temporarily stolen by Stephen's arrival, turned into one of the most heavenly days Hannah could remember.

Following the family breakfast, Joe sneaked up on Hannah in the kitchen as she washed the dishes, put his arms round her waist and kissed her so long and tenderly that Hannah felt she would explode. Breaking off the kiss, Joe whispered, 'Thank you for last night, it was so very beautiful, just like you, my angel. Now we've found each other for the second time, don't go away again, please.'

Hannah was floating and felt she could hardly breathe as she whispered in reply, 'No, never, my darling Joe. I can't believe this is happening.' Tears fell down her cheek and onto Joe's shirt. 'I'm so happy, so indescribably happy.'

Close to tears himself Joe said, 'I feel just the same. I love you so much. Forgive me if you feel I am being too forward, but... darling Hannah, will you do me the great honour of becoming my wife?'

Hannah was almost speechless with emotion. 'Yes, oh yes, Joe. How I love you!'

Joe cupped Hannah's face in his hands and was kissing her gently on the lips when Ella breezed into the kitchen, humming a Christmas carol. On seeing Joe and Hannah, she stopped short. 'Oh, er, sorry to interrupt.'

She made her way back to the door as Joe said, 'No, it's alright, Ella.' He smiled at Hannah and, as he took her hand, said, 'We've got some good news!'

Hannah was almost bursting as she continued Joe's sentence. 'Yes. We are now a couple, and Joe has asked me to be his wife... and I said, yes!'

Ella went over to them and hugged them both, her face glowing. 'Oh, that's truly wonderful news. I couldn't be happier for you both. Can we tell the others?'

Joe and Hannah looked at each other and both said 'yes' simultaneously.

And so, just as everyone was preparing to leave the dining room, Ella asked them all to please sit down as Joe had something to say. Looking round at the expectant faces of his family, Joe suddenly felt rather shy. Hannah went and stood by his side, and as they both smiled happily at each other, Joe said, 'Hannah and I would like to announce that we are a couple, and plan to spend the rest of our lives together.'

Everyone broke into a round of applause. Archie called for a toast, and went off to get some of his home brew. As he passed Jane, who had been upstairs with the children, and on hearing the applause had come down with the little ones to see what the excitement was all about, he quickly conveyed the good news to her. And with face beaming she went into the dining room to congratulate her son and Hannah. On seeing his children, Joe realised that he had not even asked Hannah about taking on the responsibility of looking after them. Hannah caught the look on his face and reading his thoughts whispered in his ear that she would love to be Thomas and Merrily's mother, and that she loved them both dearly.

Joe took both her hands in his. 'Thank you, my darling Hannah. You will be the most wonderful mother to them, I know. As Gran would say, love is the most precious gift you can have. And we have it in abundance!'

Smiling at Joe, Hannah replied, 'Yes, that's true. And as my own dear Mum would say, you can't give all your love away.' Joe kissed her on her forehead. 'And I'm never gonna try!'

Joe and Hannah had taken time with Thomas and Merrily to explain that they would all be living together and that Hannah was going to be their new Mummy. As Hannah had been part of their daily life for some time and both liked her very much, they accepted the news happily. Merrily, who was now nineteen months old, clapped her hands, wriggled down off of her father's knee and ran off to pick up her teddy bear. Thomas, now six, was more serious and pondered on the news for a while. One of his school friends had also had a new mother and then, a few months later, a baby sister, and so, upon hearing that Hannah was going to be his new mother, asked if this meant that they would have a baby.

Joe and Hannah had struggled to keep a serious face, then Joe said, 'Maybe, Thomas. We will have to wait and see.'

After announcing to Joe's family the breaking news of their wedding, Hannah and Joe had gone straight away to see Hilda. She was simply overjoyed, gave them both her blessing, and said she would be very pleased to make the wedding cake.

Once they had time to think things through, Joe and Hannah decided to have a simple wedding in the local church at Woodleigh. Neither wished to make a great fuss or for the family to have any extra expense, and so Hannah suggested to Jane that she wore the pretty outfit she had worn for Peter and Ella's wedding. Jane agreed, but said she would make a new hat. The date, which couldn't come quick enough for Joe and Hannah, was set for the end of February, when Joe would have his next leave.

As Hannah was still working at the nursery, Ella said to her friend that she was very happy to continue to look after Thomas and Merrily during the daytime until the war was over and Hannah could be released from her job. Hannah and Joe were so thankful to Ella, and prayed that the long-awaited day of peace would soon be upon them.

Although their wedding day dawned dull and misty, nothing could dampen the spirits of Joe and Hannah as they got ready for their big day.

Ella, who was Hannah's maid of honour, helped her friend to get dressed, and as she slipped into her cream wedding dress, which she had made herself, Hannah could not have looked more radiant. Ella's eyes sparkled as she looked at her soon to be sister-in-law.

'You look so beautiful, Han.'

'Thanks, El. So do you!'

The two friends smiled at each other, then, hearing Peter's voice calling up to them, they giggled and made their way down the cottage stairs.

By the time the young couple came out of church the mist had burnt off and the sun was shining brightly. As part of their wedding present, Peter and Ella offered to pay for a photographer, and Mr Worthington from Sandham was on hand to capture the newlyweds and their family as they gathered in front of St Michael's Church.

Back at Rylands a delicious meal had been prepared by Ella and Natalie and was thoroughly enjoyed by everyone. Keeping to the bride and groom's wishes for a simple day, the entertainment was provided by music from the gramophone; and Joe and Hannah were first to take to the intimate dance area in the drawing room at Rylands, dancing to *It had to be You* among other popular hits. After they had put the children to bed, they left for a honeymoon in Bath, where they shared a blissful forty-eight hours.

CHAPTER EIGHTEEN

As the winter merged into spring, hopes of the war ending grew with each passing day, and this in turn gave Jane, Archie and all those who had been evacuated from Downside Alley hope of returning to their homes.

In the end, the wonderful news came suddenly. After almost six years, on May 8, 1945 the war in Europe was finally over. Church bells, which had been silenced throughout the war, apart from the time when there was a threat of invasion, rang out all over the country in celebration of freedom. Words alone can never describe the relief felt by everyone, and, of course, there was much sadness, too. Millions of men in their prime had died, leaving families without fathers and husbands. But in spite of the tragedies, the relief of being freed from Hitler's grasp was immeasurable. The whole country was in a buoyant mood and there were celebrations everywhere. Woodleigh estate was no different.

Thankfully, Hilda was quickly released from her job on the railway and happily she was soon employed as chief cook at Rylands, with Natalie as her assistant. Although Peter, Joe, Violet and Florrie were still away, Ella, with Hilda and Natalie's help, organised a huge party for everyone on the estate. This was held on the village green, with the village hut being close by in case of rain. All the ladies of the village joined in with the catering and the children were entertained by a local magician and conjuror. The men of Woodleigh put out tables and benches from the hut, and in the evening the local band from Sandham played some lively music. Almost everyone danced. The atmosphere on the green that day and evening was electric and palpable. Everyone was in high spirits.

Ella had assumed that when the war was over, Peter would be home almost immediately. But on his first leave after the war ending he told Ella that he would be going to Norway as planned. This was a great disappointment to Ella, who was desperate to have Peter home with her and to bring their plans for the estate into fruition.

'I know it's frustrating, darling, but it could be so much worse. When all of us airmen had to queue up for news of our postings, some went to the left, as I did, and those who went to the right were sent to the Far East, poor devils. Now, where's that lovely, dimpled smile, eh?' Peter tilted her head towards his and kissed her. Ella responded warmly and, as they broke away, she smiled tenderly at Peter.

'You've done it again! Always turning a negative into a positive. Where would I be without you, my darling Peter?'

Before he had a chance to answer his wife, Georgia came running into the room, shouting at the top of her voice, 'Daddy, swing me!' Peter and Ella turned to see their daughter's pleading expression.

'I'll be there in a moment, sweetheart. I just need to talk to Mummy first.'

Georgia looked from one to the other, then turning to go she called out, 'Bye, bye, Daddy!' She ran out into the garden and helped Joe to push Merrily on the baby swing.

As Ella and Peter watched their daughter laughing at Merrily, Peter said, 'You see how fortunate we are?'

'I do. And I thank my lucky stars every day.'

Peter smiled. 'I know you do, my darling.'

'Now what else were you going to say before Georgia came running in?'

Peter looked thoughtful. 'Ah, yes. Two things really, not related. When I was having a late breakfast this morning, Hilda, and by the way it's marvellous to have her back with us, asked if she might have a word. She wondered if I'd seen the list of the local men who had been killed in the war. Apparently it was in the local evening *Herald*. I told her that I hadn't and asked if she knew anyone on it.' Peter looked down. 'Bless her, she blushed, and then went to the drawer, brought out the *Herald* and handed it to me. As I scanned the list of names, the only one I really knew was that of Charles Harrington.'

Ella took a sharp intake of breath. Peter continued. 'I know. Just reading his name was shock enough.' Peter went over to Ella and cuddled her in his arms. Hearing Charles's name was enough to start Ella shaking. Peter held her tighter and said, 'It's alright, my darling. He can't hurt us now.'

After a few moments, Ella composed herself. She wasn't sure how she felt. She knew as a caring person she should be sad that he had lost his life, and yet she could not. As she calmed down it suddenly dawned on her that she would never, ever have to see him again, and that thought gave her more comfort than she could possibly have imagined. As she pulled herself together, she said, 'Thank you for telling me, Peter. And did you say there was something else, my love?'

'Yes, I was thinking that I need to meet the Public Relations Officer from the War Office to find out about Downside Alley, and when the folks can return. I could probably do it on my way back from leave, as I guess I will have to meet him in London.'

'Let's hope it's soon. Archie will be over the moon to go back to his birthplace, and Jane, too.'

'I know. But it may take a while. The Army used it for target practice, so there will be a few unexploded shells to be removed! Anyway, let's go and push our darling Georgia on the swing first. Then I'll phone the War Office and make an appointment.'

In order to secure a meeting, Peter had communicated to the secretary that he was the owner of the adjoining estate to Downside Alley. A meeting was arranged for a few days later, a meeting that was short and to the point. Although Peter had sought some positive reassurance as to the future of Downside Alley, he was told that none could be given at the present time.

As he travelled on to Scotland to rejoin his fellow airmen, Peter felt deeply disappointed. And due to the journey being long and tiring, he decided to telephone Ella the next day. Although telephones are a marvellous means of communication, when there is bad news to convey, the Bakelite mouthpiece seemed an inadequate tool to do so, and Peter wished that he was there with Ella when he told her that no one could return to Downside Alley, at least for the present.

Ella was more disappointed for all the evacuees, especially Jane and Archie, than herself. She wondered how best to tell the latter without upsetting them too much. She decided to choose her moment carefully, but, while waiting, Jane, who was anxious to get back to her cottage at Downside Alley, broached the subject when she came to help with the children two days after Peter's meeting.

'I was wondering, dear, if you have heard

from Peter regarding when we can go back to Downside Alley?'

Ella had no option but to tell her the truth. 'Peter did manage to see someone from the War Office. But sadly he was offered no reassurance.'

'Oh! What does that mean?'

'Just that at the moment there are no plans for the evacuees to return. I'm so sorry, Mum.'

Jane was visibly shocked. 'Goodness. That is a shock. Whatever will Archie say... well, I don't know.'

Although Archie was shocked, he tapped into his inner strength and his original disbelief of the assurance given. 'What did I tell you? The words written on that letter... well, they are, as Hardy said, wind, just bloody wind.'

Jane could see that Archie was working himself up into a state. 'Don't upset yourself, Arch. At least we have a comfortable home here.'

Archie began to pace up and down. 'But thass not the point, Jane. We was promised.'

'They haven't said we can't go back.'

'No. And by all accounts, they 'aven't said that we can!'

Jane poured her husband a brandy, which he downed without realising.

'Look. You always say how blessed we are. And when you think of the other evacuees, poor souls who have been flung all over the county, we're very fortunate.'

After drinking another brandy, Archie

calmed down and became more rational. 'I know what you be saying is right, my dear. But 'tis not really to do with how fortunate we be, but how scheming t'others be!'

'I know just how you feel, Arch. But we need to keep strong, and remember that 'tis not over yet.'

'No. But if we don't go back, 'twill be a real injustice. An' thass all I'm saying on the subject fer now.'

When the latest news of Downside Alley reached the other evacuees it was as if a cloud had descended over the whole area. For three long years they had waited to move back to their village, and now, with the war being over, the war which had robbed them of their homes, they were told that there were no plans for them to return, and were given no date as to when they possibly could.

On VE day, when Germany had surrendered, Norway, which had previously been taken by Germany, came under that surrender, which, as the Allies had demanded, was unconditional. Peter's time in Norway was much more relaxed than any of his previous positions. For one thing the clement weather gave everyone on the camp a good tan and all looked as if they had been on holiday.

Their destination was Kristiansand and the journey had taken several days. They arrived at the camp to find that the SAS had already rounded up the German prisoners and taken them to a PoW camp. Their vicious Alsatian guard dogs had been shot by the commanding officer. Although bereft of the German soldiers, the camp was full of Russian PoWs, who had now been freed. Britain had ordered that the Russian soldiers be given some clothing, but with a short runway the aeroplanes could not land and so dropped the parcels of clothes from a height. Peter recalled to Ella that one poor man had been impaled by this dangerous procedure.

Much later, and not long before he returned home for good, Peter recorded in his letter to Ella that he had travelled from southern Norway to Oslo, where they were all billeted in a big house. Proudly the RAF men took part in a parade in the palace grounds and were addressed by King Haakon of Norway, who himself had recently returned to his country after being evacuated to the relative safety of England for the duration of his country's occupation.

In August 1945 came VJ day, when Japan ceased fighting. Finally, the World War was over. Now followed the slow process of rebuilding the country and gradually getting everything back to normal, which would take some time. The servicemen were demobbed by age and length of service, the older men with a shorter service time being demobbed first.

Joe was due to be home in February 1946, but taking off his owed leave, he hoped to be home by Christmas 1945. Peter, who had joined early in 1939, had signed on for seven years and was unlikely to return until early 1946.

Both Ella and Hannah read the news of their husbands' respective homecoming dates with disbelief.

'Just when I thought we could make our plans to move into Woodleigh House, and now it's to be delayed again!' Ella said in exasperation.

Hannah, who had now been released from her job at the nursery and was working at Rylands full time, had been reading her letter from Joe and nodded her head in sympathy.

'I know how you feel, El. Joe won't be home until the end of the year. I'm just thankful we have each other for company, and to have a good moan too!' When Ella saw Hannah smiling mischievously at her, she quickly shook off her negative thoughts.

'You're right, Hannah, where would we be without each other? It's just a bit disappointing though.' Ella changed her voice to an exaggerated American accent, then continued, 'Cos I miss my man!'

Hannah gave a saucy laugh. 'Me too! Those Samways boys are rather addictive, to say the least.'

'My sentiments entirely! Ah, well, we can't sit around here all day mooning over our absent men. I need to get on with the bills for the estate.'

Hannah looked at her watch. 'And I need to go and pick Thomas up from school. Life goes on, eh? Men or no men!'

The two laughed at each other and went their separate ways.

Jane received letters from both Violet and Florrie to say they were safe and well, and their expected demob dates would probably be at the beginning of the New Year. Violet's letters were full of news of a soldier she had been seeing. His name was Angus, and he came from Scotland where his family ran a farm. She asked her mother if she might bring him home to meet the family, adding, this was providing that they could both get leave together. Jane spoke to Archie about it, and they both agreed that it was high time she had a boyfriend, and looked forward to meeting him and hearing all about farming life in Scotland.

Florrie's letters were always more reserved

and formal. She spoke about Melanie, who was in the same unit as her, but no mention of a boyfriend.

'Our Florrie always was very choosy,' Archie remarked as he peeled the potatoes for his wife.

'As long as she's happy, my dear, that's all that concerns me.'

The following month, Violet and Angus came to stay at Woodleigh. As Myrtle Cottage was rather small, Peter and Ella offered them the use of the west wing of Rylands. This contained two bedrooms, a sitting room, kitchen and basic bathroom, the latter being the second to be installed on the estate, with Woodleigh House having had the first inside bathroom there in the 1920s. The bedrooms looked over the fields towards Woodleigh woods and beyond, and the sunsets from those windows were often stunning. Violet squealed with delight as she went from room to room.

'This is magical,' she said to Ella, who was showing her round while Peter and Angus were discussing farming matters in the kitchen. 'Thanks so much for letting us stay here!' Violet's eyes sparkled bright as she surveyed the bedroom with its pretty curtains and matching bed cover. 'Oh, my goodness! What luxury this is, El, after those hard, narrow bunk beds.'

Ella laughed at her sister-in-law's face, which looked as if it was about to burst with happiness. 'We're delighted to have you with us.' They filed into the second bedroom, which was more subdued.

'Do you think this will be alright for Angus?' Ella asked. She realised fully that they would probably end up in Violet's room, but, not wishing to openly say this, kept a straight face. Violet, who had not thought that far ahead, mainly because she imagined that they would stay with her mum and dad, answered, 'Course it will. It's very nice.'

Ella smiled happily as the two made for the kitchen. 'Good. Shall we see how far the men have got with putting the farming world right?'

Soon Angus had met the children and was helping them to make aeroplanes from paper. When Hannah came in to take them for a walk, all three children wanted Angus to join them.

Sometime later, once the adults were alone and enjoying some of Hilda's homemade shortbread with a cup of tea, with a little prompting from Violet, Angus began to talk about his family and background. His enchanting Scottish accent soon had them all captivated, and Ella could see how Violet had fallen for this imposing, yet gentle man with huge brown eyes and engaging smile.

Angus and Violet shared a loving look before he began to speak. 'Well, my family have been farming in Ayrshire for at least two hundred years, so you see it's in the blood! I have seven brothers.' He stopped momentarily. 'Or should I say, had. Very tragically my youngest brother, Andrew, was killed in the Dieppe raid in 1942. I cannet imagine how he knew, but it seems he must have had some knowledge of just how dangerous the raid was going to be, because when he was on his last leave, he told his friend, Horace that he would not be coming back.'

Pausing, he looked at Violet, who squeezed his hand, before he continued in a lower voice. 'Mother never told us until after his death, but apparently he told her that if he should not come back, she was not to mourn, but to hold her head up high.'

Angus's pain was felt by all of them in the room. The silence that followed was all consuming. Everyone instinctively knew that Angus's story was not yet finished, and they all took a sip of their tea, including Angus, who then continued, 'My parents have always treated us boys alike, but being the youngest of us all, and coming late in life to my parents, my mother thought the waarld of Andrew, and always had an extra soft spot for him, which we all understood. And so the shock of his death was totally devastating for her, and she suffered a stroke as a result.' Angus looked up at the concerned faces of Violet's family.

Ella smiled kindly at the young man, before

saying, 'I am so sorry to hear that, Angus. How is she bearing up now?'

'For a wee while we thought we were going to lose her. She told us that the pain inside was unbearable... and that she wanted to join him.'

In a quiet voice, Violet said, 'Tell them about the vision, Angus.'

Angus looked at Violet with great affection. 'O, ay, the vision. One night about a month after Andrew's death, Mother said that she hadn't been in bed long when a white cloud appeared at the end of the bed, and as it cleared, Andrew's face emerged before her, and behind him were two flags. As she stared at her son, he said, "Mother! You're not doing as I asked. Please don't mourn for me any longer, and hold your head up high." Then his face gradually faded. From that day she began to improve and is now able to go out and about in a wheelchair.'

Ella, who was always quick to offer help and support, said, 'Well, that's wonderful news, Angus. Please tell your mother that if she would like a holiday, she and your father will be most welcome here anytime. We'd love to have them stay, wouldn't we, Peter?'

'Yes, we certainly would. And as much as I would love to talk farming and country matters with your parents, I know that my father would love to share some tales about farming in the old days. He was always so set in his ways, but since the forced evacuation and having to move twice in a short time, well, his outlook has broadened considerably.'

Angus was taken aback by such a generous offer. 'That is so very kind of ye both. I will indeed tell them, though I doubt that they would undertake the long journey, certainly not yet for a wee while. And, er, I look forward to meeting your parents this evening, Peter.'

'Thank you. It should be a happy gathering, and with all of the Samways clan seated round the table,' Peter laughed. 'Well, I hope it won't be too much of an ordeal.'

Now feeling much more relaxed, Angus replied, 'I'm sure it won't. If I can handle Violet, I'm sure I can handle her parents and siblings!' He winked at Violet, who gave him a mock glare.

The evening meal was a great success, the whole family embraced Angus as one of their own, and Archie, who could be very critical at times, liked him very much, and he was on top form as he chatted away to Angus after the delicious roast beef dinner.

'Now then, young Angus, I normally tell my children that they should be beware of strangers and that, when considering a partner, they should get to know the colour of his roots. But you have changed all that. And I can well understand why our Violet likes you.'

Coming from Archie, this was praise indeed, and having been told by Violet how parochial her parents were, Angus took Archie's words as a compliment, and, combined with the extraordinary kindness he had received from everyone in the family, felt that he had been unequivocally welcomed into the fold.

The weekend visit was a great success and Angus was invited down for Christmas, if he was free and not going home.

The fields and lanes on the estate were soon glowing with the vibrant hues of autumn, and once again blackberries were being gathered in the warm afternoon sunshine, which, as the sun was lower in the sky, was now more intense than on many of the summer days, piercing into the back of the gatherers like a hot iron.

As the chilly October mornings melted into glorious afternoon sunshine, Ella and Hannah, after picking Thomas up from school, would take the children on nature walks, where they would spot the last of the bees, butterflies and dormice before they hibernated for the winter. These halcyon days were treasured by them all and stored in their memories.

One day in mid November, after returning from one of their nature walks, they met the postman who was delivering the afternoon post. Touching his cap to Ella, he placed some letters and a small parcel into her hand. The parcel was addressed to Ella, and, in anticipation of what might be inside, she tore at the brown paper excitedly.

The carefully wrapped parcel was marked as delicate and much to her surprise she found a neatly wrapped present with a Christmas label tied to it, with the words 'Thank you for making me so welcome. Please open on receipt! Best wishes from Angus'.

'Oh, how kind,' she exclaimed, and tearing off the Christmas paper found a haggis neatly wrapped inside its own dish. 'Well, isn't that lovely? I've never tasted it before, so it will be something completely different! Let's put it straight into the larder, Han, to keep it cool.'

As they all pulled off their boots and entered the kitchen, Hannah said, 'I wonder if that means he's not coming here for Christmas then?'

'Well, maybe he's waiting to see if Violet is off or not.' Hannah looked at the other post, which Ella had put on the table. 'Maybe one of the envelopes is a card from the girls.'

Ella picked up the pile of letters and started to open them. 'I hope so.' She paused as she read the first letter, which was from Florrie, saying she would be on the five o'clock train arriving at Sandham station on Christmas Eve, and please could someone meet her. Ella looked at Hannah. 'Well, that's good news. One down and one to go!'

Ella passed two letters to Hannah. 'Would you like to open those, Han, while I open these two?'

Hannah took the letters and relayed the gist of them to Ella. 'Oh, marvellous news! This is from Violet. They're both off for Christmas and would love to take up your offer of staying over the Christmas holiday.' She looked at Ella. 'How brilliant is that?! It goes on to say they will arrive at Rylands early evening on Christmas Eve, and that they can't wait to see us all. Marvellous! Two more pairs of hands in the kitchen, El.'

Laughing, Ella replied, 'I like the sound of that!' Then, looking down, and speaking in a more serious tone, she said, 'I just pray that our men will be with us too.'

'I know. I didn't want to say anything. But it's time we heard from them.'

CHAPTER NINETEEN

During November when the leaves had finally left the trees and the ground was scattered with a profusion of colour, the children went with Ella and Hannah along the lanes and into the woods, where they picked up the multicoloured leaves and tossed them into the air in playful mood, while the adults gathered hazelnuts and chestnuts, which were available in copious amounts.

Although most of the nuts were stored away for Christmas, later that evening Ella and Hannah roasted some chestnuts by the fire, and, as they relaxed with a glass of wine, giggled to themselves as they recalled the afternoon when, as they made their way from one group of trees to another, Georgia, who was trying to keep up with Thomas, cried, 'You don't wait for me for half a tiny little second!'

'She'll catch up with him one day,' Hannah mused as she carefully manoeuvred some more chestnuts from the fire.

'Yes, bless her. It's nice that they'll all grow up together on the estate,' Ella said, adding thoughtfully, 'How things have changed for us all in the past three years, eh?'

'I know. It's all incredible, El. And the way things have happened, which really have been beyond our control, well, it makes you wonder about predestination and all that. Don't you think?'

'Yes, I do. When I really think of all that has happened to me since I came to Downside Alley, well, all I can say is I do believe in a greater power, and that, as your mother told me when I was in my darkest place, things do have a way of working out, and we must always believe that, whatever happens.'

Cracking another nut, Hannah said, 'Umm. It's true. She's a wise old soul, my mum. And I'm glad she could help. Just look what's happened since then? I mean, if you'd run off or something, look what you'd have missed!'

'I never thought of it like that, Han,' Ella said as she popped another chestnut into her mouth. 'As they say, every experience teaches us something, and I think you and I have grown up considerably since we first met.'

'Too right we have. Look, we're both mums now and running houses! Who'd have thought that a few years ago?'

Ella laughed at her friend's expressive face. 'Who indeed? Now, how about a cup of cocoa before we go to bed?'

With that a cry was heard from the bedroom. 'Oh, there's Georgia. She seems to be having a few nightmares lately. No doubt it will pass. I'll just go and settle her, Han. If you'd like to put the kettle on, that would be great.' With that Ella disappeared upstairs and Hannah went into the kitchen to make the cocoa.

Festive preparations had been under way for some while at Rylands, and since late November, Ella, Hannah and the children had begun to make paper chains to hang round the rooms at the Samways' abode. Thomas and Georgia had even made some homemade sweets with Natalie, which were so delicious that they only lasted a week.

Some weeks before the festive season, Ella decided that Natalie, Mavis and Hilda would have the three days off over Christmas, but all three had an invitation to join the family for Christmas dinner. Hilda thanked Ella for her kind thought but said she would be happier helping in the kitchen. Although both the other two ladies enjoyed working at Rylands, they were very pleased to think that they could have an easier time for a few days.

On the day Ella told them the news, Mavis had an extra reason to celebrate. She had had a letter from her mother, Lily, asking if she could come and stay for a few days early in December. Mavis was thrilled and had spoken to her Aunt Jane about it, who was very pleased that her sister had managed to get some time off from her factory job and was travelling down to

Woodleigh. As Vine Cottage was quite small, Jane said that Lily could stay with her and Archie. Ella, who was also pleased to hear the news, said that they must all come to tea at Rylands one day.

On her first day at Woodleigh, Lily and Mavis joined Jane and Archie for the family meal. It was a very happy occasion, and after they had eaten, all played some card games as had been customary in Jane and Lily's family home before the sisters were wed. The following day, Lily and Jane spent some time together catching up on family news. Lily, who had seemed to be in good spirits up to now, broke down in front of Jane as she told her that her son, Jack had been badly injured when serving in France. The soldier in front of him had trodden on an explosive, which had killed him and badly wounded Jack. He had been on a hospital ship for a month, and was, after many medicals, now discharged.

Jane was very sad to hear all this, and comforted her sister as much as she could. 'He will recover in time, our Lily, and no doubt will pick up his life again. I'm sure he'll be alright.'

With that, Lily wiped her eyes and smiled at Jane. 'I know you're right. It's just that the shock of it all has been building up inside of me. I've kept it in at home, but... I'm sorry, my dear, I let it out with you.'

'No need to be sorry, Lil. We're sisters, that's what we're here for, isn't it?'

Lily nodded in agreement. 'I think it's seeing

our Mavis alright, too. You know, it's real affected me that folk can be so kind.'

'Peter and Ella were only too pleased to help, Lil.'

Lily wiped her eyes, and said, 'Bless them. An' you're right about things picking up for Jack. The BBC has said that his job is still there for him when he is fit enough to go back.'

'Well, that is wonderful news! That must have given him a boost?'

'It did. Once he can walk with a stick, he'll be back in the office again.'

'You send him our very best wishes. And if he ever wants to come and visit, he'd be most welcome.'

After blowing her nose, Lily said, 'That is kind. You are all of you so very kind. I must count my blessings and not look back.'

'That's it, our Lily. Don't look back. There's nothing there, the past with all its horror has gone, thank goodness. Look forward now, it's the only way.'

Lily gave Jane a peck on the cheek. 'Thanks, Jane. Now, I believe we've got an invitation to tea at Rylands!'

As Jane led Mavis and Lily into the hall at Rylands, squeals of joy could be heard coming from the kitchen. The hoots and squeals came from Hannah who had just received the good news that Joe would be home a few days before Christmas. As Mavis entered the kitchen she witnessed Hannah doing a little jig round one of the chairs in a display of sheer happiness.

Ella, who had laughed at Hannah's impromptu dance, greeted her guests with enthusiasm, pleased to have something to take her mind off the fact that, as yet, she had had no news of Peter's demob date.

Even though he knew that he might still be away, Peter had suggested to Ella the idea of giving all the estate workers and their families a party around two weeks before Christmas. Ella had agreed wholeheartedly, and with this being the first Christmas of freedom since the end of the war, she planned to make it an extra special celebration for them all.

Although the war was over, food rationing was not, but with some careful planning and imaginative recipes, concocted by Hilda, and with help from Ella, Hannah, Natalie and Mavis, the party was a huge success. The Christmas tree, which was guarded by Tommy, one of the younger farm workers, who had a bucket of water by his side, was lit by candles and looked simply magical as it glowed and flickered brightly in one corner of the hut. All different coloured jellies, which wobbled on their plates, were soon devoured by the children, along with the homemade ice cream that Hilda doled out to each child as they appeared before her with expectant faces. A delicious selection of sandwiches and various scrummy cakes went down a treat. Many children there had not tasted such food since the war began, and some, never.

The afternoon had started with the local school's performance of their nativity play. Thomas was very proud to play Joseph, while Georgia, who although not at school yet, had been invited to be an angel. Rather excited to be on stage with Thomas, she smiled broadly at Ella every time she caught her eye. After the feast, the children sat on the floor and their parents on wooden benches as the church choir, led by Reverend Morley, sang carols, which everyone sang.

Just before the end of the afternoon, a banging was heard on the wall of the village hut. The vicar took charge, and said, 'I wonder who that can be, children?'

One of the bigger boys, who somehow had inside knowledge, shouted, 'It's the man from the pub!' But before he had spoken the last words, the knocking came again, and the vicar spoke with enthusiasm, 'Let's find out who it is, shall we children?' As the children gave a roar of ascent, Bill Bradley came in dressed up as Father Christmas, with a full sack on his back. The children all cheered excitedly, with some shouting at the top of their voices, 'It's Father Christmas!' as Bill walked round the hall, waving at them all.

In order of age, with the youngest going first, one by one the children went up to see Father Christmas. Some were very wary, as they had not seen him before; others quite boldly told him what toy they would like Father Christmas to bring them. Some even sat on his knee and whispered their wishes into his ear. Bill, who had not experienced anything like it before, was rather touched by the children's innocence and trust. Every child left with a present in their hand, all carefully chosen by Ella, Hannah and the children's mothers.

On a dark, wet afternoon in mid December, on his second delivery, the postman brought the frustrating news that Peter would not be home until January. Although Ella tried to tell herself that it was only a short time to go now, the disappointment of not having him with her and thinking that his face would be the only one missing round the Christmas table was too much to bear, and she broke down and wept.

Hannah had been out when Ella received the letter, but when she came through the door and heard Ella crying, she rushed to comfort her, praying that it was not bad news.

After holding each other for a minute or so, Ella broke off, blew her nose and wiped her eyes.

'I'm alright, Han, just being a bit silly, really.'

'What's happened, El?'

'Oh, I've just heard that Peter won't be home with us at Christmas. I won't see him until sometime in January.' She blew her nose again. 'You must think me daft for getting so upset? Especially after all the trauma we've been through.' Ella paused. 'This setback seems so minor.'

Hannah took her friend's hand. 'Of course I don't. After all the waiting and planning, it's only natural. I tell you what. I'd be climbing the walls if Joe had told me that he wasn't home 'til next year! If you ask me, you're doing bloomin' marvellous to cope with everything as you have.'

Hannah's down-to-earth reply made Ella smile. 'Where would I be without your pragmatic thinking? Thanks, Hannah.'

'That's what we're here for, isn't it? To help each other. I know it won't be the same without your Peter, but we'll make the most of it, eh?'

By now, although she was bitterly disappointed, Ella was feeling ashamed of her momentary self-pity, which was so out of character. Smiling brightly, she said, 'We certainly will. Now, shall we have a cup of tea before getting on with writing the Christmas cards, as we'd planned to do?'

When Joe returned to Woodleigh Cottage on December 23 he found that Hannah was still at work. As he walked across to Rylands to find her, he noticed that the barn was stacked full of logs. As he was wondering who had put all the man hours into achieving such a marvellous sight, Archie came out from the barn with an axe in his hand. It was one of Archie's jobs to cut up the trees that had fallen down on the estate, something he was well used to doing from when he lived at Downside Alley.

As he always had done, he made his own explosives with which to crack the trees open. This to him was second nature, and he did the job effortlessly, and was then able to chop the broken boughs into usable-sized logs. Now that the weather had suddenly turned very cold, and with the fires being lit from early in the morning, Archie was very pleased that he had worked the extra hours to ensure everyone had a shed full of logs.

When he caught sight of his son, Archie put down his axe and walked over to him. 'Ah, Joe. 'Tis good to see you safely home, son, and in your demob suit too!' The two shook hands.

'Thanks, Dad. I can't tell you how wonderful it is to be here.' He turned his eyes to the barn. 'Did you chop all those up?'

Archie's face was beaming. 'I certainly did, and a few more, too. Your shed is full up and so is ours!'

'Crickey! That's brilliant. We'll all be warm this Christmas then?'

'Ah, an' well fed too, I reckon. I had a few extra birds from last week's shoot to add to the festive table.'

Joe put his arm round his father's shoulders. 'Plenty of home brew too, I hope?'

Archie winked at Joe. 'Too right, son.'

Joe, who was so relieved at finally being home for good, said, 'I think it's gonna be my best Christmas ever!' With that, Hannah rushed out of the door, gave a whoop of delight and flung herself into Joe's arms.

Archie scratched his head, and said, 'I think you're right there, son.'

After witnessing Joe's rapturous welcome, Archie went back to the barn and continued chopping the rest of the wood. Elated to have Joe home, Hannah led him by the hand to their cottage, where once inside the door they wrapped themselves in an amorous embrace. Hungry for each other, they started to undress as they went up the stairs and were soon making sweet, passionate love. When their fiery lust had been fulfilled, they lay back in each other's arms, feeling as if they were floating on air. Speaking words of love to each other, Joe was taken to new heights as Hannah told him that she was three months pregnant.

That evening it was the family Christmas service at St Michael's Church, and the local place of worship was beautifully lit by many candles. The Samways clan arrived just as the five-minute bell stopped ringing, and they managed to squeeze into the back row.

Looking proudly at all of the family, Joe whispered, 'Being squashed together has its good points... we can all keep each other warm!'

Two of the older, quite staid-looking parishioners turned to Joe and gave him a glare, which he thought was far from Christian like. Catching their warning stare, and smiling at her husband, Hannah put a finger over her lips in a bid to silence him.

The children hadn't been to an hour's service before and Ella and Hannah were slightly anxious as to how they would react. They had brought some soft toys to amuse them in case they got restless, and hoped the singing of carols might engage their interest. As it turned out they were all very good. Thomas, who had already been to the church with his school, joined in with some of the hymns, which made him feel quite important. Georgia and Merrily pushed their soft toys up and down the pew for a while and then were happy to be picked up by Ella and Joe, mesmerised by the flickering candles and the singing congregation.

After shaking hands with the vicar and some of the familiar faces from the village, the family walked home over the fields, singing *We Three Kings* at the top of their voices, their way being lit by a moonlit sky, which sparkled with a billion stars.

When they reached Rylands, Ella and Hannah went straight into the kitchen to serve up the supper, which had been slowly cooking in the AGA while they were in church. The others settled in the sitting room where the fire was still ticking over and giving out a welcome heat. After a delicious supper of roast pheasant and vegetables with a glass of wine, followed by treacle tart, Archie and Jane said they should be going, and, after thanking Ella for a lovely supper, said their goodnights and made their way home.

The children, who by now were over-tired, were gathered up and taken to bed where Joe read them all a story. Merrily was asleep before the second page, while Georgia fought it out until the middle before succumbing, and Thomas, who stayed awake for the whole of the Christmas story, gave his dad a huge hug, before cuddling up to his teddy and drifting off to sleep.

Joe then went outside to bring in some more logs, and then joined Ella and Hannah for a glass of wine. Hannah, who had waited to tell

Joe first of her exciting news, was bursting to let Ella know, too. She took Joe's hand before announcing, 'Joe and I have some very exciting news, El. We're going to have a baby in June!'

Ella jumped up from her chair and gave Hannah a big hug. 'Oh, Han!' She looked at Joe. 'I'm so thrilled for you both. This is truly wonderful news.'

Joe grinned triumphantly. 'It's the best Christmas present I could ever have!'

Ella went over to the sideboard. 'This calls for a brandy!' She poured out three tumblers and offered a toast. 'To you all!'

They all chinked glasses and offered up a united 'Cheers!' as they each took a sip of brandy. Hannah, who was beside herself with total joy, took Joe's hand and said, 'It's all we ever wanted. And now, thanks to you and Peter, Joe has a job and we have a home. We couldn't ask for more.'

'Hannah's right, Ella, we feel so fortunate. And I've been thinking, if it's alright with you, I thought I would make a start in the office tomorrow?'

Ella smiled at them. It was just so wonderful to see them both so blissfully happy. 'Well, that is kind of you, Joe. But tomorrow is Christmas Eve!'

'I know. But I feel that I would like to make a start. That is, if you don't mind?'

'I don't mind at all, Joe.' She looked at Hannah. 'Hannah and I will be busy getting the last-minute bits ready for Christmas. But, no, you carry on by all means. I will be on hand, should you need me.'

'Thanks. I'm sure I'll be fine. There's a mound of old paperwork to look at first, I believe?'

Ella put down her glass. 'Yes, that's right. Should keep you busy for a day or two, I guess.' Ella winked at Hannah.

Joe put his arm around his wife. 'Well, I don't think I'll be working Christmas Day. But I'll have to check with my boss.'

As she laughed, Ella said, 'Of course you won't. It's gonna be an extra special celebration this year. Hannah and I have been working like I don't know what to make it so. Haven't we, Han?'

Hannah, who by now was almost falling asleep, replied, 'Sure have! It's gonna be just simply wonderful.'

Joe, who had learnt from Hannah about Peter's news, said, 'We shall miss Pete, though.'

Ella had promised herself that she would not get down by her husband's absence, and replied, 'Well, when he does come home, it will be an excuse for another family party, eh?'

'Absolutely!' Joe looked at his watch. 'Do you know, it's almost midnight?' He stood up and offered Hannah his hand and pulled her up. 'Come, my princess.' Then, as he picked her up in his arms, added, 'Your carrier awaits!'

Feeling totally relaxed, Hannah giggled and sunk into her husband's arms, then blew a kiss to Ella who followed them to the door. Before leaving, Joe turned to Ella and gave her a kiss on the cheek. 'See you in the morning, Ella. Thanks for everything. Night.'

With that Ella locked the door, then, as she turned, paused momentarily to reflect on Joe and Hannah's baby news. Looking wistful, she whispered, 'Why are we not blessed, too?' Then, shaking off her fleeting sadness, she put the guard around the fire and went to bed.

CHAPTER TWENTY

The villagers of Woodleigh awoke to an icy Christmas Eve morning. As Joe made his way to the office in the courtyard, which lay at the back of Rylands, he stopped to admire the sun glistening on the frost of the Georgian roofs and to breathe in the pure fresh air. Was it the amazing news that he was going to be a father again, which made him want to rejoice in every aspect of nature that morning? Or was it that he felt so fortunate to be living in Woodleigh? The perfect place to bring up the children. A combination of both, he thought. Of course, the icing on the cake would be to return to Downside Alley, the home of his childhood and his father's and grandfather's, too. But what made Woodleigh more appealing, he reasoned, was that Peter was his landlord, whereas at Downside it would be Squire Harrington again, who was not very fond of spending money on his properties.

One of his last memories of living in Downside Alley was seeing some old sacking put down by the door of the Cutler's cottage. The bottom of the door had rotted away and was letting in the wind and rain, and all Squire Harrington could say to his tenants was, 'Throw some sacking at it', which was pitifully inadequate. But Joe didn't want to dwell on any negatives that morning.

For Joe, that morning was the first day of his new life, and it had started in the most joyful way, for when he awoke he found that Hannah and he were entwined around each other as one. They had both slept deep and long, and only awoke when they heard the dairyman calling some of his cows, which had strayed into the lane by their cottage. Realising the time, they gently untangled themselves from each other, and, after some tender kisses and caresses, Joe got up and made a cup of tea for them both, taking Hannah's up to the bedroom for her.

As she drowsily whispered her thanks, she added, 'I must be the luckiest girl in the world!' Shortly afterwards, Thomas and Merrily peeped through the bedroom door and, after an encouraging smile from Hannah, leapt onto their parents' bed, jumping up and down with squeals of delight.

After watching the happy scene, Joe kissed Hannah and the children, then replied, 'And I'm the luckiest boy! See you all later, my darlings.' With that he was gone, taking those memories with him and the ones from the previous night, when he had thought he must have died and gone to heaven.

Ella had already unlocked the office, and as Joe entered the brick-clad building he was pleased to find the kettle on the old range was near to boiling. Cups, tea, coffee and milk fresh from the farm were all on a small table, along with some of Hilda's shortbread biscuits. 'What a girl! She's thought of everything,' Joe murmured as he gazed round the rather cluttered room, where shelf upon shelf was overflowing with musty old books, files and papers.

His desk was covered in mounds of various shabby files, and after trawling through a pile of old papers, some of which, by the look of them, had not been touched for many a long year, he thought it best to begin with those dating back the furthest. And so, after making himself a cup of coffee, Joe began his duties as the estate manager.

He became fascinated by the old papers and documents. Many related to tenants and tenancies, and some of them were over one-hundred-and-fifty years old. Immersing himself in the names and titles, he suddenly stopped stock-still, reading and rereading a certain document. Hardly daring to believe what was written on the musty old page, he leapt up from his chair, went across the yard and was soon knocking on the door of Rylands.

Ella, who was in the middle of making some mince pies when she heard the urgent knocking, brushed the flour from her hands and went to see who was there. She was surprised to see Joe on the doorstep and exclaimed, 'Oh, Joe! Is everything alright?'

Joe gave her an excited nod and said, 'Have you got a minute?'

'Have you found something interesting then, Joe?' Ella asked as she tried to keep up with her brother-in-law, who was almost racing across the estate yard.

The two entered the office and Joe gestured to Ella to take a seat. 'I think so. But I need you to read it for me, just to make sure that I'm not hallucinating!'

Filled with curiosity, Ella looked at the paper spread before her. Like Joe, she needed to read it a second and third time as the enormity of the words before her sank in. Joe was smiling all the while as he realised that he was not seeing things and that the information on the document was real.

Ella, who was speechless for a while, finally said, 'My goodness, Joe. This is absolutely incredible!'

Joe could not stop grinning. 'I know. I know. Imagine what Mum and Dad will say!'

'Yes! And imagine what Peter will say!'

The two just kept looking at each other, then looking at the document, until Ella finally said, 'We need to show this to our solicitor. Thankfully, we have a reasonable one. Which is more than you can say about the Harringtons!'

'I agree. But first, can we have a tot of something? My head is in such a spin!'

Ella could not stop smiling. 'Of course! Why didn't I think of that? We'll toast your amazing find, and then I'll call Mr Robson.' Ella decided to have a coffee instead, but poured Joe a tot of brandy. As they chinked cup and glass together, Ella asked, 'I know this sounds a bit weird, given the whole exciting magnitude of the revelation, but can we keep this to ourselves until I have spoken to Peter? He is phoning me at five o'clock this evening.'

Knocking his brandy back in one, Joe replied, 'Of course, Ella. I understand. But it's gonna be mighty hard to hide my excitement though!' He placed the glass on the table. 'But what can I do now?'

'Well, just wait until I have phoned Mr Robson, and we'll take it from there.'

'Sure. Good thing it's a Monday and not Sunday, eh? It would drive us mad having to wait any longer.'

'Yes. And a good thing the office is open on Christmas Eve.' Ella went over to the filing cabinet. 'Now, where is his telephone number?' She rummaged in the drawer and pulled out a piece of paper. 'Ah, good, here it is. And the number of Mr Etherington, who I guess Mr Robson will also need to contact.'

Without further ado, Ella phoned her solicitor, who said he would need to check certain facts and asked if she could take the document to his office.

After Ella had relayed the solicitor's conversation to Joe, he said, 'Good, let me take you to him right now.'

'Thanks, Joe. This is so exciting. I just hope it's true.'

'Of course it's true! The writing on the paper confirms that.' He checked his pocket to make sure he had the car keys. 'Okay, young lady. Let's go.'

Without further ado, Ella picked up the relevant papers and the two headed for Joe's car. Half an hour later they were sat in Mr Robson's reception area, while Mr Robson went into his office to read the paperwork.

Looking at Ella over his half-rimmed spectacles he said that if he found the document to be genuine, he would then phone Mr Etherington, the Army's Public Relations Officer.

Ten minutes later, Miss Scott, Mr Robson's secretary, told them that Mr Robson was awaiting a telephone call from Mr Etherington, and maybe they would like to get some fresh air and come back in an hour's time.

And so Ella and Joe strolled down Sandham's high street. To pass the time they decided to call in at Kathy's Cafe and have coffee and cake. Feeling revived, they then wandered further down the high street and as they passed the grocery and provision store, Ella said she could do with buying some more candles. Entering the large high-windowed shop, which had the peculiar combined smell of strong cheese, paraffin and moth balls, Ella walked over to the counter with Joe at her side.

Suddenly, Mabel White came and stood next to her. Eyeing Joe up, she said to Ella in an acerbic tone, 'Husband still away is he?' and much to her chagrin, Ella answered her cheerfully, 'Yes.' With that Mabel took her change and left.

Ella and Joe looked at each other and laughed. 'You'll never change people like that, Joe,' Ella said. 'They thrive on causing problems. Sad really, isn't it?'

Joe agreed. 'You wonder what they gain from it, don't you?'

Ella took her bag of wrapped candles from the shop assistant, and as Joe held the door open for Ella, she said, 'Nothing, Joe. They gain nothing. Well, except a callous heart. Anyway, enough time spent on that woman. Let's go and see what Mr Robson has to say, shall we?'

Thankfully, Mr Robson had some good news. As he offered them a seat in his rather drab office, he pulled off his spectacles and smiled at them both as he confirmed that the information on the document was completely genuine. As Ella and Joe smiled with relief and happiness the solicitor continued with a caution. He explained that although everything was perfectly legal, there was another matter relating to the terms, which he needed to clear up. He assured Ella that he would get straight on with the business and would call her at home as soon as he had news.

He shook Joe's hand and thanked him for bringing Ella to the office. Then, turning to Ella, he congratulated her and told her how pleased he was for both her and Peter. After exchanging festive wishes, he shook Ella's hand and said goodbye.

Ella and Joe almost floated out of Mr Robson's office. The morning's revelation had been quite extraordinary, and the two linked arms as they headed for the car.

'I just hope Mrs White is watching,' Joe exclaimed.

Ella's face was radiant. 'I don't give a jot about Mrs White. This news is so amazing, Joe. I can't wait to tell Peter when he phones this evening. He'll be just over the moon. The possibilities are endless!'

When they arrived back at Rylands, it was past lunch time and Ella quickly made them both a sandwich. Hannah had taken Georgia and Merrily to pick up Thomas, who, after performing in the school nativity play, finished for the day at two o'clock.

As Joe munched his way through his tasty sandwich, he said, 'I don't know how I'm going to contain my excitement, Ella!'

'Me neither. But it's only 'til I speak to Peter, then we can tell everyone. What a Christmas present for us all, eh?'

'I should say so! A Christmas present to change our lives forever, that's for sure!'

By the time lunch was over it was half past two, and before long Hannah came back with the children, who were so excited about Father Christmas coming that night that they went to check in the study to see that the chimney was clear for him to come down. The fire was not to be lit in that room specifically for that reason.

Hannah was pleased to hear that Ella had given Joe the afternoon off and, with the last-minute presents to wrap, she asked her husband if he could look after the children. Joe was more than happy to do this and asked them if they would like to go and collect some holly and ivy to decorate the houses. A resounding 'yes' came from Thomas and Georgia, and Merrily, who did not like to be outdone, joined them a few seconds later with her own 'es'.

Just as they were returning from their adventure in the woods, armed with copious amounts of holly and ivy, Violet and Angus drove up the drive, tooting their horn as they waved out of the car window. After whoops of jubilation and lots of hugs, Violet and Angus took their cases into their bedrooms, which looked charmingly festive as Ella had thoughtfully hung some of the paper chains and the children's bells and angels round the rooms. Once settled the young couple joined Ella in the kitchen for tea and a catch up, and, much to Ella's surprise and delight, Angus gave her a toboggan, which he had made for the children and said he hoped that they may be able to use it over the holidays.

'That is so kind, Angus. Archie did say he thought snow was on the way, so it may be used sooner than we think! Oh, and thank you for the haggis, too.'

Angus's eyes sparkled. 'What did ye think of it?'

Ella couldn't lie. 'Uh, well, all I can say is it must be an acquired taste!'

Angus laughed. 'You cannet judge it by one tasting. When you've tried it meybe a few more times, you'll get to love it.' He turned to Violet. 'Won't she, lassie?'

Violet smiled lovingly at Angus, then looked at Ella. 'Yes. Angus is right. Maybe we'll try some on New Year's Eve, if the local butcher sells it.'

Ella laughed. 'That's a big if, Vi. He's had hardly any decent meat for ages.'

Angus shrugged his shoulders. 'Ah well, ye cannet expect a butcher this far south to have such a thing! Meybees you'll join us in Scotland one day, and we'll show you some real Scottish hospitality, in repayment for your own?'

'Oh, Peter and I would love that, Angus. Thank you.'

During the late afternoon the sky became increasingly heavy, and the snow, which Archie had predicted at lunch time began to fall. Looking out of the sitting room window, the children were both excited and bewildered by the strange white world outside, which was becoming whiter by the minute. Watching their excited faces, Joe asked them if they would like to go and play in it, and have a ride on the new toboggan. Their excited screams could be heard all over the house, and within a few minutes the three children and Joe and Angus were warmly dressed for the chilly, but picturesque world outside.

Gently padding their way over the snow-covered drive and into the lane, they were soon on the top of Woodleigh Hill, where the delighted children spent some time sledging down the hillside; then, after having a few rides each, with help from Joe and Angus they made a lovely snowman. As they were wondering what to use for the eyes and mouth, Joe pulled out some carrots and coal from his pocket, which he had hastily popped in there just before they left home. And so, with squeals of delight the children helped to put them in place.

As they all stepped back to admire their handiwork, Georgia fell over in the snow and began to cry. Scooping her up in his arms and pacifying her, Joe said that as the light was failing and everyone was getting cold they should be making their way home where they could all warm up in front of the roaring fire.

Hannah had said she would collect Florrie from the station, and as she went to leave that afternoon the first flakes of snow began to pitch on the ground. She was glad that it had only just begun, as she wasn't sure how well Trixie would handle the roads in snowy conditions, and having had no experience of slippery roads as yet, wasn't sure how she would handle it either.

As the clock turned half past five, Ella was a little on edge. Peter had not yet phoned, and he was always punctual. Joe, who was relaying to Ella the details of the afternoon walk and how excited the children had been when making a snowman, said not to worry, there must be a reason, and he was sure Peter would be in contact soon.

The station at Sandham was busy with people coming and going, and Hannah had to push through the crowd to find a space on platform two where she could easily see Florrie alighting.

It was a very chilly evening and Hannah was thankful when she saw the gates close and the down line signal giving the all clear for the south-bound train to halt at the station. As the passengers disembarked, Hannah searched for Florrie's purple felt hat, which she always wore in winter time. She quickly spotted her sister-in-law and went up the platform to meet her.

As their eyes met and they made their way towards each other, Hannah noticed that Florrie had an unusually bright smile on her face, and it was then that she noticed someone else walking closely behind her. It was Peter, with an even wider smile on his face. Running towards them for the last few yards, Hannah held out her arms in sheer joy. Soon all three were hugging each other, with tears of happiness falling on their cheeks. As they made their way towards the car, Peter explained to Hannah that the orderly staff at Folkingham in Lincolnshire, where he was stationed while awaiting his demob number, had miscalculated his owed leave and that he was actually due two weeks extra than had at first been thought. He added that when his number was finally called he had to walk through a long hut, where, after being measured up, he was handed a cardboard box with a pin-stripe suit in. He was also issued with a trilby hat, which he said he would give to Archie.

'Ah, so that's what's in your box then! I did

wonder,' Hannah said, smiling cheekily at her brother-in-law as the three of them piled into the car. 'Ella is going to be absolutely over the moon,' she added, as she pulled out of the station car park.

'And I can't wait to see her!' Peter replied. 'Poor love will be worried as I was due to phone at five. I had no chance to let her know. When I heard the news, I just had time to catch a train to London, and then jump on the connecting train, which was bound for Sandham.'

Florrie smiled and joined in, saying, 'I just couldn't believe it when Peter walked by my carriage. And I had to wait until we got to Southampton before I could talk to him, else I would have lost my seat.'

'Yes, thankfully someone from Florrie's carriage got out at Southampton, and I managed to sneak in.'

'Funny how things work out, isn't it?' Hannah said as she crashed the gears. 'Whoops, sorry about that.'

Peter and Florrie laughed. They were almost home, it was Christmas Eve and it was snowing. Could life get any better?

In spite of Joe's reassurance, Ella was feeling very anxious, and when Peter walked through the door she fell into his arms and cried with relief.

As Peter cuddled her tenderly, he whispered, 'I'm so sorry I couldn't let you know, my darling. But I would have missed my train if I had delayed any longer.'

Ella, who was so overjoyed that he was home and safe, simply said, 'You're here, and that's all that matters, my love.'

Regaining her composure, she offered everyone a glass of mulled wine and suggested they go into the sitting room where it was warmer.

After stepping inside the spacious hallway, Florrie had taken time to admire the very tall Christmas tree, which was beautifully decorated with homemade angels and bells. And after taking the glass of mulled wine from Ella, she entered the sitting room and was enchanted to see how beautifully decorated it was, with swathes of holly and ivy everywhere, and a few sprigs of mistletoe, too.

Archie's logs were burning away on the huge hearth, and as Florrie took a seat in a comfy armchair, Georgia came up to her and scrambled onto her knee. 'Are you going to hang up your stocking for Father Christmas, Aunt Florrie?'

Florrie looked at the sweet, innocent face before her and replied, 'Of course, Georgia! Shall we leave him a drink and biscuit, too?'

Georgia nodded and then, wriggling down, ran over to Thomas, who was trying to put an angel back in place after it had fallen from the tree.

Soon the family were gathered in the south-facing sitting room, sipping mulled wine and nibbling on Ella's mince pies. With such exciting news to impart to her husband, Ella asked Hannah if she would mind keeping an eye on the meal, which was cooking slowly in the Aga, as she needed to have a catch up with Peter.

'Course not, El. I'll give the children their meal first, then while Joe and the girls are helping the little ones hang up their stockings, I'll pop the veg on.' She checked the clock before adding, 'It's only six o'clock now. So why don't we delay dinner for an hour or so and eat at, say, seven thirty?'

'That's a brilliant idea, Han. We'll do that then. Jane and Archie will be here soon, so if you can entertain them, Joe, that would be great.'

Joe realised the importance of Ella talking to Peter and, as he winked at his sister-in-law, said, 'My pleasure, El. Take your time.'

CHAPTER TWENTY ONE

An hour later Jane and Archie were sat down by the fire and enjoying the Christmas refreshments along with the rest of their family, and while Hannah finished off the meal, Violet and Florrie helped the children, who were now in their nightwear, to hang up their stockings. Then, full of excitement and chatter, Thomas, Georgia and Merrily had piggy backs from Joe, Angus and Archie as they went up the stairs to bed. Once all tucked up and calmed down, they listened to a Christmas story from Joe and were soon fast asleep.

Just in time, Joe joined the rest of the family as they took their places in the dining room to enjoy a tasty meal of local lamb with all the trimmings, followed by apple tart and cream.

Before eating, Ella said grace and offered a prayer of thanks for the ending of the war and for the safe return of their family, to which everyone said a heartfelt 'Amen'.

As everyone ate their meal the conversation flowed freely and the atmosphere was happy and relaxed. Once the dishes were cleared away and the wine glasses refilled, Peter and Joe, who were both in ebullient spirits, said they both had something to say.

Joe spoke first. During his fairly short

speech he thanked Ella and Hannah for the wonderful meal, and Peter and Ella for their kind hospitality. Then, as he turned towards his brother, he said, 'And now I'll hand over to Peter, who has, I know, some very good news to convey.'

Peter stood up and, thanking Joe for his words of appreciation, looked round at the smiling faces of his family, cleared his throat and proceeded with his hastily formed speech, which he had jotted down on a piece of paper.

'I would like to start by saying how wonderful it is to have you all here with us this Christmas Eve. When you think that it's seven years since we shared a Christmas free from the anxieties of war, it makes this one very special indeed.'

As he paused to look round at his family, murmurs of 'Here, here' were heard.

'I was at home in Downside Alley when the announcement of war came on the wireless, and as I looked round at you all that night I felt that whatever the challenges were, you would all face them admirably, and you have.'

Archie shouted, 'And so have you.' Peter waved his hand in modest response, then continued.

'I am very proud of the fact that we all share a belief in what is good. This belief, this total faith, has helped nurture us all through those dark days and family tragedies, and, along with family love and incredible miracles, has brought us here, to where we are this evening. Please forgive my indulgence, but if you don't mind I would like to take a few minutes of your time to try to put into context what I am ultimately coming to.'

Ella stood up. 'Before you go on, darling,' she looked round at everyone, 'Would anyone like some more wine, or a hot drink?' The general consensus was a top-up of wine, of which Joe took charge.

With everyone settled and rather curious as to what Peter was coming to, he continued. 'My childhood, like that of my siblings, was everything a childhood should be. During those years I had love and kindness shown by my amazing parents, who disciplined me by example and taught me the importance of manners and respect. My leisure hours on the farm and common gave me the freedom which all boys desire, and, being surrounded by animals and wildlife, I learnt about life and death. All these important factors contributed to my strength of character... or so I thought.' Peter looked down at his notes and cleared his throat.

'Life is not easy, and goodness knows how people who did not have my upbringing cope. For when I was confronted by a real crisis, I almost buckled. Yes, almost, but not completely. Miraculously, through the appearance of Edward, who seemed like a guardian angel to me, everything began to change for the good. And I quickly learnt that you can't run away from life.'

Peter paused to take a sip of water. Everyone in the room was entranced and wondered where this was going.

'The list is endless. Firstly and most importantly, Ella forgave me and accepted my proposal of marriage... without doubt, the very best thing to have happened in my life!' He turned and smiled at Ella. 'Then, on our wedding day, we heard of Edward's incredible legacy, which was the most staggering revelation. And it's even more wonderful because I get to share it with all of you. As I said before, life is not easy, and at this particular time I know that one sadness for Mum and Dad is the uncertainty of Downside Alley, the place that holds so many happy memories for us all, well except Angus, that is.'

Everyone broke into laughter, and looked at Angus.

'Now, where was I? Ah, yes, I was talking of miracles, and belief and trust, and not giving up when things get tough, which, sadly, I almost did. I truly believe that whatever the future may hold, if we just hold on to our faith, somehow things do work out.' He paused once more to take a sip of water.

'As you know, Joe is taking on the job of estate manager for the Woodleigh estate, and what he has discovered just today is quite incredible. Now, I'm gonna give my voice and you a break and hand over to Ella, who can fill you in on the finer details.'

Ella stood up. Her face was beaming as she looked round at her family. 'I also need to ask you to bear with me, as we feel the news needs to be fully explained to you all. Today was Joe's first in his new position, and oh boy, I don't think we will ever forget it! About ten o'clock, he came to my door asking me if I could go to the office with him.'

Joe smiled in remembrance and raised his glass of wine to Ella, who winked at him before she continued. 'There on the table he showed me a small piece of dusty paper, which was besmeared with large sprawling handwriting. We, both of us, had to read the information a few times before taking it fully in.'

Looking round at his family's entranced faces, Joe could not stay silent any longer. 'Just wait till you hear this folks.'

Ella's eyes sparkled as she smiled at everyone. 'It sure is exciting, my dears. In fact it is indescribably amazing! In short, it said that Downside Alley and the whole of the Downside estate had been leased to the Harrington family in 1840 for one hundred years. The lease was signed by Edward's great grandfather, Clarence Spencer, who, along with the Woodleigh estate, was the rightful owner of the Downside estate at that time.'

Violet gasped. 'Well, I never, that means...'

'Yep, you've guessed it, Vi. Well, Clarence in turn willed it to his son William, and from there it had been passed down through the family until Edward willed it to Peter.'

There was a collective 'huh' from everyone in the room. Hannah and Violet, who were sat next to each other, hugged, then went and kissed everyone in the room. The atmosphere was buzzing with bonhomie and words of joy as Ella continued.

'After speaking to our solicitor, Joe drove me to his office, where we handed the document over to Mr Robson.'

Joe stood up. 'Yea, and he managed to prolong our agony a bit longer!'

Ella grinned. 'Well, frustrating though it was, he had to take time to check it all carefully and then speak to Mr Etherington from the Army. And so, after going away for an hour, Joe and I returned to the solicitors, where we were summoned to Mr Robson's office.'

As Ella paused to take a sip of water, Peter stood up and put his arm round her waist, then asked her to continue the amazing story.

'Well, the stunning news was that he was able to confirm that the document was genuine and that Peter was the legal owner of the Downside estate. One small problem was that, as we all know, the Army had taken over the estate in 1942 for the remainder of the war. Mr Robson pointed out to Mr Etherington that when Squire

Harrington signed the paperwork handing the estate over to the Army, he was not the legal owner, the lease having expired in 1940.'

Archie clapped his hands together. 'Well, fancy that. You ought to charge him for some rent then, Peter!' As everyone laughed, Archie looked at Ella. 'Sorry, my dear. I couldn't help but see the funny side of that. Do carry on wi' your story, 'tis wonderful to hear.'

Ella's face was aglow as she continued. 'That's alright, Dad. A very valid point! Anyway, Mr Etherington, who obviously felt rather embarrassed by the whole situation but at the same time wanted to save face, told Mr Robson that the Army had previously hoped to keep the estate indefinitely for training purposes.'

Before Ella could continue, Archie burst into speech once more. 'There, what did I tell you?'

Ella, who had felt equally as shocked when she heard this news, smiled at her father-in-law. 'I felt just the same, Dad. But thankfully this tangled web of fate, which the author Robert Service wrote about, has overruled all the hazards and given us Downside Alley.'

Archie looked a little sheepish. 'You're right, my dear, it's just that I hate being lied to. But as you say, 'tis all come right. Now, do tell us exactly how it did.'

'Well, after Mr Etherington spoke to his superiors they decided that due to the dubious legalities of the lease, they had no choice but to hand it back to the legal owner, adding that they would continue their training on Salisbury Plain.'

As Ella paused to have a sip of wine, Peter continued. 'Thanks, my darling, just one more thing to say really. And that is, because of the unexploded shells, we will not be able to have access to the estate for at least six months.' Mutters of 'Six months!' echoed round the room.

'Umm, I know. Sadly, some of the houses have been badly damaged, but others hardly at all.'

Peter looked adoringly at Ella. 'Thankfully, Ella had the sense to ask Mr Robson if Mr Etherington could pinpoint some of the worst damaged houses, and, after checking, he phoned Ella back late this afternoon to say that Downside House was in ruins, and also the cottages by the sea, being near the main target area, have been badly damaged. But as far as he knew, the houses in Downside Alley were unscathed, which is miraculous!'

Peter looked round again at all his family. 'This news today is something we never asked for or expected, but it is truly wonderful, and will change all of our lives for the better. And it only reiterates the belief that everything is possible if we don't give up.'

He paused and looked at Ella. 'I think that's enough of me for tonight. Except to say, thinking of all that's happened, I do believe there is a greater power that shapes our destiny. I mean, after having to leave Downside Alley in such grim circumstances, we could never, ever have imagined such an outcome!'

Looking at the large wooden clock on the mantelpiece, he added, 'My goodness, it's just on midnight! A very happy Christmas to you all!'

As everyone began to speak about the stunning news, Archie felt he had to say just one more thing. Looking at Peter he said, 'I hardly know what to say, son, except thank you for telling us the good news. I've never given much thought to miracles. All I knew about was survival. But this news...,' he paused and wiped his eyes, 'be quite remarkable. To think that we can really go back to Downside Alley!'

He looked at Peter. 'And that you, Peter, are the rightful owner, well, that is...,' he turned to look at Jane, who was also in tears, 'an answer to our prayers, and all we could ever ask for.'

As Archie paused to take a gulp of beer, he looked round at his family's smiling faces. Feeling the full impact of his new status, with a huge smile on his face and a glint in his eye, he added, 'I always used to call Downside Alley our ancestral home, and now it is! An' to think of all the generations of our family that 'ave gone before, all toiling the land for their living, an' now with this yere turn of events, well, finally, we be 'stocracy!'

As everyone laughed at Archie's humorous

words, he lifted his glass, and raising their glasses too, all joined him in a rousing toast of 'Cheers!'

By the time Peter and Ella had cleared the dining room in readiness for the morning, it was gone one o'clock. It had been an emotional day for them both and they were shattered.

Before getting into bed they took time to gaze out of the window and take in the beauty of the white world, which stretched before them over the fields and woods of Woodleigh.

Peter, who was standing behind Ella, put his arms round her waist and, speaking softly, said, 'Isn't it magical, darling?'

Ella turned her face towards him, kissed him gently and said, 'Yes, just like the day we've had.'

They held each other in a warm embrace, then Ella looked up at her husband, feeling so proud of him, and whispered, 'Tonight was so special, being all together and sharing the wonderful news.'

'Yes, it was very special indeed.' He lifted her up and carried her to the bed, and, laying her gently down, said, 'Just like you.' He kissed her tenderly, before adding, 'I love you so much.'

'I love you too, my darling Peter.'

Then they hastily undressed and tumbled into bed, but, tired as they were, sleep eluded them. And a few minutes after saying goodnight, Ella wanted to talk, and as soon as she began talking about Downside Alley, Peter was wide awake, too.

'I've been thinking, darling, once the Downside estate has been declared safe, we can go and assess what the actual damage really is.'

'Of course we can,' Peter laughed. 'And you know what I was just thinking?'

'What's that?'

'Maybe Dad was right, and I should send old Harrington a bill for illegally living on the estate and for taking the rent for five years!' For a split second, Ella looked horrified, until Peter said, 'Only kidding, my angel.' He kissed her on the forehead. 'Now, Mrs Samways, tell me your sensible thoughts.'

Looking excited, Ella said, 'Well, it just occurred to me that perhaps we could rebuild the cottages down by the cove and use them as holiday homes for underprivileged families.'

Peter smiled lovingly at his wife. He loved it when she was inspired by a project. 'That is a good idea, my love. But we will need to let all the evacuees know that they can return to their homes if they wish to. And we can point out to the folk whose houses have been badly damaged that it will be some while before they can return.'

'Of course! I hadn't thought about that... but if any should be left empty, then maybe we can consider using them for holiday homes for those most in need?'

As Ella laid her head on Peter's broad chest, he stroked her beautiful long hair, which flowed down her narrow back. 'That's an inspired idea, and so typical of my Ella.'

Ella's mind was still whirring. 'Thinking about what you said about the evacuees, I suppose I had better write to my father.'

'I guess so. What will you tell him?'

'I certainly won't tell him that you own two estates! I will simply say that we are married and have a daughter, and that the house and surgery are available to him, if he chooses to return.'

Peter had mixed feelings about having Godfrey back on his patch. 'Are you sure that is wise? I mean, once he knows about the inheritance, he will be insufferable.'

Ella was thoughtful for a few seconds. 'Maybe; it's a chance we have to take. It's my bet he won't even return. He doesn't like country life at all. Only came because of the war.'

'Umm, he never really settled in, did he?'

'No, my love, he didn't.' Ella made to get up. 'I don't know about you but I'm really thirsty. All that wine, I guess. Shall I make us a cup of tea?'

'Wonderful idea! Thanks, sweetheart.'

Ella went down to the kitchen and was pleased to find that the kettle was still hot. Ten minutes later they were both sitting up in bed sipping a refreshing cup of tea. As Ella snuggled into Peter's arms once more, she said, 'Now, where were we?'

'At Downside Alley I believe!'

'Ah, yes. While I was making the tea, I thought that maybe we could have some open days on the Downside estate and use one of the barns for a museum, which could illustrate the history of Downside and the evacuation. What do you think?'

Peter loved the idea. 'That's brilliant, Ella. And as Dad is more rooted in the landscape than anyone else, perhaps he could talk about the history to the visitors and share some of the old tales!'

Ella was excited by this. 'He'd love that, and so would the visitors. Hey, and you will be able to finish your notes on Downside Alley and publish them.'

'Crickey! With all the horror of the last few years, I'd forgotten about my notes. So, yes, maybe, and something else people would love to see is pictures of how the village used to look. They could be included in the book. Dad has some lovely old postcards, and I remember when some of them were taken in the 1920s. I was quite small but have a vivid memory of the photographer standing in the middle of the road... hardly any cars then, you see. As he assembled his apparatus and pulled a big dark cloth over his head, and then a huge flash and bang as the scene was captured, well, I thought he was some sort of alien!'

Ella giggled. 'And I know what else we could do. We could have outdoor theatre performances, just like the ones I went to see at the Minack Theatre in Cornwall. And the money raised could go to the refuge, and the publicity would highlight the work of it, too!'

As he propped himself up on the pillow, Peter took her hand. 'Umm. I like that. And while you were brimming with ideas over the teapot, I was thinking about your hopes for a refuge. Now that I'm home we can put our ideas into action.'

Ella ran her fingers over his hand. 'Tell me your ideas, my love?'

Peter looked slightly awkward. 'What I'm about to say is very sensitive. Do please forgive me if you think it inappropriate, but I feel I really must put it to you.'

Not sure what to expect, Ella said, 'Sounds intriguing. Go on.'

'Well, having no money worries, I wondered whether you would consider having Downside House rebuilt and turned into the refuge for battered wives, their children, and all those young girls and women who find themselves pregnant and homeless, that you have long dreamt about?'

Ella was quiet for some while, then, as she turned to her husband, quietly said, 'I think that is a wonderful idea, Peter. It would be the fulfilment of my vision. And thinking of what happened to me inside those walls, and the lives that could be completely transformed there... well, it would be something good coming out of bad. Such a miracle that we have the money to facilitate it.'

Pulling Ella closer to him, Peter said, 'Darling Ella, I hoped that's what you would say. And something else I thought about was the possibility of calling the refuge Edward House.'

'My God! That's the perfect name for it, Peter... and the ultimate tribute to dear Edward.' Ella touched his cheek tenderly. 'The past with all its sham and pain has gone. This rebuild will be a rebirth.'

Peter smiled at her determined expression. 'Yes. Let's tie a bow on the past, and look forward to the future and its unknown challenges with fortitude and excitement.'

As she nestled into Peter's arms, Ella said sleepily, 'When you think of all the dramas and heartache we've been through, it's amazing to think that, in spite of everything, we've come safely through it all.'

Wrapping the blanket over Ella's bare arm, and with a smile of contentment on his face, Peter said, 'Yes... and so has Downside Alley!'

The End

APPENDIX

1. The Royal Military Police is referred to as this due to the scarlet covers on their peaked caps and scarlet coloured berets.

2. Robert W. Service (1874 to 1958) was a British-Canadian poet often called the Bard of the Yukon.

3. The Navy, Army and Air Force Institutes.

4. No 151 Wing Royal Air Force was a British unit, which operated with the Soviet forces on the Kola Peninsula in the northern USSR during the first months of Operation Barbarossa, in the Second World War.

5. a privy or outdoor toilet in which earth is used as a covering or as an absorbing or deodorizing agent.

6. someone whose occupation is pushing or driving carts.

7. vertical poles located around the perimeter of a sailboat and are used for installing lifelines around the boat's deck to keep people safe.

8. GI are initials used to describe the soldiers

of the United States Army and airmen of the United States Air Force and general items of their equipment.

9. Press gangs were well-known for the physical force they used in recruiting men into the Royal Navy during the seventeenth and eighteenth centuries.

10. Rococo emerged in France in the 1720s and remained the predominant design style until it became unfashionable fifty years later. It was excessively flamboyant and characterised by a curved asymmetric ornamentation and a use of natural motifs.

11. Women's Auxiliary Air Force.

12. Henry Robert Hall, CBE (1898 to 1989) was an English bandleader who performed regularly on BBC Radio during the British dance band era of the 1920s and 1930s, through to the 1960s.

13. Extremely happy; a sandboy was a boy hawking sand for sale.

BIOGRAPHY OF LESLIE BURT JP

Born in 1921 on a remote farm on the northern edge of Lulworth, Leslie (pictured) was surrounded by the natural world, which he loved. Son of a farm labourer, he was proud of his farming roots. His family moved to East Knighton when he was four, and he started  school soon after, where he did well. When he was fourteen, the local farmer said there was a job at the farm for him, where he worked in the dairy for two years. One day he rode to the RAF base at Warmwell, and as he watched the young men parading round the ground, said to himself, 'I can do that.' After answering an advertisement and passing an examination at Bristol he was part of the RAF. Following his training at Uxbridge, he was based at Calshot for two years, where he was made Corporal. Then came the overseas posting. After some weeks at sea a message came, 'Lessons will be given in Russian.' He didn't realise it at the time, but he was on the very first Arctic convoy from the UK to Russia. Their mission being detailed in the postscript of this book. He returned to the UK on HMS Berwick and was stationed at RAF Ouston near Newcastle-upon-Tyne, where, on New Year's Eve 1941, he and two fellow airmen walked in to a pub and saw three young ladies. He instantly fell in love with Ada (pictured), and soon proposed. They were married for 61 years. Years later he often said to his family, 'It really was, From Russia with Love.'

Leslie and Ada married in 1942. Leslie was posted to Wales where he became Sergeant. They were delighted when their daughter Yvonne was born in 1944. They lived in Newcastle for the first five years of their marriage, but the call of Dorset was too great, and the family moved to East Knighton in 1947.  By now Leslie had left the RAF; he had signed on for seven years in 1939. They found lodgings in East Knighton with Jane Cox, a wise and intelligent lady in her 70s, who had a great influence on Leslie. She was loved by all the family, and known as 'Granny.' Leslie worked at Bovington Camp in the salaries department. Their second daughter, Devina was born in 1952, and with her parents used to visit Granny every week. In 1958, Leslie began work in the personnel department at the United Kingdom Atomic Energy Establishment at Winfrith. Sadly, Granny died in 1962, but a year later they were able to buy her cottage, which made them very happy.

In 1967 Leslie became a councillor for Winfrith Parish Council, later becoming chairman. He loved serving and helping his community and felt very honoured in 1968 when he was sworn in as a JP for the county of Dorset, where he also became chairman of the juvenile panel, and served on the Lord Chancellor's advisory committee.

After he retired from Winfrith in 1986, Dorset Police asked him if he would be able to swear in all the new recruits to the Dorset Police Force. This was something he really enjoyed and always offered the young recruits some sound advice. He continued in this role until he was eighty-five. How delighted he was in 1995 when he heard about the reunion of the 151 Wing. Many happy meetings followed at the Imperial War Museum, London, where the veterans received many medals from the Russian Ambassador. His growing family gave him much pleasure, and he would regale them with his tales of the old days.

He had an unshakeable faith, which meant he never had to worry about anything, and would often recall the words of Granny Cox after he had visited her in his lunch break one day in the late 1950s, and had emptied her toilet bucket. When Granny caught him doing this, she admonished him for doing that in his smart clothes, adding, 'I can't reward you, my son, but you will be rewarded.' Reflecting on his life years later, he would say how true her words were, and that his life had been truly blest.

POSTSCRIPT

Set during the years of World War II, Stronghold of Happiness tells a story with both fact and fiction at its core.

I am delighted – and privileged – to be able to highlight the astonishing Royal Air Force operation that is the fact at the heart of the story.

In 1993 I was Defence and Air Attaché at the British Embassy, Moscow. I was asked to help with a handful of RAF veterans, about to make their first visit to Russia since 1941. Back then they had been among the 600 airmen – including the author's father, Leslie Burt – sent to Russia as the 'cargo' of the very first Arctic Convoy of the Second World War. Hitler had reneged on his Treaty with the Soviet Union, and invaded on June 22, 1941. Churchill's response was as swift as could be achieved in those difficult days. The RAF's No 151 Wing, with 40 Hurricane fighters, and those 600 men to maintain and fly them, was in Russia in little over two months from first call.

Based in Murmansk, the Wing came immediately into action, defending that port, through which the Arctic Convoys would keep Russia supplied. The aircrew and ground crew had a secondary mission, which was to train the Russians how to operate those Hurricanes. The

Wing's aircraft would be left behind. They would be the nucleus of some 3,000 more to be supplied by following convoys. The men were delivered home to Britain in Christmas 1941. Only three were lost in action.

The veterans' numbers inevitably dwindled until the last man passed away in April 2023, aged 102. But until then, and with their families maintaining contact still, an RAF Association had kept them together, able to share their memories, and to enjoy the publicity that a film and several books have brought them. This novel adds to the record, and gives the veterans' reputations another boost. I am glad to have been able to support them and their Association since my first contact with them 30 years ago. I am proud to have helped tell their remarkable and indeed unique story.

Air Commodore Phil
Wilkinson CVO RAF (Ret'd)

THE PAUL CAVE PRIZE FOR LITERATURE

The Paul Cave Prize for Literature, established in 2023 by Tim Saunders Publications, is in memory of Paul Astley Cave-Browne-Cave (1917 to 2010), a hugely inspirational magazine and book publisher. In 1960 Paul founded Hampshire the county magazine, running it for over 40 years. Paul was keen to help those who had the drive and determination to succeed, which is what this prize is all about.

What we are looking for:
All forms of poetry: haiku, free verse, sonnet, acrostic, villanelle, ballad, limerick, ode, elegy, flash fiction, short stories and novellas in any genre except erotic. Work must be new and unpublished. International submissions welcome.

Guidelines
Poems
should not exceed 30 lines

Flash fiction
should not exceed 300 words

Short stories
should not exceed 1,000 words

Novellas
should not exceed 10,000 words

Prizes
Best Novella - £100
Best Short Story - £50
Best Flash Fiction - £25
Best Poem - £25

Winners of each category will have their work published on this web page and will receive a complimentary copy of The Paul Cave Prize for Literature 2023 book to be published by the end of 2023.

All approved submissions will feature in The Paul Cave Prize for Literature 2023. Each writer who submits a piece of approved work is guaranteed to have it published in the book.

How to enter
1. email your submission(s) to tsaunderspubs@gmail.com
2. send payment by Paypal to tsaunderspubs@gmail.com

For more information visit:
tsaunderspubs.weebly.com

Devina Symes

When I was twelve years old my father showed me a poem by William Barnes, the Dorset dialect poet, and I immediately became hooked, and soon began writing my first dialect poem.  Then Dad showed me some of the works by Thomas Hardy, and, again I loved it. I had always liked reading stories and poetry, and when I was fourteen, I wrote my first standard English poem, Autumn, which won me first prize in The Young Soldier magazine. Over the following years I continued to write poetry about life and the seasons. In the year 2000, when, looking forward to the bicentenary of William Barnes in 2001, I penned a play about his life called, A Life in Rhyme. The play, which was in aid of the William Barnes Society, was, thanks to the cast and crew, a great success.

My friend, Norrie Woodhall, the founder of The New Hardy Players amateur dramatic group, knew that I had written the play about William Barnes, and asked me if I would like to write a play about Thomas Hardy's life with her. Having known Hardy, she was able to write the last scenes, which was invaluable. The play, A Life of Three Strands, was performed at various venues throughout Dorset in 2007, raising money for the Weldmar Hospice. In 2008, Norrie asked if I could adapt Hardy's, The Mayor of Casterbridge, for the 2009 production, saying that the original Hardy Players had not performed that one. An intriguing novel with so many twists and turns, I wanted to do it justice. Norrie's special request was to include the country characters, which Hardy loved so well, which I did. After seeing the success of The Mayor of Casterbridge, Norrie asked me if I could adapt, Tess of the D'Urbervilles for the 2011 production. As I typed away on the computer, I was excited to see it all come to life. Tess was performed at eleven venues, and was greatly enjoyed, especially by Norrie. In 2023 Saltbeef TV Productions asked me if they could use my Dairy Maids scene from my Tess of the D'Urbervilles script, which is being produced by Martin Clunes and Mel Giedroyc for a TV programme to be screened in the autumn of 2023. I gave my permission and look forward to watching it.

BOOKS

In 2002 I wrote and self-published a small guide book, The History and Mystery of Corfe Castle, where I had worked for eight years. It was a fast facts guide and was illustrated by James Langan.

It sold well and I followed it by writing The History and Mystery of Lulworth and The History and Mystery of Brownsea Island. The National Trust then asked me if I could write a book on The Red Squirrels of Brownsea Island. Liz Poulain, a member of the New Hardy Players, started up her own publishing business in 2018 and asked me if I had any children's stories. I said I did have one, which needed polishing up a bit, and set about writing three short stories of Grandma's adventures with her visiting grandchildren, which is set on the Dorset coast. The Adventures of Grandma's Gang, which Liz illustrated, was published in 2019.

Early in July 2023, I read of a poetry competition run by Tim Saunders Productions and decided to enter. On reading more I was intrigued to find that they also publish books, and decided to email Tim about the possibility of publishing Stronghold of Happiness. I was overjoyed when he said this was just the sort of book he likes, and after emailing him the first chapter, the rest is history. My hope is that as you engage with the multifarious characters you will feel that you know them intimately, and that you too are a part of the Stronghold of Happiness.

Printed in Great Britain
by Amazon